NIGHT NIGHT, SLEEP TIGHT

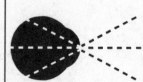

This Large Print Book carries the
Seal of Approval of N.A.V.H.

NIGHT NIGHT, SLEEP TIGHT

HALLIE EPHRON

THORNDIKE PRESS

A part of Gale, Cengage Learning

Farmington Hills, Mich • San Francisco • New York • Waterville, Maine
Meriden, Conn • Mason, Ohio • Chicago

GALE
CENGAGE Learning®

Copyright © 2015 by Hallie Ephron.
Thorndike Press, a part of Gale, Cengage Learning.

Thorndike Press® Large Print Basic.
The text of this Large Print edition is unabridged.
Other aspects of the book may vary from the original edition.
Set in 16 pt. Plantin.

LIBRARY OF CONGRESS CATALOGING-IN-PUBLICATION DATA

Ephron, Hallie.
  Night night, sleep tight / by Hallie Ephron. — Large print edition.
    pages cm. — (Thorndike Press large print basic)
  ISBN 978-1-4104-7955-6 (hardcover) — ISBN 1-4104-7955-2 (hardcover)
  1. Beverly Hills (Calif.)—Fiction. 2. Large type books. I. Title.
PS3605.P49N54 2015
  813'.6—dc23   2015005982

Published in 2015 by arrangement with William Morrow, an imprint of HarperCollins Publishers

Printed in Mexico
1 2 3 4 5 6 7 19 18 17 16 15

For Molly, Naomi, and Frances Louise

ACKNOWLEDGMENTS

One of the pleasures of writing this book was taking a trip back in time, remembering what it was like to grow up in Beverly Hills. A special thank-you to the folks in the "Beverly Hills in the 50s & 60s" Facebook group for sharing their remembrances, as well as to friends Jodyne Roseman and Ellen Kozak. For a sanity check on Hollywood and the movie business, thanks to my sister Delia Ephron.

Thanks to Lee Lofland for help on police procedure; to Deb Duncan on insurance fraud; to Paula Shelby on the workings of a Harley dealership; to Susannah Charleson on arson investigation; to Clarissa Johnston, MD, on trauma; and to Michelle Clark on death investigation.

For help working my way out of plot holes, thanks to generous fellow writers Paula Munier, Roberta Isleib, Hank Phillippi Ryan, and Jan Brogan.

I am deeply indebted to my agent, Gail Hochman, and my editor, Katherine Nintzel, for their clearheaded critiques and encouragement. Seriously. Thank you. Thanks to assistant editor Margaux Weisman for help shepherding this manuscript through to publication.

Thanks to Joanne Minutillo, Danielle Bartlett, Tavia Kowalchuk, and the other amazing folks in publicity at HarperCollins for their talent and enthusiasm launching this book.

Thanks to Jim and Anne Hutchinson, whose generous donation to Raising a Reader purchased a character name for their son Jack.

And finally, thanks to my husband, Jerry. Without his patience and forsaken weekend outings, this book never could have been written. He, more than anyone, was glad to see it finished.

■ ■ ■ ■ ■

FRIDAY,
MAY 23, 1985

■ ■ ■ ■ ■

CHAPTER 1

Arthur Unger slides open the glass door and steps out onto his flagstone patio. He's had a few drinks but he doesn't feel them. It's late at night, and though the sky is clear and there is no moon, there are no stars, either. There never are. Between ambient light and air pollution, he'd have to drive to Mount Baldy to see Orion's Belt.

The sky is . . . He gazes up at it. *Opaque? Inky? Like warm tar?* His ex-wife would have nailed it. She was great at narrative description and dialogue. And of course, she could type. He was the plotmeister. Arthur takes a final drag on his cigarette, the tip glowing in the dark, and stubs it out in one of the dirt-filled, terra-cotta planters in which Gloria once cultivated gladiolus. Or was it gardenias? Something with a *G.*

He picks up one of three cut-glass tumblers sitting on the table on the patio, left over from tonight's unpleasantness. Why does he have to rehash what was agreed on and settled years ago? He did what he promised. DEBT PAID IN FULL should be stamped across his forehead, and he has the paperwork to prove it.

He raises the glass in a toast. *To the end of old debts and life without gardenias.* He knocks back lukewarm, scotch-flavored ice melt, then reaches into the house and flips a light switch. The water in the pool — it's just twenty-five meters long, not the size to which he feels entitled, not what he expected to have earned by this point in his life — glows radiant turquoise against a row of coral tiles above the waterline.

Arthur imagines his yard is a movie set. A camera dolly backs up in front of him as he strides across the lawn in terrycloth slippers, an open Hawaiian shirt, and bathing trunks. A pair of amber-tinted swim goggles hangs loose around his neck. He reaches to unlatch the gate in the utilitarian chain-link fence surrounding the pool, but it's already open. Careless. He once had to scoop a neighbor's Chihuahua from that pool, and he has no desire to fish another dead animal from the water.

He slips through the gate and latches it behind him. Tosses a towel over a chaise longue made of aluminum tubing and white vinyl strapping. Takes off his shirt and drapes it there, too.

Arthur is in his late fifties, conscious of once taut muscles in his chest that sag if he exhales and relaxes at the same time. Even alone in his own backyard he tries not to let down his guard. Tonight he looks tired, the dark pouches under his eyes echoing the flab in his gut. He needs his thirty laps to drain away anxiety, get his blood flowing, and make him feel sufficiently worn out to fall asleep without a Valium and another scotch.

The pool has been skimmed, at least. That's supposed to be his son's job, but Henry rarely notices that it needs skimming. Rarely notices much at all, in fact. Henry seemed stunned when Arthur told him the house has to go on the market, though this would be patently obvious to anyone living here and even minimally aware of anyone's needs but his own.

Time to grow up, baby boy.

That's a line from a musical comedy Arthur and his wife wrote. *Show Off* was supposed to star Judy Holliday and Dean Martin, but she dropped out to have throat surgery. And then, of course, there was the breast cancer. Tragic for her. Tragic for

13

audiences to lose such a brilliant comedic talent.

Arthur first met Judy way back when . . . He closes his eyes and tries to remember. He must have been working as assistant stage manager at the long-ago razed Center Theatre in Manhattan, a gorgeous art deco ark at Forty-Ninth and Sixth. Late nights, after the show, he'd take the subway down to the Village where Judy performed a cabaret act with Betty Comden and Adolph Green, accompanied at the piano by fellow unknown Leonard Bernstein. They were all so young. So talented.

Show Off could have been big. Should have been big. Would have kicked his and Gloria's career back into high gear. Plus he'd have scored a producing credit and points on the back end. Even with the studio's creative bookkeeping, eventually it might have earned him a decent-sized pool and enough in the bank that he could have offered to help out his kids when they needed it.

But he's not out of the game yet. His book could catapult him back onto the A-list. It's the quintessential Horatio Alger story. He'll write the screenplay. Direct the film version. Cast a great actor in the lead. Someone capable of nuance. Subtlety. A little comedic

14

flair. Maybe he'll give himself a walk-on cameo.

Arthur runs his fingers back and forth through his hair, still dark and thick and curly, about the only good thing that both he and Henry inherited from Arthur's father. Then he stretches, arms wide, fingers splayed. Inhales deeply. Coughs. He tries to imagine his girls, *ingenues* as they were once called, perched around the edge of the pool. He sees the camera panning from one to the next, sliding appreciatively across cleavage and shapely leg, then over to him as he smiles benevolently back at them.

Give a little, get a little. That's always been his motto. Only lately he's been getting just that. A little. And sometimes not even that.

He adjusts his swim goggles over his eyes. His girls, if they were really there, would be a golden blur now. The camera dolly would have faded into murky darkness. He imagines it tracking him as he steps slowly, deliberately to the deep end of the pool. The wall of his garage, lit by a wavery glow, makes an eerie backdrop as his shadow creeps up it, nearly reaching the windows of his second-floor office. In a film, it would feel like foreshadowing. Very dramatic. Perhaps a bit melodramatic — at least that's what Gloria would have said, and she'd have been right.

Arthur faces the pool. Centers himself. Three long strides and he feels the concrete apron around the pool under his bare foot. A leap and he's airborne, outstretched and arcing in a racing dive. He lands more heavily than he'd like and the water is a lot colder than he expects, but the initial shock quickly recedes.

He swims, stroke after stroke after stroke, a turn of his head to take a breath. He reaches the far end, barely pausing before pushing off and surging in the opposite direction. Back and forth. He's nearing the zone, the place where his mind lets go and muscle memory takes over. He starts to review his work in progress the way he used to work through a movie script, running the maze of major and intermediate plot points; unpacking the emotions, goals, and obstacles that drive them; probing at knots and dead ends until he'd worked them through.

But what rises to the surface, like the taste of a bad oyster, is last week's phone call and tonight's meeting. Arthur feels his shoulders tensing up, his breathing begin to labor. If he wanted to be dictated to, told what he could and couldn't write, he'd be working on a screenplay.

He's not looking forward to tomorrow's meeting with the Realtor. She advised him to list the house at 899K. Apparently nine hundred is a barrier for buyers, and even though the market is hot, his house is not. How did she put it in the ad copy? *A classic open-plan home with lots of possibilities.* In other words, a dump. But hey, it's Beverly Hills, even if it is in the flats south of Sunset, and Arthur is determined to list his house for an even mil. Let them underbid and think they're getting a bargain. One thing he's learned: you don't ask, you don't get.

His daughter, Deirdre, agreed to drive up from San Diego tomorrow and spend a few days helping him get the place ready to go on the market. He called to remind her before coming out for his swim, but she didn't pick up the phone. Probably sleeping — Arthur loses track of the time. It's no big deal because Deirdre has never needed reminding. Even when she was little, she got out of bed and dressed for school without having to be coaxed. She did her homework. As grueling as the physical therapy was, she just did it, never complaining, even when it was clear that it wasn't going to make any difference.

Once he'd have taken Deirdre for granted.

But having someone he can depend on is something he cherishes now. Especially since he hasn't exactly earned her undying loyalty. She blames him for the car accident that crippled her, and how could she not? It's the kind of thing that apologies can't fix, though Lord knows he's offered them up.

Apologies. Excuses. Anything but the truth. It really wasn't his fault, but he can't tell her that, because if it wasn't his fault, then whose was it? He can't go there. Not yet, anyway. Maybe never. Besides, it's the last thing Deirdre wants to hear and it won't bring her the peace he wishes he had to give her.

He strokes across the pool. Turns.

He means to thank Deirdre properly this time. Maybe send flowers to that art gallery of hers. Her constancy is such a support these days. Henry seems incapable of fulfilling even the smallest commitment unless it involves one of his dogs or his muscle bikes. Gloria left years ago. Oh sure, they talk on the phone, though only occasionally, and not since Gloria began a monastic retreat. Tibetan Buddhist, shaved head, vegan diet, the works.

He tries to let go, to push away unfinished business as he pushes off from the end of the pool. As he strokes, he tells himself, *There's always tomorrow.* A wrong-answer buzzer goes off in his head. As Gloria often chided him: *Focus on the now.*

In this moment, as he swims in a steady rhythm, he is the star of his own movie, his life story brought to the silver screen, his backyard the set. The director, hidden in darkness behind the camera, has long ago called for *Quiet! Roll camera! Action!*

Fade in.

All attention is focused on Arthur as he turns again at the far end of the pool.

A beat.

He plunges back in the opposite direction, stroking powerfully toward the spotlight where . . . Who? Billy Wilder and Elizabeth Taylor, he decides, are waiting for him to surface and accept a golden statuette with his name engraved on the base. Recognition of his lifetime achievement, something even his kids can feel proud of.

Ready for his close-up, Arthur reaches the opposite end of the pool, raises his head, and hangs there for what he thinks will be just a moment, basking in the illusion that he's the star of his own show. Realizing too late that the spotlight he sees through the goggles — a yellow, water-streaked glow — is real and getting bigger, until it's bright and blinding and right in his face.

He blinks and looks away, and in that split second the light goes out. And we hear the sound that Arthur can't — the thud of heavy metal connecting with Arthur's head, his prefrontal cortex to be precise, the part of his brain responsible for a lifetime's worth of lousy decisions and selfish moves.

It's a wrap.

■ ■ ■ ■

SATURDAY
MAY 24, 1985

■ ■ ■ ■

CHAPTER 2

By the time Deirdre Unger reached the Sunset Boulevard exit off the San Diego Freeway, her stomach burned. The Egg McMuffin she'd wolfed down an hour and a half ago had been a mistake.

Used to be this was an easy turn, but traffic had grown heavier over the years. As she waited, she took a sip of what was left of her coffee. It tasted mostly of waxy cardboard and only made her stomach seethe. She set the cup back in the drink holder and foraged with one hand in her messenger bag, feeling for an errant Rolaid or Life Saver and coming up with only lint.

"How hot is it, kiddies?" The voice on the radio sounded maniacally overjoyed. "So hot trees are whistling for dogs!" A buzzer sounded, then hollow laughter. "Seriously, it's hot out there, so drink plenty of water. Red flag warnings have been issued for today and tomorrow. Heat and dry winds are expected to turn Los Angeles and Ventura County mountains and valleys into a tinderbox."

Yippee. Deirdre snapped the radio off and gripped the wheel. Another reason to have stayed in San Diego.

At last there was a break in the traffic and she turned onto Sunset. Why on earth was she doing this? Couldn't Henry for once in his life have stepped up to the plate? She wondered, what would he do after the house sold? No way he'd want to live with Arthur in a condo complex filled with actual grown-ups. He'd have to find a place for himself and Baby and Bear — those were his rottweilers — and his Harleys. She had no idea how many bikes he had at the moment, but she wouldn't have been at all surprised if he'd named them, too.

It was a shame about Henry. He'd wanted desperately to be a jazz guitarist, and if he'd worked at it, he might even have made a career of it. But freshman year of college he dropped out, stopped playing, and moved home. Not that he'd done badly after that. He made a good enough living selling bikes for a Harley dealership in Marina del Rey. Problem was, he "invested" his earnings in vintage bikes, Stratocasters, and the best pot that money could buy. Girlfriends came and went so fast Deirdre had stopped asking. Henry seemed to be allergic to any kind of personal commitment.

A loud *blat* came from a passing car. Deirdre realized she'd nearly sideswiped it. She jerked her car back in its lane. *Get a grip,* she told herself. Her father had asked for her help. He'd mellowed a lot in his old age, and even took the occasional break from his monologue to ask what she was up to. And it was just a weekend, not a lifetime.

She'd intended to drive up last night, but at the last minute her business partner, Stefan Markovic, got a call from an arts reporter for the *Wall Street Journal* who wanted to meet with him to talk about the new arts district that was taking shape in San Diego. She and Stefan had agreed it was potentially great publicity. But that meant he wasn't there to help install their new show, so she'd been at the gallery with the artist's assistant until after midnight. By then it was too late to start driving to L.A., so Deirdre had gone home. Before she went to sleep she'd turned off her phone's ringer. Her father had a nasty habit of calling at all hours of the night, using her silence as permission to rattle on about his latest brilliant idea or vent his spleen, depending on how much he'd had to drink. When he was done, he rarely said good-bye. He'd just hang up, and she'd end up lying in bed for an hour, trying to fall back asleep.

Deirdre crossed into the left lane and accelerated. Power surged and her Mercedes SL automatically downshifted and shot forward, hugging the road as she pushed it around a bend. She braked into the curves and accelerated coming out, weaving between cars on the winding four-lane road. Forty, forty-five, fifty. The end of her crutch slid across the passenger seat, the cuff banging against the door.

The car drifted into the right lane coming around a tight curve and she had to slam on the brakes behind a red bus that straddled both lanes and poked along at twenty miles an hour, idling just outside walled estates. STARLINE TOURS was painted in slanting white script across the back.

Deirdre tapped the horn and crept along behind the bus, past pink stucco walls that surrounded the estate where Jayne Mansfield had supposedly once lived. It had been a big deal when the actress died, had to have been almost twenty years ago. And still tourists lined up to gawp at her wall. Breasts the size of watermelons and death in a grisly car accident (early news reports spawned the myth that she'd been decapitated) —

those were achievements that merited lasting celebrity in Hollywood. That, or kill someone. It was the same old, same old, real talent ripening into stardom and then festering into notoriety. Deirdre sympathized with Jayne Mansfield's children, though, who must have gone through their lives enduring the ghoulish curiosity of strangers.

Buses like the one belching exhaust in front of her now used to pull up in front of her own parents' house, passengers glued to the windows. Most writers, unless they married Jayne Mansfield, did not merit stars on celebrity road maps. And in the flats between Sunset and Santa Monica where her father lived, notables were TV (not movie) actors, writers (not producers), and agents, all tucked in like plump raisins among the nouveau riche noncelebrity types who'd moved to Beverly Hills, so they'd say, because of the public schools. You had to live north of Sunset to score neighbors like Katharine Hepburn or Gregory Peck. Move up even farther, into the canyons to an ultramodern, super-expensive home to find neighbors like Frank Sinatra and Fred Astaire.

Arthur Unger had earned his spot on the celebrity bus tour through an act of bravery that had lasted all of thirty seconds. It had been at a poolside party to celebrate the end of filming of *Dark Waters,* an action-packed saga with a plot recycled from an early Errol Flynn movie. Fox Pearson, the up-and-coming actor featured in the film, either jumped, fell, or was pushed into the pool. Sadly for him, no one noticed as the cast on the broken leg he'd suffered a week earlier doing his own stunts in the movie's finale dragged him to the bottom of the deep end. Might as well have gone in with his foot stuck in a bucket of concrete.

A paparazzo had been on hand to immortalize Arthur shucking his shoes and jacket and diving in. Fox Pearson's final stunt, along with its fortuitous synchronicity with the movie's title, earned more headlines for the dead actor than any of his roles. Suddenly he was the second coming (and going) of James Dean, a talent that blazed bright and then . . . cue slow drumroll against a setting sun . . . sank below a watery horizon.

When talking about it in private, Arthur liked to quote a line from *Sunset Boulevard.* "The poor dope — he always wanted a pool. Well, in the end, he got himself a pool."

Deirdre used to dress up in her mother's silver fox stole and wave at the bus from the window seat of their dining room. She perfected an open handed, tilt-to-tilt wave like one of those gowned-up girls in the Rose Parade. Back then she could dream of being in the royal court. Queen, even. But beauty queens didn't have withered legs.

Finally the bus pulled over so that Deirdre and all the cars backed up behind her could pass. A few minutes later she cruised past the familiar brown shield, its message printed out in gold letters: WELCOME TO BEVERLY HILLS. After that, the twisty road straightened into a divided parkway and the speed limit dropped to thirty, as if chastened by the wealth surrounding it. There was not a single pedestrian on the sidewalks. Not a soul in the crosswalks or waiting at bus shelters.

A half-dozen blocks farther along Deirdre turned south. Two blocks down, she pulled over and parked in front of the house where she'd grown up: stucco façade, front courtyard, and arched living room window screened by an elaborate wrought-iron grille. That was Henry's black Firebird parked in the driveway. Arthur kept his red TR8 in the garage. To the casual observer the house seemed the same as it had for years. Decades, even. She could imagine the ad: *Charming one-story Spanish colonial, three bedrooms, two and a half baths, in-ground pool.*

Deirdre sat there for a few moments, listening to the car's engine tick in the silence and wishing she wasn't such a compliant daughter. Then she reached for her messenger bag, looped the strap over her head and across her chest, and grabbed her crutch. She climbed out of the car and leaned against the door. Heat seemed to pulse off the macadam. She put on her sunglasses and took a harder look at the house. Terra-cotta roof tiles were missing, and the once white exterior was more the color of weak tea. Deirdre doubted it had been painted since her mother left, the last time for good, nearly twenty years ago. Maybe that real estate ad should include the chipper warning: *Fixer-upper.*

Not that everyone fixed up Beverly Hills houses these days. Parcels of land had become so much more valuable than the houses on them, why bother? Buyers tore down and started over, erecting new houses that looked like they were worth the million or more you had to shell out to get an address with a 90210 zip.

Case in point: Across the street from her father's house, where there had once been a gracious, one-story Spanish colonial, there now sprawled a house worthy of a southern plantation. Two-story columns and Palladian windows flanked a magnificent pair of coffered front doors: Tara with vertical blinds, and badly out of scale for its third-of-an-acre lot.

Several more properties on either side of the street had been similarly perverted, and another was in process. Her father's house, once typical for the neighborhood, had turned into an anomaly.

Deirdre popped the trunk and slammed the car door. She eased her arm through the crutch's cuff and grasped the grip to which she'd duct-taped an extra layer of foam padding. She stumped to the back of the car and pulled a small duffel bag from the trunk. She'd packed light.

As she crossed the lawn she felt the rubber tip of her crutch sink into the grass. It made a little popping sound as she pulled it out. The courtyard was a tad cooler, shaded by a leaning olive tree. The ground under it was awash in rotting olives, some of them squashed and bleeding red slime on the gray stepping-stones. Deirdre knew from experience they could be treacherous to her crutch, so she picked her way carefully around them.

Many of the blossoms on the pair of camellia trees, one planted when Henry had been born and another about a year later for Deirdre, had turned brown and rotten, their season ended, though Deirdre's tree still bore white camellias. Once smaller than she was, the tree was now about ten feet tall. It was probably the only thing she wanted to take when the house was sold. She hoped it could survive being dug up and transplanted in the backyard of her little bungalow in Imperial Beach.

Deirdre tried the front door. It was locked, so she had to ring, which set off Henry's dogs. She didn't have a key to the house because Arthur kept forgetting to send her a set. That was his way, everything always and forever at his convenience.

When still no one answered the door, Deirdre knocked again, then rang some more. The dogs were going bananas. None of it roused anyone. Now what?

She dropped her duffel on the front step and walked back across the courtyard, trying not to slip on the olives or get the tip of her crutch stuck in the pillowy moss that grew between the stones. On the driveway the air was fifteen degrees hotter. A shovel was lying behind Henry's car. Deirdre picked it up, leaned it against the two-car garage, and peered in through one of the little windows in the overhead door. Motorcycles, at least two of them, were lined up in one bay. Her father's car was in the other. Which meant he had to be there, too. He was probably in his office up on the second floor of the garage.

Deirdre tried the overhead doors. They were both locked. Then she tried the regular door that led to the stairway. It was locked, too. She knocked. Hollered. Whistled. Was he asleep? She ought to just go over and bang on Arthur's bedroom window. It was nearly noon, for heaven's sake.

She was crossing the yard when she noticed the gate to the pool was open — wide enough for a pet or a child to easily slip through and fall in. Keeping that gate secured was one of the few things that her parents had agreed upon. She was about to go over and shut it when the dogs started up again. There they were, on the other side of the living room's sliding doors to the patio, their claws scratching the glass.

Deirdre went over to them. "Hi there, knuckleheads," she said. Bear whined and wagged his butt where there was the stump of a tail. Baby, who was a little smaller and had a bit more golden brown over her eyes and around her muzzle, woofed and stood up, her front paws resting against glass

33

smeared with doggie saliva. She was nearly as tall as Deirdre.

Deirdre tried to slide open the door, but of course it was locked too. "Dad! Henry!" she shouted. "Would one of you please get out here and open a damned door so I can come in, preferably before one of the dogs has a heart attack. Come on! It's hot as hell out here."

She waited. Someone had been out there not all that long ago: on the patio table sat a cut-glass tumbler with a bit of pale amber liquid at the bottom of it.

The only vestiges of Gloria, who'd long ago walked out on Arthur, were barren terra-cotta pots surrounding the patio. Once they had contained her collection of scented geraniums. Now they held only dried-out soil and the skeletal remains of weeds.

How her mother used to fuss over her prized *specimens,* as she called them, picking off dead leaves and pruning the branches into striking, bonsai-like shapes. Now she grew herbs and taught serenity and was well along on "the path," as she termed it, in the midst of a Buddhist retreat that required her to shave her head and — something Deirdre could barely imagine — remain silent. Deirdre had known her parents' marriage was over when her mother started carrying *malas,* prayer beads, that she fingered in quiet moments as she meditated and whispered mantras under her breath. When she'd moved to the desert commune near Twentynine Palms, she'd taken only one plant with her, a rare hybrid that smelled like smoked chili pepper, abandoning the rest to Arthur's inevitable neglect.

Deirdre turned back to the pool. Her mother had detested that pool and the chain-link fence that surrounded it. She'd tortured Arthur with plans for turning the entire backyard into a Japanese-style garden of raked stones and koi ponds. He'd wanted a sauna and hot tub. It made Deirdre wonder: If it hadn't been for their success as a screenwriting team, would her parents have stayed together even long enough to have had Deirdre?

That's when Deirdre noticed Arthur's favorite Hawaiian shirt draped over the chaise longue by the pool and his slippers on the ground beside it. She couldn't remember him ever swimming laps in the morning.

Behind her, the dogs quieted. She turned back. Henry was there on the other side of the glass, bare-chested and wearing a pair of drawstring sweats that rode low on his hips. The thick gold chain he wore around his neck reminded Deirdre of the choke chains he used to train the dogs. He yawned and rubbed his grizzled face, then unlatched and slid open the door.

The dogs burst from the house and ran joyous victory laps around the yard. Bear leaped for the knot at the end of a rope Henry had tied to a tree branch and hung there wriggling and snarling. Baby circled back to Deirdre, who crouched and let Baby lick her face. She buried her face in the soft ruff around the dog's neck. Whatever else you could say about Henry, he raised the sweetest dogs.

"Yo, Deeds," Henry said, offering his hand and helping her up. He gave her an awkward hug, then stood back and yawned, exhaling stale beer breath. "What are you doing here?"

Deirdre forced a smile. She knew it wasn't fair — after all, how could he have known she was coming if she or Arthur hadn't told him — but the question annoyed her. "Dad asked me to come up and help him with the house." She couldn't resist adding, "He's selling it, you know."

"Yuh." Henry crossed his arms. "I know. Whyn't you ring the front?"

"I rang. I knocked. *Whyn't* you answer?"

"I was sleeping. And besides, Dad's here.

Why didn't he —" He turned and bellowed into the house. "Yo, Dad! Where the hell are you?"

Deirdre listened with him, but when the house remained silent, Henry said, "Well, I thought he was here." He shuffled off in the direction of the bedrooms, only to reappear moments later. "So . . . where is he?" He stepped out onto the patio. "Is his car here?"

"Parked in the garage."

"Maybe he's up in his office."

"It's locked. I knocked. And yelled. Looks like he took a swim. He left some stuff out here." Deirdre pointed to the shirt and slippers.

She edged a few steps closer to the pool, then stopped. Her neck tingled and she smelled blood in her nose as she realized that there was a shadowy shape submerged under the water at the deep end of the pool.

CHAPTER 3

Deirdre felt as if, for a moment, the iris of a camera closed and opened again in front of her. *Click.* She dropped her messenger bag and stumbled across the patio, onto the grass, cursing the crutch that made a lousy substitute for a good leg. She was a strong swimmer if she could ever get to the damned pool.

Henry flew past her. In seconds he was across the yard, through the gate, and diving in. He took two strokes underwater and then surfaced, driving the body that Deirdre knew was her father to the side of the pool.

Deirdre reached the edge and sank to her knees. "Oh my God. Daddy?"

Henry held on to the tile edge of the overflow channel, gasping and trying to lift what was surely dead weight. Deirdre grabbed her father under an arm. Between her pulling and Henry pushing they managed to lift him out onto the concrete apron.

Time seemed to slow down as Deirdre shivered and backed away, then sank into a crouch. Her father lay on his side, his back curled and knees bent, hands stiff in front of him as if the water had returned him to the womb. His eyes were open, their surfaces clouded over, and the skin on his hands had shriveled like loose latex. She knew CPR, but anyone could see that her father was well beyond help.

Bear licked her hand. Beside him, Baby was down on her haunches like a sphinx, coat glistening, her massive head tilted, staring at Arthur. Henry was ashen, holding on to the edge of the pool. His lips moved, and she knew that he was saying something, but it felt as if rushing water filled her head.

He was dead. Her father was dead. If only she'd gotten there sooner. If only she hadn't stopped for that Egg McMuffin. They had to call an ambulance. Or the police. Or the fire —

"Deirdre!" Henry's voice penetrated. "Are you okay?"

Deirdre tried to speak, but the breakfast sandwich was backing up in her throat. She burped and her mouth filled with acidic coffee.

"Stay here. I'll call 911," Henry said and

hoisted himself out of the pool.

"I'll go," she said, reaching for her crutch.

Her weak leg was folded under her. She struggled to her feet, threw Henry the towel from the lounge chair, and clumped as fast as she could, hand over her mouth, through the gate, across the yard, and into the house. She reached the bathroom just in time.

Afterward, she stood at the sink, splashing water on her face and then drinking from her cupped hands, trying to wash away the nasty aftertaste. She looked into the mirror. Her long dark hair was wild around her face, like Medusa's snakes in the Caravaggio portrait, her father's haunted eyes staring back at her. She shivered, realizing that her dark leggings and top — an oversized T-shirt with XENO ART, the name of her gallery, silk-screened across the front, the neck artfully torn out — were completely soaked.

All she could find to dry her face was a ragged hand towel. She blew her nose and grabbed a few extra tissues for later, tucking them into the waistband of her leggings.

Numb, moving like a defective robot, she limped into the kitchen. The phone hung on the kitchen wall. She punched 911 and sank into a chair at the kitchen table, trying to collect herself.

An operator picked up. "Beverly Hills 911.

Where is your emergency?"

Where? Deirdre wasn't expecting the question. It took her a moment to come up with the address of the house where she had grown up.

"Thank you. What's the emergency?"

"My father. He drowned in the pool. He's dead." Her voice sounded as if it were coming from someone else's throat.

"Are you sure he's dead?"

Deirdre closed her eyes. She could see Arthur's stiff, clawed hands. "He's dead."

"Is anyone there with you?"

Deirdre squeezed the receiver. "Please send someone."

"They're on their way. Are you alone?"

"My brother . . . He's —" She stood and gazed through the window, past white ruffled café curtains that she'd helped her mother hang. Her vision blurred. She had to call her mother.

"Hello?" The dispatcher's voice sounded far away. Deirdre was trying to remember where she'd written the phone number her mother had given her months ago, before she'd checked into that Buddhist retreat. It had to have been in her datebook. Which was . . . she tried to recall where.

She hung up the phone, belatedly registering the dispatcher's "Please stay on the

41

line . . ."

She must have dropped her bag on the patio. She went to look. Sure enough, there it was. She opened the sliding door and shouted to Henry, "They're on the way. I'm calling Mom."

A minute later she was dialing, even though she knew no one would answer — it was a *silent* retreat for God's sake. At least she got an answering machine. "Cho Bo Zen Buddhist Temple. Please leave a message. *Gassho.*"

After the beep, Deirdre said, "This message is for Gloria Unger. I'm her daughter. Please tell her —" What? That something had happened and to please call back at once? No. Her mother would worry that something had happened to Deirdre or Henry. So she just said it: "— Arthur died. Suddenly. He . . ." Deirdre pulled the handset away from her face and stared at it, then put the receiver back to her mouth. "Mom?" Her eyes misted over and her throat ached. "Daddy drowned."

Deirdre ended her message with "It's Saturday," because who knew if there was a date stamp on the phone messages or how often the monks checked the machine. "I'm staying at the house. Henry's here. And I wish you were here, too."

42

The doorbell chimed just as she managed to croak out, "Please, call back." *Could the police have gotten here that fast?*

Deirdre hung up the phone, wiped her eyes, blew her nose, and went to answer the door. She expected to find paramedics or grim-faced police officers outside. Instead, a woman about her own age stood there, arranging a white bow at the neck of the blouse she had on under the jacket of a dark pantsuit that was a size too small.

"I'm here to see Arthur Unger," the woman said. Her gaze traveled to the crutch Deirdre was leaning against. Deirdre was used to that.

Was that a siren in the distance? Deirdre looked past the woman.

"Deirdre?" The woman wiped away beads of sweat that had formed on her upper lip. She seemed vaguely familiar. Maybe an actress? Arthur was always having hopeful young women over to the house to *read lines,* even when everyone knew that Arthur's only lines were the ones he used to convince the world that he was still a player.

"You don't remember me, do you?" the woman said.

Finally Deirdre really looked at her. Auburn hair. Sloping eyes. Pale soft flesh and freckles like sugar sprinkled across her nose. Deirdre did remember her. Of course she did.

"Joelen?" *Joelen Nichol.* Deirdre hadn't seen or spoken to her in what, at least twenty years? Not since high school. Not since that night. She was the daughter of glamorous Elenor "Bunny" Nichol, a movie star known for her spectacular silhouette, electric blue eyes, and lousy taste in men. Joelen had confided to Deirdre that her father's name was Joe. That explained her unusual name, pronounced *Joe-Ellen* — a combination of Joe and Elenor.

Joelen had her mother's incredible aquamarine eyes, luminous complexion, and radiant smile with dimples on either side. "It's so good to see you." She grasped Deirdre's arm, oblivious to the sirens that were growing louder. "This is so amazing. I had no idea you'd be here, too. Did he tell you that we had an appointment?"

"He?"

"Your father. I have a meeting with him this —"

"No." The word came out louder than Deirdre intended. Joelen recoiled. "I'm sorry. He . . . he can't see you now. It's too late. He's —" Deirdre couldn't finish it.

"What? Did he change his mind? Is this a bad time?" Joelen started to back away, trip-

44

ping over her own feet. The siren was screaming now. "I can come back. No problem. Another time?" She pulled a card from the outer pocket of her briefcase, lunged forward, and gave it to Deirdre. "Tell him to give me a call and —" Joelen broke off midsentence when the sirens fell silent. She turned and stared out toward the street.

Deirdre brushed past her. She moved through the courtyard, jerking her crutch loose when it got stuck between the paving stones. A police cruiser was parked in front of the house, lights flashing. Pulled up behind it was a red truck with gold lettering on the side: BEVERLY HILLS FIRE PARAMEDICS.

Deirdre was dimly aware of Joelen scurrying from the house, crossing the street, and getting into a dark compact car as Deirdre pointed two paramedics to the backyard. One of them carried an oxygen tank. Another maneuvered a wheeled stretcher that clattered up the driveway. A pair of uniformed police officers raced around ahead of them. Deirdre trailed behind. Henry was waiting at the gate to the pool. He'd wrapped up in the towel and, in spite of the heat, was shivering. He had the dogs on tight leashes, sitting tensed at his side.

The EMTs raced for the pool. Henry

45

watched them for a moment, then led the dogs back into the house. Deirdre waited on the patio for him to come back out. She crossed her arms, feeling stiff and chilled as she watched one of the paramedics kneel beside her father. The oxygen tank lay abandoned on the ground.

A police officer stood by the pool, talking on a radio. All Deirdre could hear were bursts of static. The officer belted the receiver, exchanged a few words with one of the paramedics. He crouched by the body, then lingered there a few moments longer, looking into the pool.

Slowly, he got to his feet and took in the yard and the back of the house, then shifted his gaze over at Deirdre and Henry. He crossed the grass to the patio. He was an older man with the boyish intensity and short sturdy stature of Richard Dreyfuss.

"I'm Officer Ken Millman." He offered Deirdre his I.D., just like in the movies, only this wasn't a movie. "I'm sorry. He's gone."

Deirdre knew full well that her father was dead, and yet she felt as if the air had been sucked out of her. She groped for a chair and sat. Tears filled her eyes, her stomach clenched, and her mouth opened in a silent scream.

Chapter 4

Deirdre barely heard Henry's "Are you okay?" Or the police officer's "Do you need a glass of water?" She tried to say *I'm fine,* to wave them away, but it was another few minutes before she could even lift her head. She found the tissues she'd stashed in her waistband and wiped her eyes. Blew her nose. Sat some more, just trying to wrap her head around what had happened.

At last, she found her voice. "Sorry."

The police officer whose name she'd already forgotten was crouched in front of her, his eyes searching hers. "The county coroner will be here soon." He was speaking slowly. "It's routine in an unattended death. Do you understand what I'm saying?" He waited for her nod, then continued, "I need to collect some information. Are you okay with that? Can you answer a few questions?"

Deirdre blinked. Henry put his hand on

her back.

The officer stood. He pulled out a note-book and flipped it open, then thumbed to a fresh page and jotted a few notes. "The victim's name?"

"Arthur Unger," Henry said. "He's our dad."

"He lives here?"

"Yes. I live here, too. Deirdre lives in San Diego." Henry gave the officer his name and phone number. Deirdre gave him hers.

"Can you tell me what happened?"

"We don't know what happened," Henry said. "My sister got here and found him floating in the water."

Not really floating, Deirdre thought. Arthur had been barely suspended above the bottom of the pool, beneath the surface, like a fly in amber. She choked at the memory.

"How long ago?" the officer asked.

"Not long," Henry said. "Fifteen, twenty minutes maybe."

"I called it in right away," Deirdre said.

The officer drew a rectangle on his pad, and around it a larger dashed rectangle with a gap that Deirdre realized was meant to represent the chain-link fence. "Can you show me approximately where your father was when you found him?"

Her hand trembling, Deirdre pointed to a

48

spot near the edge in the deep end.

The officer drew an X. "Then what?"

"My sister called 911."

"You're both wet." The officer squinted at Henry, then looked over at Deirdre. "I'm guessing one of you went in after him."

"Of course," Henry said, looking more annoyed than chastened. "I did. I thought . . . Actually, I didn't think. I mean, it was just a gut reaction. He might have had a heart attack or a stroke. Or fallen in and hit his head, for all we knew."

"I see." The officer gave Henry a long look. Deirdre had the distinct impression that he didn't think Arthur had just fallen in. "Thank you. That's all for now. I need you both to wait in the house until we finish up our investigation out here."

Henry hesitated a moment, then turned and started for the house.

"And I need you to leave that where you found it," the officer said, indicating the tumbler that Henry had picked up from the table.

Deirdre sat at the dining table, watching the activity through the sliding glass doors. Investigators had constructed a makeshift tent over Arthur's body. To protect him from what, she wondered. A photographer took pictures — not just of Arthur but of the entire pool area.

"You want anything?" Henry called out from the kitchen.

"No thanks."

He came out with an open bag of potato chips and set it on the table in front of her. "I found this on the floor in the front hall," he said, snapping a business card down on the table. "You know anything about it?"

Deirdre picked up the card. It had Joelen's name on it. "She was here this morning."

"I didn't know you two kept in touch."

"We didn't. Did you?"

"Why would I?" Henry said. "I barely remember her."

Deirdre let it go, but she knew that Henry remembered Joelen Nichol. Remembered her well, and not just because she'd made headlines. Henry, who'd never wanted Deirdre within fifty feet of him and his friends, used to hang out with her whenever Joelen came over. Once she'd discovered the pair of them making out on the musty sleeper sofa that her parents stored in the garage.

Sometimes, on nights when she was sleeping over at Joelen's, Henry would show up late and toss pebbles at Joelen's bedroom window so she'd come down. One night Henry's pebble missed Joelen's window and hit Bunny's instead. Bunny's boyfriend, Antonio Acevedo — the man everyone called "Tito" — had come whaling out of the house, armed with a baseball bat. Lucky Henry had ridden over on his bicycle and could get the hell out of there before he got hurt.

"She wasn't here to see me," Deirdre said. "She was here to talk to Dad."

Henry's look darkened. "Why'd she want to talk to Dad?"

Deirdre pointed to the setting sun logo and SUNSET REALTY above Joelen's name. "Just guessing. She's a Realtor. He's selling a house."

"I thought he already talked to a Realtor."

Deirdre shrugged. "All I know is she was here. She said she had a meeting with him. She freaked out when the police arrived."

"I'll bet she did."

"Don't be mean. I remember, you liked her."

"Sure I liked her," Henry said. "We had fun. Fooled around. But it was never serious. I haven't talked to her since she killed —"

"Supposedly killed."

Henry stood at the glass door and looked out into the yard. "Hey, she confessed."

CHAPTER 5

The story had made national news —
DAUGHTER KILLS STAR'S BOYFRIEND.

It had happened on a night when Deirdre
was sleeping over at the Nichols' house, late
after one of Bunny Nichol's lavish parties.
Bunny's boyfriend, Antonio "Tito"
Acevedo, was stabbed to death in her bedroom.

Deirdre didn't find out about the murder
for days after because she was in the hospital. Her father — he and Gloria had been
among the guests at the party earlier — had
come back in the middle of the night to take
her home. He'd carried her, half-asleep, out
to his car. On the way home, his car skidded off the road and she was thrown out.

She'd spent weeks in Northridge Hospital
— Arthur had insisted the ambulance take
her there because of their excellent reputation rehabbing Vietnam vets. After multiple
operations, skin grafts, and physical therapy,

the doctors finally conceded that the damage to her femoral nerve was permanent. She'd never be able to move her hip or bend and straighten her leg. She'd never feel heat, or cold, or pain, or even a gentle touch on the front of her thigh. Over time, the muscles would atrophy.

No one had warned her how much she'd come to cherish what she'd once been — unremarkable and nearly invisible. Instead, her mere presence would attract uneasy stares.

Desperate for anything to distract her from the pain and uncertainty of her ordeal, Deirdre had found a newspaper someone had left in the hospital visitors' lounge and read about the murder. After that she watched the nightly news, first from her hospital bed and later from the living room couch, as the story of the murder, photographs of the crime scene, and the lives of Bunny and Joelen Nichol and Tito Acevedo were endlessly dissected and fed to an audience ravenous for every sordid detail. Later, when Deirdre was strong enough to visit the public library, she surreptitiously tore news articles from the public copies of the *L.A. Times* and stole away with them so she could read and reread their accounts of the murder and inquest that followed.

The cause of death was a single knife thrust to the solar plexus; apparently Tito had dropped like a stone. "I did it," Joelen had told the police, who must have arrived at the house after Arthur drove off with Deirdre.

At the hearing, the coroner made a big deal about the lack of defensive wounds. Why hadn't he tried to protect himself? But that didn't seem at all far-fetched to Deirdre. Tito Acevedo, who carried a roll of hundred-dollar bills and a silver monogrammed gun-shaped Zippo lighter in his trouser pocket, would never have seen it coming. He wouldn't have been the slightest bit afraid when Joelen came at him, all of fifteen years old, a hundred pounds, dressed in that flowered cotton granny gown she wore whenever Deirdre slept over.

"He ran into my knife," Joelen told the coroner's jury.

That ten-inch kitchen knife was scrutinized, as was the nightgown Joelen had been wearing. An expert who testified was skeptical. Why wasn't there more blood? he wanted to know. From the wound Tito suffered, there should have been more.

But far more compelling than the presence or absence of blood evidence or defensive wounds was the dramatic testimony of

Joelen's tearful movie star mother. Bunny Nichol sat in the witness box wearing a dark suit and a blouse with a ruffled collar that swathed her neck like a bandage. Her jet-black hair was pulled back in a severe French twist. In the black-and-white television images, there were bruises under her eye and over her jaw, livid against skin that was otherwise flawless as bone china. She answered each question posed to her in a calm, quiet voice. It had been odd to see Sy Sterling, whom Deirdre had known forever as her father's best friend, performing his courtroom role on TV, a scaled-down Perry Mason.

"Why did you stay with a man who beat you?" Sy had asked, just a trace of his Russian accent surfacing: *bitt you.*

"I was afraid," Bunny said, staring down and kneading her hands together. "I had to do anything and everything he wanted or he said he'd ruin my face. He said I'd be sorry if I ever tried to leave him. He said if I told anyone, he'd get me where it hurt most. I knew what he meant." She'd paused and her audience, including Deirdre, had leaned into the silence. "My daughter. He would have killed us both."

Deirdre had heard Bunny and Tito fighting some nights when she'd slept over.

Angry shouting matches. Breaking glass. She could easily imagine herself in Joelen's place, listening to Tito's escalating threats and growing more and more terrified. Formulating a plan. Creeping downstairs to the kitchen. Pulling open a drawer and selecting the longest, sharpest, pointiest knife she could find. As she climbed the stairs, had Joelen thought about what would happen after? Did she hesitate as she approached the closed bedroom door? Did she have second thoughts as she stood in the hallway, screwing up her courage? Something must have spurred her to act at the moment that she did. Maybe it had been the sound of furniture breaking. Or a fist slammed into a wall. Or Bunny crying out.

It hadn't taken the coroner's jury long. After a few hours they ruled. Justifiable homicide. It wasn't *not guilty,* but it wasn't *guilty,* either. The verdict kept Joelen from being indicted for murder.

A real "David slays Goliath tale" was the verdict rendered by the TV newscaster Deirdre watched, lying on the living room sofa recovering from her first operation. She tried to call Joelen after the hearing but no one answered. She wrote to her but got no response. She begged her parents to drive her over there but they said there was no point to that. Bunny had left town. It was as if Deirdre's friend had vanished into thin air.

For months after, Bunny Nichol kept an uncharacteristically low profile too. Then came the news that she was back in town and married to a handsome young TV soap opera star, Derek Hutchinson. A few months later, the papers ran a photograph of the happy couple with a baby. Reporters were a tad more discreet in those days: Deirdre didn't remember the press commenting on the obvious fact that Bunny Nichol had been pregnant when she'd had her final fight with Antonio Acevedo. Pregnant when she testified on nationwide TV. No one was surprised that the baby boy, with his head of dark hair, olive skin, and dark eyes, resembled Antonio Acevedo a whole lot more than he resembled Derek Hutchinson, who was slender and fair. But those rumors were a gentle breeze compared to the shit storm that got kicked up a few years later when Derek Hutchinson died of AIDS, one of the sad first wave that took out so many of Hollywood's most talented.

Deirdre was finally well enough to return to school near the end of the academic year. At least she walked back into class on crutches, not in a wheelchair. Even the high and mighty Marianne Wasserman was friendly and solicitous, organizing a posse of her friends to carry Deirdre's books between classes. It made Deirdre queasy now, remembering the small amount of celebrity status she'd found herself basking in simply because she'd been Joelen's friend. Even as she'd traded on her friendship with Joelen, it had occurred to her how toxic notoriety could be.

CHAPTER 6

In the late afternoon, the pool was still cordoned off. Officers were searching the bushes surrounding the yard. Again. They'd taken samples of pool water and collected Arthur's discarded towel and clothing, the pool's leaf skimmer, and the tumbler that had been on the patio table.

It seemed awfully thorough for an accident investigation, so Deirdre wasn't surprised by the arrival of a man in a suit who climbed over the crime scene tape and talked with a few of the officers, including the one who'd questioned Deirdre and Henry. The newcomer crouched and looked under the tent that covered Arthur's body. After a pair of attendants zipped Arthur into a dark blue L.A. County Coroner's body bag, the man stood and approached the house.

He beckoned to Deirdre through the glass, and she slid the door open. "Miss Unger?

I'm Detective Sergeant Robert Martinez." He showed her his badge and gazed at her from under dark eyebrows. "I'm sorry for your loss."

Henry came up behind her. "Detective?"

"Detective Sergeant Robert Martinez, sir." The detective's gaze shifted from Deirdre to Henry. His skin was dark, with the leathery texture of an aging surfer.

"Do they always send a detective out?" Henry said. "This was an accident."

"Unaccompanied death. It's not unusual. Mind if I come in the house? I have a few —"

"We'll come out," Henry said, nudging Deirdre out in front of him. He followed and slid the door firmly shut.

"Mr. Unger was a strong swimmer?" Martinez asked when they were settled at the table on the patio.

"He swam every day," Henry said. "Like clockwork. Thirty laps."

"He often swim late at night?"

"Sometimes."

Martinez shot Deirdre a questioning look.

"Sometimes," she said. "Henry would know better than me. I don't live here."

"When did you last see your father?"

"In person?" Deirdre tried to remember the last time she'd been there.

"You came up for his birthday, remember?" Henry said. "January."

"Right," Deirdre said. That had been months ago.

"And the last time you talked to him?" Detective Martinez asked.

"Last week. He asked me to come up and help him."

"Help him what?"

"Get the house ready to go on the market."

Martinez's eyebrows rose a notch. Deirdre followed his gaze up to the sagging awning over the patio, across the paving stones with their cracked cement riven with weeds, and over to the peeling paint on the frame around the sliding doors. "Was anyone with you last night?" he asked her.

"No," Deirdre said.

"Anyone see you leave your house this morning?"

"No, I don't think so. I —"

"Oh, Christ," Henry said. "You can't think —"

"What about you, sir?"

Henry's mouth hung open for a moment. "Last night? I was here. This morning? Asleep until a few hours ago. And no, no one was with me. Just my dogs."

"And when did you see your father last?"

"Last night." Henry blinked. "No. Yesterday morning. Before I left for work. I didn't get back until late. After midnight. I went straight to bed. I just assumed . . . Oh my God. You don't think he's been out there all night?"

Martinez gazed impassively back at Henry. "We'll know more when the coroner has finished examining him. Yesterday morning, when you last saw your father, how did he seem?"

"He seemed fine," Henry said. "Normal. He was griping, you know. He liked to complain. And he was hungover."

"Your father was a drinker?"

"He liked a few drinks at night. And he could get maudlin."

"Maudlin?"

"Not wallowing in self-pity or anything. Just kvetching. Short stick. Half-empty glass. But it wasn't like he was about to kill himself."

Suicide? Deirdre hadn't even considered it. After the way her father had already screwed up her life, she couldn't believe he'd arrange for her to be the one to find him. But if it wasn't suicide, and it wasn't an accident . . . "What are you suggesting?" Deirdre asked.

"What we know for sure is that your father

died most likely sometime last night. It's not clear how it happened, or even where it happened. We don't know for certain that he drowned. But if he was upset —"

"I told you, he wasn't upset," Henry said.

"I'm sorry. I know this is painful."

"He was not upset," Henry said, his voice cold and emphatic.

"Was your father seeing someone?" The detective directed the question at Deirdre.

"I have no idea. Was he?" Deirdre asked Henry. Arthur rarely talked to her about his lady friends and for that she was grateful.

Henry rolled his eyes. "No. He was not seeing anyone."

"You sound sure of that."

"I live here. I knew when he was seeing someone."

"He was divorced?"

"A long time ago," Deirdre said.

"They get along?" Martinez asked.

"At a distance," Henry said.

"It couldn't have been her," Deirdre said. "She's on a retreat."

"Huh." Martinez started to get up, then paused. "Just one more thing. You say it wasn't unusual for your father to swim late at night. It seems odd that he didn't turn on the lights in the pool."

"Lights?" Henry asked.

"There are no outside lights on now," Martinez said. "Maybe you turned them off when you got here?" he asked Deirdre.

"I . . ." Had she? She'd been in such a state. Then she realized she couldn't have. "No. The light switch is inside and I couldn't get in."

"What about you?" Martinez asked Henry. "Last night when you got home? Or maybe this morning?"

"Maybe." Henry thought for a moment. "No. I'm sure I didn't."

"Hmm. Maybe the lights are on a timer and they went off automatically?"

"No," Henry said.

"And the lights are working?" When Henry shrugged, Martinez added, "Can you check?"

Henry slid open the glass doors and reached for the light switch just inside.

"Hang on." Martinez crossed the yard and stood inside the fence to the pool. "Okay, give it a try."

The lights on the patio wall above Deirdre's head came on. The light in the pool must have come on, too, because Martinez flashed a thumbs-up and called out, "Thanks."

Martinez stared out at the water, one arm across his chest, the other propping up his chin. Deirdre knew what he was mulling. Would Arthur take a nighttime swim without turning on any lights? And if he had turned them on, then who turned them off? Because by the end of his swim, he'd have been incapable of doing so.

Chapter 7

"That's it for now," Detective Martinez said. "The investigators should be done soon. Mind if I take a quick look around inside?"

It was the second time he'd invited himself into the house. "Inside?" Deirdre said.

"Just to be thorough. Then we won't have to come back."

Henry edged Deirdre aside. "No way, José."

Deirdre cringed but Martinez barely raised an eyebrow. "Okay, then. We'll be leaving soon, but we're not done. Your father's remains should be ready to be collected tomorrow or the next day. You should line up a mortuary. They'll know how to proceed. And here." He took out a business card and gave it to Deirdre. "In case either of you needs to reach me. If you think of something." He offered a second card to Henry, who stared at it for a moment. "Or find something you think we should know about," Martinez added.

Henry took the card.

Later that night, Deirdre was curled up on the couch, Henry sprawled in Arthur's favorite chair, a leather recliner. The wind had picked up, and the occasional gust set roof tiles chattering. Deirdre put the nub of a nearly smoked-out joint between her lips, inhaled, held her breath, and handed the joint back to Henry. They'd been eating from boxes of Chinese takeout that Henry charged to Arthur's credit card.

Deirdre had called Westwood Memorial Park. Darryl Zanuck was buried there, along with Natalie Wood. The undertaker Deirdre talked to on the phone had a deep, resonant voice that reminded her of Orson Welles. Of course, he said, they'd care for Arthur's *remains*. The term seemed appropriate. What she and Henry had pulled from the pool had barely been their father. By the time the coroner and the mortuary got done with him, he'd have been examined and dissected, his fluids drained away, his hubris along with his wit and warmth. People would come to the service and say what a swell guy Arthur Unger was. As he'd once remarked of a particularly foul-tempered studio executive, *You never look as good as you do at your own funeral.*

"At least Pedro didn't say don't skip town," Henry said, taking a pull on the joint.

"The detective's name is Robert," Deirdre replied, releasing her breath. "And maybe that's just something they say in the movies." Deirdre had no intention of leaving town. She'd called Stefan and left a message saying that it might be days before she got back. He'd be on his own with the new show — hard to believe she'd installed it just twenty-four hours ago. "So I guess you didn't want him snooping around inside the house," she added.

Henry started to laugh, choking on a final drag. He sputtered as he stubbed out the butt. "No way. Not with this shit in the house. You can bet he won't find a trace of illicit substances when he comes back."

"*When* he comes back?"

"Oh, he'll be back. You bought that crap about how they send out a detective whenever there's an unaccompanied death?" Henry scowled, making a face like the petulant thirteen-year-old he'd once been.

"Poor baby. Pushed your buttons, didn't he? What's the matter, you don't like cops?"

Henry threw a pillow at her. She caught it and sank back into the couch and let her gaze wander around the room. Arthur was everywhere, from the stack of *Variety* and *Life* magazines to ashtrays that still overflowed with the remains of her father's Marlboros to a glass cart with an ice bucket and a half-empty bottle of Dewar's. She hauled herself to her feet and, unsteady without her crutch, limped over to the piano. Open on the music stand was "Rhapsody in Blue." Shelved nearby was her father's cherished collection of LPs.

She edged over to the turntable. The record on top was *Ella and Louis.* She started the machine and set the needle. Closed her eyes to listen to the piano introduction, then Armstrong's easy, bluesy voice, having *that feeling of self-pity* . . .

"We should be drinking Dad's scotch," Deirdre said, turning back to Henry.

"Help yourself."

"I didn't say I wanted any. I'm not crazy about the stuff." Besides, on top of pot, hard liquor would be a very bad idea. "But it was his drink. And this is his music."

Henry stood and offered her his hand. He lifted her off the ground, set her feet on top of his, and rocked back and forth to the music. Deirdre closed her eyes and sang along. *"A foggy day . . ."* The words were muffled in Henry's shoulder, his shirt damp

69

with her tears. "He taught me to waltz. And the Lindy," she said.

"You were a good dancer, Deeds. All he taught me to do was smoke. And drink. And drive too fast."

"Mmm, driving too fast. I can blame him for that, too."

Henry helped Deirdre back to the couch and then sat down again himself. He poked his chopsticks into the take-out box and took another mouthful. A Singapore noodle stuck to his chin. Deirdre imagined what he'd look like as a Chia pet with noodles instead of grass growing out of his head and started to laugh.

Henry reached across, tweezed a spear of broccoli from her takeout box, and popped it into his mouth. Brown sauce dribbled down his chin to meet the noodle.

The room started to spin. Deirdre closed her eyes, which only made her feel worse. She lurched back upright.

When the phone rang, neither Deidre nor Henry moved to answer it. The machine picked up after four rings, and their father's voice echoed into the room. "You've reached Arthur Unger . . ." Deirdre flopped over and pulled a cushion over her head. When she heard the beep, she lifted the cushion.

"Hello? Henry, Deirdre? Are you there?"

Hyello. Deirdre recognized the slightly accented voice before he added, "It is Sy." Sy Sterling, attorney to the stars, was the closest thing Deirdre and Henry had to an uncle from the old country. "I heard the news. I cannot believe this is happening. I talked to your father just the other day. Yesterday, for Chrissake. And" — he paused; his voice turned raspy and his accent thickened — "we were saying how we had to get together. Pick up some corned beef sandwiches and go to the track."

Henry lurched from the chair, dropping the box of noodles, which exploded onto the Oriental rug. He cursed, then tripped on the rug's raveled edge halfway to the phone and cursed again. In seconds, Bear and Baby had Hoovered up the spill.

"One of you call me back as soon as you can? I am in my car right now but I will be home later. Two seven six —"

Henry finally grabbed the phone. "Sy? It's Henry." Henry sounded winded. "Thanks for calling. Yeah." He paused, nodding his head a little. "I don't know. He was in the pool when Deirdre got here this morning. The cops were here most of the day. They think he died last night." Henry listened. "Are we okay?" He looked across at Deirdre. "I guess." He listened some more. "Of course I didn't let them into the house."

Henry turned his back to Deirdre and walked toward the window. The phone cord stretched from coiled to straight until it wouldn't stretch farther. Henry stood quietly, listening, a long silence with just the occasional "Uh-huh," "Sure," "Okay."

Deirdre got up again. She limped over to the wall of bookshelves and picked up a framed photograph of all four of them, scrubbed and polished and posed against a backlit scrim of blue sky and palm trees. Ten-year-old Deirdre wore a demure black velvet dress with a white lacy collar, her hair skinned back in a ponytail. Henry, a year older, looked downright military in his little suit. What you couldn't see was that he'd been wearing flip-flops. That year he'd refused to wear real shoes.

Alongside the family portrait was a framed black-and-white photograph of eight-year-old Deirdre in a sparkly leotard and skirt of layered ruffles. Deirdre knew the ruffles were pink, and the black patent leather tap shoes had been bought a size too big for her so that she could "grow into them." More girls in similar getups stood posed behind her looking supremely bored as Deirdre danced her solo.

She turned the picture facedown on the shelf.

Behind the pictures were videocassettes, each with a handwritten label — some her mother's careful printing, others her father's scrawl. Also lined up was a row of their leather-bound movie scripts, the titles embossed in gold on the spines. Deirdre ran her hand over the leather. Gloria had let Arthur keep all their scripts when she'd walked out. She'd left behind most of her clothes and jewelry, too, along with her perfume and cosmetics. She'd probably have shed her skin and left that behind if she could have.

The shelved scripts were in chronological order. There was *Lady, Be Good,* their first movie, a remake of a 1920s silent film of the Gershwin musical comedy that was long on jazzy score, glittery costumes, and dance numbers and short on plot. Next to it, *A Night in St. Tropez.* Deirdre opened that script and paged through hand-typed pages until she got to one of the nine-by-eleven, black-and-white glossies that were bound into the book. Carmen Miranda winked at the camera, wearing ropes of pearls and a skirt that looked like it was made of bananas.

At the end of the row were two copies of

Singing All the Way Home, the last script her parents wrote together, and one of the last romantic musicals in an era that had been full of them.

"Really?" Henry was saying into the phone. "All right then!" Deirdre looked over at him. He was smiling. Some good news?

Deirdre pulled one of the copies of *Singing All the Way Home* off the shelf and opened it. There were no pages bound into it. Instead, tucked inside was a pocket folder that held a sheaf of papers — an unbound manuscript, carbon copies on onionskin paper. Centered on an otherwise blank first page were the words "WORKING TITLE: ONE DAMNED THING AFTER ANOTHER," and below that, "by Arthur Unger, 1985."

Deirdre turned to the next page and read.

CHAPTER 1: EXIT LAUGHING

The writing was on the wall of our office at Twentieth Century Fox when the secretary didn't show up and the phones disappeared. We were screwed. Shafted. Sucker-punched. Time to strike the set.

Deirdre smiled. She could hear her father's voice. For a moment her chest tightened and her vision blurred.

Beneath the opening paragraph, text was formatted like the slug lines and stage directions of a movie script.

INT. TWENTIETH CENTURY FOX — SCREENWRITERS OFFICE — DAY (1963)

ARTHUR UNGER opens the door to his office and starts to enter. He's trim, middle-aged, wears a suit and holds his hat. Stops. He looks surprised. Dismayed.

His secretary's desk is empty. Disconnected phone wires are coiled on the floor.

ARTHUR crosses to the window, looks two stories down to a deserted studio street where a huge movie poster for Cleopatra is plastered across a wall. In front of it is an empty phone booth.

ARTHUR raises the window. Sits on the ledge.

No, I didn't jump. Two stories up? Not high enough to kill me, and damned if I was going to let the sons of bitches cripple me for life. When I went outside to use the pay phone, I swear there were vultures circling overhead. Could've been a scene out of Hitchcock, but Hitchcock worked for Universal.

Turned out hundreds of us arrived on the Fox lot that morning to find our office phone lines disconnected and our typewriters returned to Props.

It was a clever device for a screenwriter's memoir, alternating between the idiosyncratic formatting of a screenplay and straight narrative. Odd that Arthur had kept this carbon copy tucked in the cover of a movie script. Almost like he'd hidden it there.

As Deirdre flipped to the last chapter to see how far Arthur gotten, Henry's voice pulled her off the page. "All right. Uh-huh. Sure. Don't worry, I won't forget." Clearly, he was winding up the call. Deirdre put the empty script cover back on the shelf and carried the folder with the manuscript pages to her bedroom, where she slipped it into the drawer in her bedside table.

When she returned, Henry had hung up the phone. Deirdre said, "Was that Sy?"

"*Sí,*" Henry said, deadpan.

"So?" Even if it was a wildly inappropriate time to be cracking jokes, Arthur would have appreciated the old comedy routine that he'd reprise himself whenever the opportunity presented itself. It was one of the perks, he used to say, of having a friend named Sy.

"He's coming over tomorrow morning to talk about Dad's will."

"What won't you forget?"

"Huh?"

"You told him you wouldn't forget something."

"When the police come back to search the house, there shouldn't be anything here we don't want them to find." Henry went into the kitchen and came back out with a large black plastic garbage bag, into which he dumped the contents of the ashtray.

"That's a big bag for a few ashes," Deirdre said.

"There's more. Things Dad would want me to get rid of."

"What things?"

Henry's answer was cut off by the phone ringing again. Both Deirdre and Henry froze, waiting for the answering machine to kick in. After the beep, this time they heard a woman's voice: "Hey, Zelda? You there? It's Thalia."

Deirdre might not have recognized Joelen's voice, but she definitely recognized those nicknames. Zelda, the smart but pain-

77

fully plain and geeky character who lusted after television's Dobie Gillis, was code for Deirdre; Thalia, the gorgeous, moneygrubbing blonde whom Dobie lusted after, was Joelen.

Deirdre reached for the phone but Henry stopped her as Joelen's voice continued. "Sy called and told us what happened. Gosh, I don't know where to begin. I just hate saying this to a machine." A pause. "I'm so sorry. I really can't believe it." There was a longer pause, then: "Listen, I don't know how long you'll be in town, and I know it's been ages since we were friends. But we were. Really good friends. If there's anything I can do to help, all you have to do is name it. You know where I am. Same place. Call me." Joelen recited the number. Deirdre still knew it by heart. "Mom sends condolences."

Click.

"Joelen?" Henry said.

Deirdre nodded.

"Now what does she want?"

"I don't think she *wants* anything. I told you, she rang the bell this morning right before the police. She's a Realtor. She had a meeting with Dad."

"So why is she calling now?"

"She's being nice?" Deirdre yawned and

stretched. The room had long ago stopped spinning and she felt drained and far too tired to try explaining to Henry the concept of *nice.* "I'm going to bed," she announced. She hoped there were clean sheets.

"I've got to take these guys out. Then I'll turn in, too." Henry pulled his leather jacket off the back of a chair. The dogs perked up and started yipping and circling him.

"And you'll take care of that?" Deirdre pointed to the deflated garbage bag that Henry had left on the floor. "And the things that Dad wanted you to throw away?"

"Oh yeah." Henry crouched and snapped a leash to each dog's collar. "Don't worry, it will all be gone by morning."

CHAPTER 8

The wind had died down and the house settled into an uneasy silence as Deirdre ferried beer bottles and leftovers to the kitchen. She carried her duffel bag into the room that was once her bedroom. The stuffy space had been taken over by Henry's bench press, weights, and an exercise bicycle. Judging from the layer of dust on them, they didn't see much use.

She opened the windows, but the air barely moved. On hot nights like this her father used to hose down the roof.

Her sliding closet door was sticky, but she managed to work it open. There, on the rack, hung some straight skirts and pleated skirts from high school, all of them much too long, with a few matching cardigan sweaters. A much shorter, swingy, navy blue tent dress that she'd worn in college hung there, too. She'd bought it because she thought it made her look like That Girl,

Marlo Thomas. There was the cream-colored linen suit she'd worn to her college interviews, along with a brown trench coat that she used to wear with its broad collar turned up, its belt tied at the waist in the style of Catherine Deneuve.

Way on the end was the white two-piece dress she'd worn to her high school graduation and to the dance after. She fingered the silk brocade that had gone brittle with age. The shoes that were supposed to have been her first high heels were still in their box on the closet floor. When she'd bought them she'd been optimistic that she'd be able to take a few steps, maybe even dance. Just one more thing that was supposed to happen that never did.

Deirdre tossed her duffel bag on top of some cardboard boxes stacked in the closet. Her name was written in block letters on the sides — certainly her writing — though she had no memory of boxing anything up.

She turned. On the adjacent wall hung a large framed pencil sketch of a waif with enormous, honey-dripping eyes. The little girl held a gray kitten with its own wide teary eyes. Preadolescent Deirdre had selected this awesomely awful artist-signed (Keane) piece of '60s kitsch herself. After the accident, she'd identified with that girl and begged her parents to get her a cat. She'd made up stories, none of them with happy endings, about how the pair came to find themselves in their pitiable state. Now she limped over, took the picture down from the wall, and stuck it in the closet facing the wall.

The mattress of her trundle bed was adrift in Henry's magazines: *Rolling Stone* with U2 on the cover, something called *Spin* with a sultry Madonna, *Cycle World*. Deirdre pushed them aside, unearthing Ollie, her teddy bear. The felt that had covered his paws and nose had long ago been worn away. She pressed Ollie to her face and let his sweet, woolly smell take her back to a time well before this nightmare. Her mother would have been running her a hot bath and asking if she wanted hot cocoa to help her sleep. The bed would have been made up with freshly laundered sheets instead of two naked pillows and a stained mattress cover.

Well, there was certainly no hot cocoa now. Shrugging off her old memories, Deirdre tossed Ollie into the closet where he could have a pity party with the waif and her kitten. She took a quick shower, made the bed, and got into it. Exhausted but wired, she opened the drawer in her bedside table, pulled out Arthur's manuscript, and started to read where she'd left off.

The second chapter, titled "The Bronx Is Up," recounted his childhood. He'd grown up, the youngest son of Russian immigrants, with four brothers, none of whom Deirdre had met. She skimmed the pages, through a life story told in anecdotes, many of which she'd heard Arthur tell more than once. She paused at the sound of the front door opening and dog claws scrabbling on the floor. Henry was back.

In the next chapter, "Helluva Town," Arthur flunked out of college and landed in Manhattan, found work as an assistant stage manager and a shabby room with a shared bath in Hell's Kitchen. Late nights, he hung out in Greenwich Village. Mornings he'd get up early and write plays.

Deirdre heard the front door open and close again, then the rumble of Henry's motorcycle catching, revving, and roaring off. She wondered when he was planning to take Sy's advice and get rid of anything that they wouldn't want the police to find.

Deirdre yawned. She tried to continue reading but the words swam on the page. She slid the manuscript back in the folder and tucked it into her bedside drawer. Then she plumped up the pillows and lay back. The house was silent with the occasional comforting sounds of dogs lumbering about. She stared up at the ceiling. There was a water stain in the corner. Would she and Henry have to fix the roof and get the rooms painted? Right now she was too tired to care.

The bedside clock said it was nearly one in the morning. Deirdre turned over, bunched the pillow under her head, and closed her eyes. Maybe it had been at about this time Arthur had gone for a swim. She could see him walking to the pool, his eyes slowly adjusting to the dark. Diving in.

Was that when it had gone wrong? He'd taken a running leap from the board, hit the water, and gotten the air knocked out of him. Struggled to reach the surface, flailing in darkness, propelling himself toward what he thought was sky and smashing headlong into the cement at the bottom of the pool.

Sweat broke out across Deirdre's neck and back and she sat up, gasping for breath. She imagined Arthur hanging there, a dark shadow under the water, life seeping out of him. Her fingertips tingled and her heart beat a tattoo in her chest. She smelled chlorine and death and gagged.

Breathe, she told herself as she tried to relax, counting a slow in and out, until finally the tension eased and her lungs filled completely. Shivering, she sat there for a few moments longer before sinking back into the pillow and pulling the blanket around her. The handlebars of the exercise bike looked like shadows outlined against the window. The open closet was a dark rectangle. She started to close her eyes but that feeling, like someone was chasing her and she couldn't get away, started to take hold.

Deirdre had long known that the truly scary stuff was in her own head. Doped up on Demerol after her car accident, she'd dreamed that her limbs were scattered down a hillside and she had to convince the EMTs to collect them for her. Or that she was on the table in an operating theater, a light beating down on her from above as doctors sawed off her leg, the surrounding stadium seats filled with onlookers. Or that her father was driving her home but she had to get back to the hospital because she'd left behind her hands. Even when she knew she was dreaming, she couldn't wake herself from those dreams. The memory of that paralyzing panic was far more vivid than any memory of the accident or of anything the doctors had done to her after.

She'd learned, over time, to avoid Demerol and redirect her mind. Anchor her attention on a sensation. Like the heavy sweet smell that was in the air, maybe a gardenia or night-blooming jasmine in the yard? The scent reminded her of hairspray. Aqua Net. Connect the dots and up popped Joelen Nichol, standing in front of her bathroom mirror years ago, spraying Deirdre's hair. Deirdre remembered the feel of that cool mist drying to a tight coating like a skim of egg white on every skin surface it touched.

Joelen. Who had stood at the front door hours ago and offered Deirdre a business card before bolting out to her car. Then called to offer any help she could. So she was a Realtor, not the movie star she'd dreamed of becoming.

There was a flash. A roll of distant thunder. Then the hiss of a light rain. The rain grew steadier, and the temperature dropped a few degrees. Deirdre pulled the blanket more tightly around her and let her mind drift back to a safer place, to the morning before school in sixth grade when Joelen Nichol had walked into her life.

CHAPTER 9

The sixth-grade girls at El Rodeo set their hair in pin curls and wore blouses with Peter Pan collars and circle pins. When Joelen Nichol appeared in their midst with her reddish-brown hair poufed out around her head like spun sugar, her eyes outlined in black, and mascara clumped on her stubby eyelashes, she seemed like a seismic anomaly. Her lipstick wasn't Cherries in the Snow or Coral Bells, but instead the color of a politically incorrect "flesh tone" crayon. In a world filled with Carols and Barbaras, Pattys and Nancys, even Joelen's name was exotic.

The first day Joelen came to school, Deirdre had been waiting outside for the bell to ring, her books pressed to her chest, feeling like a tree stump growing out of the concrete. As usual, the popular girls camped out at the picnic tables, their backs to outsiders, their books on the spaces between them, sending the clear message that there was no room for anyone else to squeeze in.

Deirdre didn't see Joelen walk in from the street. What she noticed was how, one by one, like a herd of prairie dogs picking up a scent, the boys shooting hoops on the other side of the fence had paused. She noticed how oblivious Joelen seemed to the stir she was creating, leaning nonchalantly against the chain-link fence that separated the picnic tables from the playground, adjusting her cinch belt, smoothing her blouse.

Maybe because they were both outsiders, doomed to perpetual orbit around Marianne Wasserman and her circle (or coven, as Joelen liked to call them), Deirdre and Joelen became fast friends. When the bell rang and the other girls gathered up their books, Deirdre fell in beside Joelen. They walked home from school together that afternoon. From that day on, they shared their lunches and talked on the phone before bed. On weekends they had sleep-overs — until the Saturday night when both their lives flew off the rails.

Deirdre turned over. It had taken her two years after the car accident before she could do that simple thing: turn over onto her injured side without aching. She'd always be uncertain on her feet without her crutch.

She closed her eyes. In her mind's eye she could walk unaided. She saw herself moving up the stairs and into the school where her friendship with Joelen had begun. She drifted through her memory of the building, down hallways and up staircases, remembering the smell of the cafeteria on fried fish day and the art room's peppermint smell of paste.

Deirdre didn't realize she'd fallen asleep until a thump yanked her awake. What time was it? Her wristwatch glowed: ten past two. She heard a shuffling sound, then a grunt. That was a person. The dogs would be growling and snarling if it were an intruder. It had to be Henry.

She tried to go back to sleep but was jarred awake by a louder thump and the sound of something being dragged. Annoyed, she grabbed her crutch and got out of bed. Paused for a moment behind the closed door and listened. She turned the knob and opened it a crack.

Henry, looking like a ninja in a black T-shirt and black pants tucked into motorcycle boots, was carrying the plastic garbage bag, which now looked to be full, from the bedroom hallway into the living room.

He disappeared into the front hall. Deirdre waited to hear the front door open and close but it didn't. Baby padded over and sniffed at Deirdre. She gave the dog a peremptory pat.

Henry reappeared. He yawned. Stretched. Turned around and scratched his head. Then he sank down on the couch and leaned back. Moments later she heard what sounded like a cow's rhythmic lowing. He was snoring.

She crept over to him. "Henry?" she said, and touched his shoulder. He collapsed a little farther onto his side, out cold.

Deirdre pulled off his boots, tilted him over onto his back, and put his feet up. Then she covered him with a plaid flannel stadium blanket that Arthur kept over the back of the couch. Warren Beatty — that was who Joelen used to say Henry resembled, and Deirdre had always been sure that Henry knew it. She'd once caught him practicing in the bathroom mirror, a Beatty-esque puckish grin morphing into a sleepy-eyed, seductive gaze. Back then he was forever pulling at his hair to get that forelock to come down over his eyes. It seemed utterly goofy and contrived to her, but girls ate it up.

These days, with his hollow cheeks and hooded eyes, his looks had sloped off into cool, sardonic Robert Mitchum territory.

She pushed his dark hair off his face and brushed his forehead with a kiss.

She'd started back to bed when she noticed that Henry had left the garbage bag sitting on the floor by the front door. She went over and poked at it with her crutch. It was folded over, not tied shut. She steadied herself against the wall and leaned over to open it. Out wafted a rich, earthy smell like patchouli. Weed, packed up but not disposed of. If the police arrived early in the morning to search the house, it would be the first thing they'd trip over.

Deirdre opened the front door. The rain had stopped and the air was much cooler. Up and down the street, outside lights were on but the windows in most of the houses were dark. In the distance a siren wailed.

Get rid of it. That was easier said than done. Where? The police would easily find it if she put it out in the alley with the trash. The trunk of her car seemed the safest bet, for the moment at least.

Deirdre took her time feeling her way over the uneven paving stones, pulling the bag across the dark courtyard and out to the street. She opened her car trunk and heaved the bag inside. Then she pressed the trunk lid down until the latch clicked. At least it was out of the house. Later she'd figure out how to dispose of its contents.

She returned to the house and crawled back into bed. This time she fell asleep almost instantly.

■ ■ ■ ■

SUNDAY,
MAY 25, 1985

■ ■ ■ ■

CHAPTER 10

The phone started ringing the next morning at eight thirty. Deirdre missed the first call and the second. The third got her out of bed. She caught the tail end of her mother leaving a message as she stumbled into the living room. ". . . I'll be there as soon as I can. By late tonight, I hope. Henry, Deirdre? I love you both."

Before Deirdre could pick up the phone, her mother hung up. Seconds later, the phone rang again. Deirdre grabbed it. "Hello?"

"Hello, Gloria?" Not her mother. A man's voice.

Deirdre took a breath. "No. This is her daughter, Deirdre."

"Ah, Deirdre. This is Lee Golden, a friend of your dad's." Deirdre knew the name. A set designer? "I just heard what happened and I wanted to reach out to you and Henry . . ." Deirdre sank into Arthur's lounge chair and held the phone away from her ear. When the phone went quiet, she thanked Lee Golden for calling and promised to let him know about funeral plans.

That was the first of a deluge of calls she took that morning. There'd been an article about Arthur's death in the paper. Callers danced around what they really wanted to know: How on earth could Arthur have drowned during a daily regimen that he claimed kept him as fit as any thirty-year-old? Deirdre thanked each caller, took names and phone numbers, and tried to get off the phone as fast as possible. Finally she surrendered and let the answering machine pick up, half listening as message after message was recorded.

None of it woke Henry, who lay on the couch in exactly the same position Deirdre had left him the night before. Deirdre let the dogs out and filled their food and water bowls. There wasn't much in the way of people food in the house other than leftover Chinese. Desperate for coffee, Deirdre found a dust-covered percolator in one of the kitchen cabinets, along with an unopened can of Maxwell House, its sell-by date long past. Soon the pot started to rumble and pop, sending out wafts of reassuring coffee aroma.

The doorbell startled her. Her first thought: the police were back. She wasn't dressed. Hadn't even combed her hair. At least the bag with her brother's pot was no longer in the house. She waited for the doorbell to chime again but it didn't. By the time she opened the door and looked out, no one was there, but four cellophane-wrapped food baskets were lined up just outside.

One by one, Deirdre carried them into the kitchen. One was from Linney's Delicatessen. Bagels, cream cheese, lox, babka, some rugelach. The card read *Condolences from Billy and Audrey Wilder.* Arthur would have been over the moon.

She poked open the cellophane wrapping and sniffed. The smell took her back to Sunday mornings when she'd stood, holding her father's hand in front of the sloping glass deli counter at Nate'n Al's on Beverly Drive, watching the clerk hand-slice belly lox from a long filet and dollop cream cheese into a container. He'd wrap up four whole smoked, bronze-skinned butterfish, which Arthur would fry the minute he got home. She remembered the feel of warm bagels through the paper bag she carried to the car.

She hooked a bagel and took a bite.

Closed her eyes. It had the perfect chewy crust, soft inside, and yeasty taste. In San Diego there was no such thing as a decent bagel, and you were lucky if you could find packaged, precut smoked salmon.

When Deirdre returned to the living room, Henry gave a phlegmy cough and turned over, his arm dropping like deadweight off the edge of the couch. He mumbled something, pushed himself up, and looked around. His expression said *Huh?*

"Morning, sunshine," Deirdre said. "Mom called."

Henry scowled. Then registered that she was eating. "What've you got there?"

"Billy Wilder's bagel." Deirdre took a bite. "Mmmmm. Delicious. Hungry?"

Henry uttered a profanity that Deirdre chose not to hear, then he rolled off the couch and stumbled toward the bathroom.

Coffee aroma reached Deirdre. She went into the kitchen for a cup and was on her way back when the phone rang again. She paused to listen to her father's greeting. *Beep.*

Another well-meaning friend of Arthur's, this time a woman, *Just calling to say how sorry I am to hear . . .*

Henry was back, standing in the doorway

and scratching his crotch. "So what did Mom say?"

"She said she'll try to get here by tonight. Take a shower, then get yourself a bagel and coffee."

"Coffee? You made coffee?"

Twenty minutes later, Henry was in the kitchen pouring himself coffee and eating a bagel. The dogs started barking and swarming the front door, and seconds later the doorbell rang.

Deirdre went to answer it. Standing on the doorstep was Sy Sterling, still trim but with a toupee where for years he'd worn an elaborate comb-over. Sy dropped his briefcase and held open his arms. Deirdre choked up and let herself be folded into a soft hug, enveloped in the scents of aftershave and cigar.

When she pulled away, Sy drew a handkerchief from his trouser pocket, blew his nose, and wiped away his own tears. "Such a pair we are."

She nodded and dabbed at her eyes with a tissue. "Everyone keeps saying it, but it really doesn't seem real."

"It should not happen," Sy said, squinting at her, his eyebrows sprouting white hairs like sparklers. "Arthur swam every damned day." He shook his head and his gaze shifted over Deirdre's shoulder.

Henry had come up behind Deirdre. He held two cups of coffee. "We're still in shock," he said. He gave Sy one of the cups and took his briefcase. Deirdre closed the door behind them as Sy followed Henry inside.

"You?" Sy said, giving Deirdre a sympathetic look. "You found him."

Deirdre's throat tightened and she swallowed a hiccup.

"You should have called me right away. I could have been here for you. They took him — where?"

"To the city morgue," Henry said.

Sy shuddered. "Of course. Unattended death. There will be an autopsy. And then?"

"Westwood Memorial Park," Deirdre said.

"Good. Your father? He would want his urn next to Marilyn's. You called Gloria?"

"She's on her way," Deirdre said.

"Good, good." Sy harrumphed. "Well, of course none of this is good. But it is what it is. Come, children." He headed for the dining table. "We need to talk." He settled into the chair at the head of the table, pulled a cigar from his pocket, and chewed on it. Then he sat back, shifted the cigar to the other corner of his mouth, and chewed on it some more. In all the years Deirdre had known Sy, she'd never seen him actually light a cigar.

"I promised your father, if anything happened to him, I would be here for you. A promise I hoped I would never have to keep." He reached across the table to clasp Henry's and Deirdre's hands. The diamond in his chunky pinkie ring caught the light. "I am here for you now. You know that? Right?" He gave Deirdre's hand a squeeze and held her gaze for a few moments, then shifted his attention to Henry. For a moment his expression seemed more questioning than reassuring. Then he sat back. "So." He undid the two straps and unlatched his battered briefcase.

Sy set his cigar on the table and took out a sheaf of papers. He handed Deirdre and Henry each a packet like he was dealing cards. Deirdre looked down at hers. On the first page, it said LAST WILL AND TESTAMENT.

"Your father? He was a dreamer, but I am afraid reality had him by the short hairs," Sy said.

"Not sure I like the sound of that," Henry said. "How bad is it?"

"There is still the house. You two will own it once the will is through probate. There is a mortgage, of course, but you will be able to get quite a bit more for the house, even" — he gestured to the water-stained ceiling — "the way it is. Your father may have already lined up a broker."

"I think he did," Deirdre said.

"Did he?" Henry said, and shot Deirdre a look. She hoped he'd let Joelen sell the house for them.

"So that is good news," Sy said. "Bad news is that between Arthur's debts and his assets, there is" — he paused, searching for the word — "overlap. When the estate pays what is owed you will be left with maybe twenty-five thousand. Of course I do not charge you for my legal services, but other expenses will have to come out of that. Burial and the funeral, of course."

"But they made a fortune —" Henry said.

"Made and spent it. And I should not have to remind you that until quite recently your father had certain obligations. Financial obligations. So some of his savings?" Sy said, looking steadily at Henry, *"Pffft."*

Henry stared back at Sy. For a moment it was a standoff.

"So," Deirdre said, "is anyone going to tell me what you're talking about?"

The dogs, who'd been lying on the rug in the living room, picked up their massive heads and started to bark, then scrambled over to the door before the bell chimed.

"Probably another fruit basket," Henry said.

The doorbell rang again, followed by a rap and a sharp voice. "Police. Please open the door. We have a warrant to search the premises."

Henry blinked. "Oh shit." He jumped to his feet, knocking over his chair, then lunged for the front hall. The dogs were in a frenzy, barking and leaping.

"Just a minute," Sy called out. "Henry, dammit, control your dogs."

Henry turned in circles, probably realizing belatedly that the garbage bag was no longer by the door where he'd left it. He shoved Baby out of the way and pulled open the door to the front closet, looking for what Deirdre knew wasn't there.

"Henry," Deirdre said sharply, gesturing her brother over. Under her breath, she said, "I got rid of it."

"Henry!" Sy said. He had one hand anchored on Bear's collar while the dog jumped up and down, oblivious. Baby was barking, standing with her paws up on the door where the finish had long ago been scratched away.

"Bear, down. Baby, down," Henry shouted. Both dogs went still. "Sit." The dogs scooted back on their haunches. Baby put her head between her paws and whined. Sy relinquished his hold on Bear and Henry grabbed the dogs' collars, one in each hand.

Multiple raps sounded on the door. Sy put a finger to his lips. He mouthed the words, *Let me do the talking,* then pulled open the door.

Four officers were on the other side. Deirdre recognized the one in the lead: Detective Sergeant Martinez.

"Officers. Can I help you?" Sy said, all traces of an accent gone.

Martinez looked past Sy to Deirdre and Henry. He glanced uneasily at the dogs. "We have a warrant to search the premises." He held up a piece of paper. "We'll need access to the garage and the cars. And, please, we'd appreciate it if you stay out of the way until we're done."

"May I see that warrant, please?" Sy asked.

"And you are?"

"Seymour Sterling." Sy took a breath and puffed out his chest, a banty prizefighter still. "I'm the family's attorney."

Henry and Deirdre nodded like a pair of bobbleheads.

Martinez handed over the paper. Sy took his time, sliding a pair of reading glasses from the inside pocket of his jacket. "Search residence," he said under his breath. "Property. Vehicles. . . ."

Deirdre's heart lurched. Would they search her car?

Sy ran his finger from line to line. "Ah, probable cause. . . ." He cleared his throat and read. " 'The Beverly Hills Police Department has been conducting an investigation into the death of Arthur Unger —' " His voice dropped again and turned to a mumble. As his eyes scanned the page, the scowl on his face intensified. He stepped aside and the officers swept into the house, Martinez taking up the rear.

CHAPTER 11

"Can they search my car?" Deirdre whispered to Sy once they were outside, getting settled at the patio table.

Sy gave her a narrow look. "Where is it?"

"Parked on the street."

"Then no."

At least that was a relief. But as Sy started going over the details of Arthur's will, Deirdre found herself barely able to follow. She strained to see over the bushes at the edge of the patio. The ground vibrated as the police investigators dropped item after item onto a plastic tarp spread out in the driveway. Crowbar. Tire iron. Shovel. Hedge clippers. Long-handled branch lopper. A candlestick lamp. All of them heavy blunt objects. Obviously they didn't think Arthur Unger's death had been an accident. He hadn't been taken ill. They were looking for a murder weapon.

Deirdre tried to make sense of it. Maybe

Arthur had surprised an intruder. He hadn't turned on any lights, so the intruder didn't realize he was out there. Arthur could be impulsive, belligerent, especially after a few drinks. Maybe he'd confronted the person. Thrown a punch, even. The intruder would have fended him off. Picked up something readily at hand. Something heavy. Swung it at Arthur and knocked him into the pool.

"Deirdre?" Sy was saying. "Do you understand what that means?"

"I'm sorry. I zoned out."

"I said, your father named you his literary executor. You'll need to go through his personal effects. His papers, letters, memos, photographs, keepsakes. Who knows what you will find. Early drafts of movie scripts. Unpublished manuscripts. He entrusted you with deciding what to preserve."

Deirdre thought of Arthur's memoir, sitting in the drawer in her bedside table. She was having fun reading it, but did it have historical or literary merit? "I'm hardly qualified —"

"Your father thought otherwise. Just take it item by item, one step at a time. First sort and cull. Then inventory what is worthy of preserving. If you are not sure, I can help. Try to imagine someone coming along a hundred years from now, trying to understand your father's Hollywood. What you are doing: conserving his piece of it. His legacy."

"Legacy." Henry snorted a laugh.

"Okay," Sy said, "your parents were not Comden and Green. But they were not hacks, either. Their films, and even some of the projects your father worked on later alone? Among the best of a certain breed. His collected works are emblematic of an era."

"Still, Mom would make a much better judge —" Deirdre started.

"You do not get to decide. Your father selected you."

It would be no small task, going through Arthur's papers. Deirdre hadn't been in his office on the second floor of the garage in ages, but she remembered it was lined with bookshelves and file cabinets. Then there was everything in the den. More probably in his bedroom. Maybe there were storage boxes. Her mother would know where all to look. It would be a huge chore, but secretly Deirdre was pleased. Flattered that her father had entrusted her with the task. "Of course I'll want your advice —" she started.

Henry interrupted. "So there are no other assets? No life insurance?"

"No life insurance."

"What about their movies?" Henry again. "Aren't there residuals?"

"There were none back then. Who knew television would be hungry for old movies?"

Henry hunched over the table, absorbing this news.

Before the police left, a technician took Henry's and Deirdre's fingerprints. Martinez explained it was to eliminate theirs from others that they lifted. Soon after that, Deirdre and Henry walked Sy out to his car.

Henry glanced up and down the street. "So Sy, is that it? Will they be back?"

"Always, they can come back. But they will need a new warrant." Sy stopped and turned to face them. "Listen to me, both of you. If the police do come back, you call me right away." He took out a business card and wrote a phone number on the back. "In case I am not in my office or in my car, here is my home phone. Anytime."

He handed the card to Henry and winked at Deirdre. Then he got into his car and rolled down the window. "I know you, Deirdre. You are a Girl Scout. You will want to help them with their investigation. But the police are not your friends. They want to fix blame and close the case. I know you think you have nothing to hide, but believe me, we all do."

As Deirdre watched him drive off she felt a chill as a light breeze rustled the leaves overhead. "So, tyell me zis," Henry said, lowering his voice and imitating Sy's accent. He put his arm around her and squeezed harder than he needed to. "Where's that bag?"

"In my car." Deirdre crossed the street and opened the trunk.

"You might have told me you'd taken it out of the house," Henry said. "Freaked the hell out of me."

"You're welcome."

"That, too." He reached for the bag.

"Back off." Deirdre pressed down with the end of her crutch on Henry's foot. Henry yelped in pain.

Deirdre opened the bag and foraged around in it, pulling out a half-dozen twist-tied baggies of loose pills. Another contained a handful of the pot she'd already smelled, along with a packet of rolling papers. She gave all that to Henry, then rummaged some more, past papers, old clothes, and what she thought at first were telephone directories but turned out to be Motion Picture Academy Players Directories, making sure she hadn't missed anything else that was illegal.

Henry was on a slow burn. "What are you going to do with the rest of it?"

"You heard Sy. I'm Dad's literary executor. I'm going take it up to his office and start executing. Maybe I'll throw all of it away. Maybe I'll keep it all. I get to decide. You just take care of that shit" — she indicated what she'd given him — "so none of it comes back to bite us."

Henry turned and stomped back into the house.

CHAPTER 12

Deirdre lugged the bag up the driveway to the garage. The door to her father's office turned out to be unlocked, so up she went, pulling the bag step by step behind her.

As kids, she and Henry had been forbidden to so much as knock when their parents were up there working, so it felt strange to put her hand on the knob and just open the door. The little apartment exhaled stale, musty air. The walls were papered with fraying grass cloth and the ceiling was waterstained. An electric typewriter with a plastic cover sat on a metal table on one side of the room. Against a wall was a sagging pullout couch. On the table next to it Deirdre spotted a dust-free circle. That's where the candlestick lamp the police confiscated must have stood. She raised one of the bamboo shades, releasing a cloud of dust motes, then cranked open one of the louvered windows.

The floor was stacked with piles of papers and videocassettes, and below a large mirror on the opposite wall stood two-drawer metal file cabinets. Deirdre pulled open a file drawer and poked through. Contracts. Correspondence. Bills and receipts.

Sort. Cull. Inventory. As Sy had said, she'd have to take it item by item, one thing at a time. It hardly mattered where she began.

She pulled out a file at random. Telephone bills starting in 1963. That had been around the year that her parents lost their contract at Fox and started using this space as their office. *Toss.*

The unlabeled folder behind it had about a dozen black-and-white stills from a movie she didn't recognize. She set it aside. *Keep.*

Another file folder contained stock certificates. One was from the DeLorean Motor Company. Hadn't they gone bankrupt? *Ask Sy.*

On top of the file cabinet Deirdre noticed a glass ashtray from Chasen's, the celebrity hangout where her parents had dined regularly. She needed another pile for personal keepsakes. Not for any literary legacy, but because she'd always loved the restaurant with its red leather banquettes, dark corners for secret trysts, and special tables set aside for moguls and stars. Even if there'd been nothing on the menu that an eight-year-old could stomach.

Four items and already she'd started four piles. She hadn't even cracked open the closet. Make that closets — there were two of them. She'd be at this for weeks, culling the trivial from the memorable from the valuable and setting aside items that signified her father's literary life.

Deirdre went out onto the landing and retrieved the black plastic bag. She sank down on the floor beside it and started sifting through the items that Henry said their father would have wanted him to throw away. Newspaper and magazine clippings, a restaurant review for a Chinese restaurant on Beverly Drive dated 1978, empty Cuban cigar boxes. All of it: *toss.*

Next she pulled out six Motion Picture Academy Players Directories, the annual compendium that listed every Hollywood actor. She'd spent hours and hours poring over directories like these when she was stuck home recuperating after the accident. In it were pages and pages of head shots of actors, most of whom could have strolled down Rodeo Drive and not turned a single head. And yet they were all members of the Screen Actors Guild. It just brought home the formidable odds against becoming a celebrity.

These were a straight run from 1963 to 1968. Deirdre opened the 1963 directory, flipped through until she found someone she recognized — sexy, sultry Edie Adams who sang the Muriel Cigar TV commercial. That ad had ended with a sly wink and the suggestive, *Why don't you pick one up and smoke it sometime,* delivered with a sensual subtlety that Madonna never could have managed. A few pages on, there was Donna Douglas, all wide-eyed with her Elly May blond curls tamed. Annette Funicello, Deirdre's favorite Mouseketeer, looking grown-up and bland.

Tucked between two pages, Deirdre came across a snapshot. She recognized the white rippled edges as an early Polaroid. She was five years old the Christmas her father got their first instant camera. He'd snapped a picture of Deirdre with her new Tiny Tears doll, Henry, and their mother, still in their bathrobes and seated on the white "snow" carpet around their tinselly tree. Deirdre had watched breathless for what seemed like forever until the second hand on her father's watch went all the way around and he opened the camera's trapdoor. Like magic, he peeled away the film and an image bloomed.

But the person in this faded snapshot wasn't Deirdre or Henry or their mother, and there was no Christmas tree. Instead it showed an attractive young woman, her collared blouse unbuttoned halfway, kneeling on the floor beside an end table and gazing at the camera with wide, kohl-rimmed eyes worthy of Keane. A mirror in the background reflected a window with a bamboo shade, and in front of it the photographer with the camera held to his face.

Deirdre realized with a jolt that the woman was kneeling in precisely the spot where she was sitting now. She turned the picture over. On the back, in red pen, were five asterisks.

The same girl's picture, much clearer and crisper, was in the Players Directory on the page where the snapshot had been tucked in. Second row from the top. *Melanie Hart,* the kind of white-bread, feel-good name — like Judy Garland or Hope Lange — that studios selected for young hopefuls.

Poor Melanie Hart. If she'd harbored any illusions that this photo session would lead to her big break, she'd been disappointed. Flipping the pages of the Players Directory, Deirdre found more faded Polaroid photographs, each with asterisks on the back. Her father favored buxom blondes and redheads, each of them photographed the same way, in the same spot.

Deirdre felt sick to her stomach. Her father had been taking advantage of young women who were desperate to break out in the film business. She stacked the photographs on the floor. They conjured the smell of My Sin and soiled sheets. At least her father had realized these needed to be destroyed. *Burn.* A pile she hadn't yet started.

Deirdre heard footsteps on the stairs and a moment later Henry loomed in the doorway. He had on a black leather bomber's jacket and badass cowboy boots. A motorcycle helmet — ice blue with an eagle sprouting red and yellow flames painted on it — hung from his hand. He tossed her a set of keys. "Here, so you can get in the house."

"Did you know about these?" she asked, pointing to the pile of pictures.

"Good God. I haven't been up here in ages." Henry took in the deflated garbage bag, then the Players Directories and the snapshots Deirdre had stacked on the floor. "Got to hand it to Dad. He was a pretty slick operator."

"You knew?"

Henry smirked. He picked up one of the pictures. "She doesn't look too unhappy, does she?"

"You can be such an asshole." She grabbed the picture back.

"And you can be so predictable. Dad was a jerk, but he wasn't Satan. That's how things were done in those days."

Those days. The 1960s had been a decade of upheaval in Hollywood. Her parents, along with most of Hollywood's "contract" talent, lost their jobs. From then on they worked project by project, from home, and didn't get assigned work unless some panel of studio honchos, usually decades younger than they, gave them a thumbs-up.

There had been upheaval at home, too. The car accident that crippled Deirdre had been in the fall of 1963. A year and a half later, she was finishing high school, Henry was flunking out of college, and their mother was making frequent trips to a commune in the desert.

"They knew," Henry said. "Every one of those girls knew the score."

Girls? *Women!* Deirdre wanted to shout back at him. "And I guess he was so proud of himself that he made you promise to destroy the evidence."

"You think this should be part of his legacy?" Henry poked a steel toe at the pictures. "If you'd just let me —" He leaned

118

down and picked up one of the photographs.

"Put it down."

Henry glared at her.

"I'm telling you now, Henry, if anything disappears without my say-so, even something like that, then I'm . . . I'm . . ."

"What'll you do? Tell Mom?"

"Don't push me. Okay?"

Henry scowled and dropped the picture. "Fine. Lucky you. What on earth are you going to do with all this shit?" He didn't wait for an answer, just turned on his heel and walked out.

Good question. What *was* she going to do with all of it?

As Henry stomped down the stairs, Deirdre picked up one of the Players Directories by the spine. Shook it. More photographs rained out. The thought of what must have gone on in this room, on that couch or on the floor, made her sick to her stomach. Her father had been luring hopeful young women with promises he'd never had the clout to fulfill.

She heard the rumble of a motorcycle starting, and the floor shook as the garage door opener beneath kicked in. A minute later, the floor shuddered again as the garage door shut.

But what shook Deirdre was that one of the photographs that had dropped out wasn't another pretty stranger. It was Joelen Nichol.

Deirdre picked up the picture. Joelen had been so young. Had Deirdre been in the house while her father was out here, indulging in this sordid hobby?

Disgusted, Deirdre shoved the picture into her pocket, grabbed her crutch, and started to struggle to her feet. She was half up when the crutch tip snagged on the plastic bag, slipped, and she went down with a howl of outrage. Dammit. Damn *him.* On top of everything else, if it hadn't been for Arthur, she wouldn't have to deal with the goddamned crutch at all. In a fury she shoved away the crutch and surrendered to what she knew was a sorry bout of self-pity. The chaos, the sheer volume of it, and the sadness of the tawdry, pathetic minutiae she'd have to paw through — it was too much.

The crying jag left her with a pounding headache and an aching chest. Defeated and deflated, she dried her eyes on the hem of her T-shirt, then tried to pull herself together as she surveyed the room. The piles she'd started. The file cabinets she'd barely cracked open. None of this had to be taken care of today, or even this week.

She scooted over so she could reach her crutch and set it carefully on the carpet, realizing as she stood that the crutch had torn a hole in the plastic bag. She bent to gather up the items that threatened to spill out of it. Among them was what looked like an armful of crumpled yellow netting, brittle with age. It was wrapped around a flat wooden box. On the box's lid was a little metal shield with the word SHEFFIELD burned into it. She opened the box. Inside, set into a red flocked cardboard inset, was a knife with an old-fashioned antler grip. The blade was long and tapered. A silver cap covering the butt was engraved with the fancy initial *n*.

N for Nichol? Deirdre felt a chill creep down her back. She snapped the box shut and began to wrap it up again, her mind lurching ahead. *Toss? Keep?* That's when she realized that the decaying netting with which she was wrapping the box was the tulle skirt of a dress with a high-necked lace bodice and long sleeves. She drew back, her hand over her mouth. The yellow satin underskirt was covered with dark stains. Blood?

There should have been more blood. That was what one of the expert witnesses had testified at the inquest into Tito Acevedo's murder. On the carpet under Tito's body. On the nightgown Joelen had been wearing when she stabbed him. On the nightgown Bunny had been wearing when she said she'd cradled him as he breathed his last. Well, here was more blood: on the dress Deirdre had been convinced made her look like a movie star when she'd borrowed it from Bunny Nichol to wear it to the party the night Tito was killed.

CHAPTER 13

Deirdre dropped the dress. She'd been fast asleep, passed out in Joelen's bedroom when Bunny's final fight with Tito had turned lethal. Hadn't she?

It had been long past Deirdre's bedtime when Bunny sent her and Joelen upstairs to bed. Instead the girls had sat at the top of the stairs and watched the party wind down. Deirdre's parents had been among the first to leave, and Deirdre had run down to kiss them good night.

After the rest of the guests had gone home, after Bunny and Tito had retired, Deirdre and Joelen had padded downstairs. They smoked lipstick-stained cigarette butts left in the ashtrays and polished off the remains of pink champagne in abandoned flutes and vodka in martini glasses. They'd staggered about giggling, stuck fat black and green olives on the tips of their fingers, and gorged on leftover crab dip, pâté, and shrimp cocktail. They'd gotten slaphappy and performed a boozy duet, an a cappella "Let Me Entertain You." They twirled. And twirled. So much that Deirdre staggered outside and puked in the bushes. After that, she lay on the grass beside Joelen and stared up at the sky. *So this is what it feels like to be drunk,* she'd thought as stars seemed to streak across the sky like meteors and the ground felt as if it were flipping her like a pancake. She rolled over and threw up again and again until there was nothing left.

She must have passed out on the lawn, because her memory of what happened after that was fragmentary at best. She did not remember going back into the house. She did not remember climbing the stairs, as she must have, to get to Joelen's bedroom. She hadn't heard Bunny and Tito fighting. She hadn't heard Joelen leave the bedroom.

All she remembered was leaving the house herself. Being guided through a dark tunnel that smelled of camphor and floor wax, down a narrow, steep staircase — not the grand staircase in the Nichols' house, which was like something you'd expect Ginger Rogers to dance down. Wondering why her father had come back to get her in the middle of the night. Shivering in her pajamas, she'd stumbled out to his car through chilly night air.

That had been the last normal walk she ever took.

She had no idea when she'd taken off the beautiful lemon-colored dress. And was this the knife that had killed Tito? How on earth had her father ended up with them both? And what was she supposed to do with them now?

Deirdre stuffed the dress and the knife back into the torn plastic bag, shoved the bag in a closet, and slammed the door shut. Then she stumped down the garage stairs and across the garden. Back in the kitchen, she washed the dust and sour smell from her hands. If only she could erase the stench that the photographs and the stained dress had left in her head. She felt like Pandora, trying to figure out what to do with what she'd found in the box.

The answering machine was flashing "Full." Deirdre half listened to the messages, intending to write down the names of people to call back when funeral plans were final. But instead she just sat there, staring at the machine and letting the voices wash over her.

Until the message that was not from a well-wisher. "This is Detective Martinez. I need to speak to Deirdre Unger." Deirdre sat forward, feeling a wave of dread. She was thoroughly rattled by what she'd found in her father's office and in no frame of mind to answer questions.

Before Deirdre could decide what to do, Detective Martinez's voice was drowned out by the dogs stampeding out of Henry's bedroom and skidding into the front hall moments before the doorbell chimed.

Detective Martinez's voice on the answering machine was giving Deirdre his telephone number as she peered out the window. A police cruiser was parked out front. She stood there, unable to answer the door, listening to her own breathing and the next message of condolence on the answering machine. Deirdre's armpits were damp, and butterflies fluttered in her stomach.

If the police do come back, you call me right away. Sy's voice came back to her. But he'd handed his card to Henry, and Henry had gone out.

At the knock at the front door, Deirdre sank down onto the floor under the window, her heart in her throat. Moments later she heard a sharp rap at the kitchen door. The dogs were going wild, racing from the front door to the kitchen. Any minute the police would come around to the back, look through the sliding glass doors, and see her

126

cowering. Were the doors even locked? Would the police try to open them? Would they break in?

Deirdre pulled a phone book from the drawer under the phone. She found the page that began STANDISH and drew her finger down the column looking for STERLING. Was Sy even listed?

And then, just like that, the dogs stopped making their racket. The knocking stopped. Deirdre peeked out the window. Martinez and a uniformed officer were getting back into the police car. Car doors slammed.

Could it be that easy? Were they just going to give up and drive off? Deirdre drew back and waited to hear the engine start. She was still waiting minutes later when the phone rang. She didn't reach for it. It had to be Detective Martinez or the other policeman, watching the house and making the call from their car phone.

But when the answering machine picked up Deirdre heard a familiar voice after the beep. "Deirdre? Are you there? I don't know if you got my earlier message. I hope the fruit basket we sent over got there —"

Deirdre picked up the phone. "Joelen?" she whispered, even though she knew the police couldn't hear her.

"Hello?" Joelen said.

Deirdre put the receiver closer to her mouth. "Hi. I'm here. Can you hear me?"

"Yes, I . . . Is everything okay? I mean, of course it's not. But you know what I mean. Is it?"

"The police are back. They want to talk to me. I'm here all alone —"

"Do they know you're there?"

"No. Maybe. My car's parked out front."

"And they're — ?"

"Sitting outside in their car. Waiting. Maybe I should just go out there and get it over with. I have nothing to hide."

Joelen laughed a not-funny laugh. "Honey, everyone has something to hide."

Deirdre thought about the yellow dress and couldn't argue the point. She heard a car pulling up in front and peered out. A bright blue van had parked behind the police cruiser. KABC-TV NEWS 7 was emblazoned on the side. A slender blonde in a dark pantsuit hopped out and went over to the window of the police car. She was chatting with Martinez's partner when a white-and-blue KNBC van pulled up and stopped across the street.

"Shit," Deirdre said. "Two news vans just pulled up."

"Okay. That's it. You need to get out of there. Now. Go out the back."

"But my car —"

"Don't take your car. I'll pick you up. Go out in the alley and start walking north. I'll be there in five."

"But what if someone —"

But Joelen had hung up. Deirdre stared at the dead handset. She remembered a moment years ago when Joelen had climbed onto the roof of her pool house and dared Deirdre to come up and join her. Henry had been there, too, and while Deirdre was screwing up her courage, Henry shoved her into the pool.

"That's what happens when you hesitate," Joelen had told her when she'd climbed out. Even now Deirdre's face grew hot, remembering how Joelen and Henry cracked up because Deirdre's white pants had turned semitransparent.

She hung up the phone, lurched to her feet, and peered outside again. A man who must have been in the first news van was filming the pantsuited woman talking into a microphone in front of the house. The passenger door of the second van opened, and a man in a suit followed by another man wearing a T-shirt and jeans and carrying a camera got out and headed up the path to the front door.

The dogs started up again. The doorbell

rang. Deirdre felt as if she were under siege. Joelen was right. She had to get out of there. Now. She grabbed her jacket and messenger bag and exited through the sliding glass doors. Crossed the yard. Took a quick glance down the driveway to where the hood of the police car was just visible.

She slipped down the narrow passageway between the chain-link pool surround and the garage. Her nose tickled with a smell, ever so faint. Was something burning? It reminded her of the once pervasive metallic smoke that backyard incinerators belched decades ago before they were banned.

It wasn't until she was in the alley, enveloped in the smells of eucalyptus and garbage ripening in the metal cans lined up behind each house, that she realized she was wearing the Harley T-shirt and drawstring pants she'd slept in. She stayed close to the edge, careful that the tip of her crutch didn't skid on the layer of grit and broken glass coating the broken asphalt, checking over her shoulder to see whether the police or the TV newspeople had picked up her scent.

She was halfway up the block when a dark sedan started coming toward her, kicking up a cloud of dust. A hand waved out the window and then the car pulled up alongside Deirdre and the passenger door opened. Deirdre threw in her crutch and hopped in after it. She slammed the door and sat back, resting one hand on the dash and the other over her chest. Her heart was pounding and she was sure she was about to throw up.

"Just breathe," Joelen said, accelerating, the tires spinning on loose gravel. "Sit back and relax." The car emerged from the alley. No cruisers or media vans were there to meet them. Joelen pulled out onto the street, stopped at a corner, and turned north. "You okay?"

Deirdre took a deep breath, held it for a moment, then blew out.

"You know," Joelen went on, "you'll have to talk to them eventually. The police. They don't just give up and leave you alone. But you can do it on your own terms."

CHAPTER 14

Deirdre stared out Joelen's car window, feeling her heart slow and the sweat that coated her forehead and neck cool. Familiar and unfamiliar houses flew past. Joelen drove with her hand resting lightly on the steering wheel. She still bit her fingernails down to the quick. Though it was more than twenty years later, she didn't look all that different from the picture that her father had taken of her in his office.

"What?" Joelen asked, giving her a sideways glance. "Have I got a booger hanging out of my nose?" And, Deirdre noted, she still said exactly what she thought.

"Sorry," Deirdre said. "Didn't mean to be ogling you. It's been a crazy day. The police came this morning to search the house and the garage. Now they're back to talk to me. In the meanwhile, I found out that I'm my dad's literary executor, which means I have to deal with all of his shit. Like, one of the things he's got? Remember your mom's yellow dress?" She hadn't meant to say any of that, but there it was.

"My *mother's* yellow dress?"

"The one she let me wear to her party . . . you know, that night."

"That . . . ?" At first Joelen looked puzzled. Then, "Whoa, whoa, whoa." She pulled the car over to the curb and stopped. She turned in her seat and faced Deirdre. "What are you talking about?"

"The dress your mother let me wear to her party that night. It was in a pile of stuff that Dad wanted Henry to throw away."

"So how did your father end up with it?"

"All I know is that he did."

Joelen stared out through the windshield, her brow wrinkled, shaking her head. "I have no idea how your father got that dress," she said at last, turning back to Deirdre. "Cross my heart and hope to die."

Deirdre took a shuddering breath. "Was I there when Tito got stabbed?"

"You were in the house."

"But was I in the room?"

"Why would you think that?"

"Because the dress. It's got dark stains on it."

"And you think — ?"

133

"I don't know what to think. I'm just asking."

Joelen held Deirdre's gaze for a long moment. "No, honey. You were not. You were fast asleep in your jammies."

"You're sure?"

"Sure as hell." Joelen looked over her shoulder and pulled away from the curb. "I was there. You were not."

Deirdre leaned back and felt the tension drain from her neck and shoulders.

After a long silence, Joelen said, "I'm sorry we didn't keep in touch."

"Me too. I tried to call. I wrote."

"I was trying to become invisible. Besides, they sent me away." Joelen stopped at Sunset, signaled right, and waited as cars streamed past.

"Where?"

"After the verdict, they sent me to juvie." She pulled into traffic. "Which wasn't really as bad as you might imagine. I met some fascinating people." She laughed. "Then the judge sent me to live with my aunt Evelyn in Des Moines, for God's sake. Not so fascinating. Fields and fields of wheat. I finished high school there. For a year I was Jennifer, so no one knew who I really was or why I was there, and I was damn well going to keep it that way. I didn't make a single friend."

"You must have gone bonkers."

"I did. A little." Joelen gave a bitter laugh. "Poor Aunt Evelyn, God bless her. She had one black-and-white television set and she had it on all the time. She was addicted to the *Price Is Right, Queen for a Day, Search for Tomorrow, Guiding Light.*" Joelen rolled her eyes. "And, oh yeah, wrestling. The only books in the house were steamy romance novels. And the Bible, of course. We went to the mall every Saturday, church every Sunday." She signaled right. "Supposedly that was more therapeutic than living with my mom. I had to stay until I was eighteen."

She turned into the familiar driveway and stopped at a metal gate that hadn't been there years earlier. NO TRESPASSING and PROTECTED BY FIVE STAR SECURITY signs hung on it. Joelen rolled down the window, reached out, and pressed a button on an intercom box.

It took a while for anyone to answer. At last a man's tinny voice croaked out, "Yeah?" "Hey, it's me," Joelen said.

Slowly the gate swung open and Joelen drove through and up the winding driveway. Deirdre turned and looked over her shoulder. The gate began to swing shut.

The rest of the driveway up to the house

looked familiar: a tennis court, then farther along a carport sheltered under a bank of bougainvillea. Alongside the carport a white fence surrounded a kidney-shaped pool and pool house. The driveway curved back on itself and climbed. From above Deirdre could see that the pool was half-full, and the water in it had turned a sickly green.

Joelen stopped alongside a motorcycle in a broad parking area in front of the house, just feet from the front door. Deirdre picked up her crutch and started to open the door.

"Deeds?" Joelen said. The familiar nickname that only Henry still called her brought Deirdre up short. "I heard about what happened to your leg," Joelen said, her eye on the crutch. "Tough break. I didn't find out until I got back from Iowa. I tried to call you, but you were already away at college."

Deirdre had spent the summer after she graduated from high school at UC San Diego and fallen in love with art history. She'd been desperate to get away from Beverly Hills, to meet people who didn't know her as either Joelen Nichol's onetime best friend or the crippled girl everyone pitied.

Joelen's look turned serious. "So why do the police want to talk to you?"

136

"All I know is Sy said if they came back, not to talk to them alone."

"Sy." Joelen blinked. "You mean, it wasn't an accident."

Deirdre looked down into her lap.

"How awful. I'm sorry," Joelen said. "But they can't think it was you."

"I don't know what they think. And I didn't want to find out when I was alone."

Joelen pushed open the car door and got out. Deirdre followed her to the columned portico. "Listen to Sy," Joelen said, "and do exactly what he tells you. I don't even want to think what might have happened to me if I hadn't."

"Is he still your mom's lawyer?"

"And friend. He's really been there for us. It's great that you've got him in your corner. And your family, too, of course. Where's your mom?"

"Living in the desert on a monastic retreat. She'll show up. Eventually."

"Here's a scary thought," Joelen said, holding the front door of the house open for Deirdre. "Marooned on a desert island with your mother and my mother. *Gilligan's Island* meets . . ."

"Dallas," Deirdre said. It was a game she and Joelen used to play, and any other time Deirdre would have added on with *wear-*

137

ing . . . or *eating* . . . or *singing* . . . But at that moment, Deirdre couldn't have come up with anything else clever if her life depended on it. All she wanted to do was talk to Sy.

CHAPTER 15

Deirdre stood for a moment in the massive two-story entryway. She hadn't been in this house in more than twenty years. The once uneven stucco walls of the entryway were paneled over with a light wood, like a patterned birch. The floor, once rich terra-cotta tile, was now inset with slabs of peach-colored marble. The generous staircase was carpeted in thick white pile, the wrought-iron handrail that had once wound up to the second floor replaced by opulent carved and gilded balusters. Hanging from the ceiling was a massive Lucite and crystal chandelier that would have been right at home in a Las Vegas hotel.

A young man, dark and handsome, looked down at Deirdre from the landing halfway up the stairs. Deirdre felt a jolt of recognition. Before she could process it, Joelen pulled her across the entryway and down two steps into a white-carpeted living room, its windows swathed in gauzy white. "Bunny!" Joelen called out as she headed for the door at the far end of the living room.

Deirdre remembered how weird it had seemed the first time she'd heard Joelen call her mother *Bunny* instead of *Mom.* Then it turned out to be a '60s thing. As usual, the Nichols were ahead of the curve and the Ungers were behind it.

Deirdre looked around the living room. It, too, had changed over time. Couches and ottomans that had once been covered in a floral brocade were now cream-colored linen. The white grand piano was still there, but many of the other furnishings Deirdre recalled — carved and inlaid Versailles-inspired credenzas, tables, and chairs; massive bucolic landscape paintings — were gone. She wondered if the odd combination of opulence and minimalist elegance was some interior designer's vision, or whether the furnishings had been sold off to pay bills.

One of the pieces that did remain was a towering portrait of Bunny, still hanging in an elaborate frame over the marble fireplace. She was sitting in one of the missing chairs and wearing a pale blue, diaphanous Greek goddess dress. Her black hair was brushed to the side, curls cascading over one shoulder. Standing at her knee was a very young Joelen looking like a stiff little soldier in a starched white eyelet pinafore.

Still there too, looking marooned in the half-empty room, was a white lacquered credenza that had held a stereo system. After school, Deirdre and Joelen used to hang out here and hope Tito would show up and demonstrate the fine points of tango. He'd been agile, electrically handsome, and he'd smelled of sweat and cigars and a musky cologne. Before he'd take Deirdre or Joelen in his muscular arms, he'd turn the stereo up so loud that Deirdre could literally feel the floor vibrate as the violin bow struck the strings. Then he'd stand tall, even though he wasn't all that tall, and stick his chest out, his silk shirt unbuttoned to reveal a large medal hanging from a thick gold chain against a field of dark chest hair. His stance reminded Deirdre of a toreador addressing a bull. He'd offer her his hand, and she'd let hers float down to meet it. When it did, he'd twirl her once, twice, and then whip her close in time to the musical flourish, his palm anchored firmly against her lower back and his thigh pressed hard between her legs. "Eess not about the esteps," he'd whisper, his voice deep and intoxicatingly accented, his breath hot in her ear. "Eess about the *co-NECK-shun*."

Later, the memory of him pressed against her had been enough to make her go all tingly. Deirdre wondered if there were still tango records stored inside the credenza on the shelf below the sound system.

"Bunny," Joelen called out again.

The door at the far end of the living room opened, and Elenor "Bunny" Nichol entered, regal in a gold caftan, her black hair piled high on her head. At first she appeared tall, but as Deirdre got closer she seemed to shrink. Face-to-face, she was actually shorter than Deirdre.

"My dear!" Bunny held Deirdre at arm's length and took in her leg, her crutch. Like Joelen, she hadn't seen Deirdre since before she was crippled, but her gaze didn't linger. She reached for Deirdre's hand. "I heard the terrible news. I am so sorry about Arthur." Her voice was low and resonant and there was real emotion in her eyes.

"Thank you. I —" Deirdre choked and the words caught in her throat. She swallowed. "Thanks, Mrs. Nichol."

"Bunny, please. You know, your mother and I were pals. We were both chorus girls at Warner Brothers. We used to play hearts in full makeup and costume during our lunch breaks on the set." Deirdre's expression must have betrayed her because Bunny said, "Does that surprise you?"

"A little. My mother didn't have many friends." Deirdre didn't add that although her mother had once aspired to act, she had come to dismiss actresses as self-indulgent narcissists. Talking to one, she used to say, was like getting trapped in a mirror.

"Your mother was whip smart," Bunny said. In other words, never made it out of the back row whereas Bunny had quickly moved front and center. "And your father was a charmer. He made friends for both of them."

Friends? Deirdre cringed. Like the women he'd photographed up in his office? Joelen saved her from a response by saying, "Bunny, the police think someone killed Arthur and they want to question Deirdre."

The words left Deirdre momentarily stunned. It was true, of course, but she hadn't let herself think about it in such stark terms.

"Oh dear," Bunny said. "How can we —"

"She needs to call Sy Sterling," Joelen said.

"Of course," Bunny said. "Come. Use the phone in my office."

Moments later, Deirdre was sitting at the glass-topped desk in Bunny's study. Bunny knew the number and dialed for her. Joelen watched from the door.

"Attorney's office." The smoker's voice of Vera, Sy's secretary, brought back a memory of the second-floor law office in Westwood Village. Open the door with the pebble glass inset and there Vera would be at her desk, a pencil stuck in her hair and a stash of crayons and drawing paper hidden in the supply closet. The smells of Vera's cigarettes and Sy's cigars mingled in the dimly lit corridor where they used to let Deirdre ride her tricycle up and down while Sy met with Arthur in his office.

Deirdre breathed a sigh of relief when Vera put her right through. "Sy? It's Deirdre. You said to call if the police came back? Well, they did. First they called and left a message that they wanted to talk to me. Then they came to the house. When I didn't answer, they just sat out front and waited. Then TV news vans pulled up —"

"Where are you now?" Sy said, interrupting. "Are you all right?"

"I'm fine. Just rattled. My friend Joelen came and got me. I'm at her house."

"Joelen?" Sy seemed surprised. "Elenor Nichol's daughter?"

"She was my best friend in high school. Dad was supposed to meet with her to talk

144

about selling the house." Silence on the other end of the line. "She's a Realtor now."

"I know," Sy said.

"Where should I go? I can't stay here." Deirdre swallowed, trying to tamp down the hysteria that threatened to envelop her. "What do the police want?"

"Probably just answers to routine questions. They are investigating a suspicious death. You discovered it. But I do not like them harassing you at the house. And I really do not like newspeople showing up. Schmucks, all of them." Sy's outrage was comforting. "We need to get out in front of this. Go in and talk to that detective." He must have covered the receiver because she could hear muffled voices, then, "Can you meet me in front of City Hall in about an hour? I will call you when I arrive."

Deirdre covered the receiver on her end. "Joelen, can you drive me over to City Hall? Not now. When Sy calls back in an hour."

"Of course," Joelen said.

"I'll be there," Deirdre told Sy, feeling relieved. She wasn't eager to talk to the police, but taking action, any action, felt infinitely better than waiting to be mugged.

"Can you find a scarf?" Sy asked. "Or sunglasses? Just in case reporters are hanging around. I don't want anyone to recog-

145

nize you on the way in."

"Recognize me?" Deirdre asked, startled. "Why would anyone recognize me?"

"There are already news vans at your house. Who do you think they are looking for?"

"My father was just a writer, for God's sake. Why do they even care?"

"Your father drowned. And years ago he failed to save Fox Pearson from drowning."

"Who remembers him?"

"No one would except that he died with so much drama. In a swimming pool. And your father tried to save him. The press loves it when history tries to repeat itself."

CHAPTER 16

"Scarf? Sunglasses? *Pffft.* Amateur hour." Bunny Nichol rubbed her hands together, wiggled her fingers, and blew on the tips. "We can do better than that." She threw open the door to her dressing room. It was half the size of the master bedroom, which itself was about the size of the entire first floor of Deirdre's house in San Diego. Out wafted the scent of orange blossoms.

Instantly Deirdre was transported back to when she and Joelen spent hours in Bunny's dressing room, sampling her skin creams and applying her lipstick — a strawberry red called Fraises des Bois — and trying on gowns and costumes. Chiffon and satin, feathers and sequins, leather and metallic lamé. Then adorning themselves with pounds of costume jewelry.

But the last thing Deirdre needed right now was a getup that drew attention to herself. "Even with a paper bag over my head I'll still be recognizable. I can't get around without this," she said, indicating her crutch.

"When I'm done with you, you'll be able to bump right into them, crutch and all, and they won't so much as blink. You'll see."

"Bunny used to be a magician's assistant," Joelen said. "She once performed with the legendary John Jasper."

"Deirdre's probably never heard of him, have you, dear?" Bunny said. "He wasn't a celebrity so much as a magician's magician. Brilliant guy. He could do anything. Make anything disappear, including the teeth right out of your mouth. He was injured doing the bullet catch onstage in Piccadilly. Died a day later. Death by misadventure. If the police had understood how the trick was done, they'd have done more investigating." She shook her head, then gave a wicked smile and a wave of her hand. "In John's early days, I was the eye candy. That's the whole point of having an assistant. To distract. Though he didn't need me. He was that damned good. But here we have the opposite problem." She pursed her lips. "We don't want you to disappear. We just want to make you appear invisible."

Invisibility. Now there was a goal worth aspiring to.

The facing walls of the dressing room were mirrored, reflecting back an infinitely repeating version of Deirdre's frazzled self. Deirdre dropped her gaze to Bunny's makeup table. It was also mirrored, and sitting on top was a gilt-framed ink-and-watercolor portrait of Bunny. She addressed the viewer with a direct gaze, a knowing gleam in her eyes, her chin resting on her curled fingers. Tendrils of silky black hair framed her face. She looked like a grown-up, worldly, and slightly naughty version of a Breck girl.

Outside the border framing Bunny's face, the illustrator had drawn a heart-shaped bottle filled with brilliant blue liquid. The word *CERULEAN* was lettered in gold on the bottle, and beneath it in script were the words *Fragrance for women.* The liquid in the bottle matched the brilliant blue the artist had used to color Bunny's eyes.

Bunny grabbed the framed picture and laid it facedown on the dressing table. "No one's supposed to see that," she said. "It's all very hush-hush, so you must promise me you won't tell a soul. They're not launching the product for a while yet, and I don't want to jinx it. But isn't it exciting?"

Joelen caught Deirdre's attention in the mirror and rubbed her fingers and thumb together. "Mom will be the official spokes-person."

"A little old-style Hollywood glamour," Bunny said. "Still sells. If Sophia Loren can do it, why not Elenor Nichol? I've still got it." She stood for a moment, chin up, hip cocked, admiring herself in the mirror.

"Yes, Mother dear." Joelen rolled her eyes. "Remember the last time Deirdre was here? You let her borrow that yellow dress."

"Did I?" Bunny said.

"Lace with a high neck," Deirdre said. "It was the most gorgeous dress I'd ever worn, before or since."

"Oh dear, that is a sad story." Bunny gave Deirdre a sharp, appraising look. "You could probably still get into that dress. I'm sure I could not."

Deirdre shivered at the thought of actually stepping into the torn, soiled dress. How different it would be from when she'd first put her arms through the sleeves on the night of her last sleepover.

That night, while the caterers were busy downstairs setting up for the party, Joelen and Deirdre sat and watched from the floor of this dressing room as Bunny got ready. First she "put on her face," as she called it. Foundation, then powder brushed on over it, then a darkish powder applied, she explained, to shorten her nose and accentuate cheekbones. Next Bunny did her eyes, painting a thick band of turquoise eyeliner on the lids — a trick, she said, to make her eyes look even bluer than they were. Over that, with a steady hand she painted a narrow black line that echoed Elizabeth Taylor's Cleopatra.

Joelen had stood behind her mother, brushed out her hair, and pinned it up in a silky French twist. Bunny artfully pulled out strands to frame her face. Then Joelen sprayed until the air in the dressing room was moist and heavy with scent.

One by one, Bunny had pulled cocktail dresses from the closet, holding each up to consider. Satin, lace, chiffon, some in saturated jewel tones like colors of the millefleur glass paperweight on the makeup table, others pastel, like eggs in an Easter basket.

Bunny had held up an emerald-green satin sheath. "Not my color," she said. She held the dress under Joelen's chin. Joelen looked past her mother at her own reflection in a mirror. Without a word, some agreement seemed to pass between them. Bunny unzipped the dress and held it open; Joelen took off her pants and top and stepped into it. Bunny unhooked Joelen's bra and Joelen slipped out of it and poured her breasts into the dress's boned bodice. Deirdre felt like one of the little mice who watched Cinderella's transformation as Bunny zipped Joelen into the dress, turned her to face the mirror, and pinched the fabric on either side of her narrow waist.

The overall effect was breathtaking. The intense green made Joelen's complexion glow, and the contrast set fire to the reddish streaks in her hair. Her soft, full cleavage swelled into the plunging sweetheart neckline.

Clap. Clap. Clap.

The sound had startled Deirdre. It was Tito, standing in the doorway and staring in at them. He was dressed in a formfitting black silk shirt that was open halfway down his chest.

Joelen blushed, and her hands flew up to cover her breasts. Tito strode over to her, put a finger under her chin, and waited until she raised her eyes to meet his. "Do not be ashamed. You are beautiful like your mother." He started to lean in toward her, as if he were about to give her a kiss, then turned and gave Bunny a peck on the cheek. "These young ladies," he said, winking at Deirdre, "they should come to the party." Then he strode off, leaving behind a wake of musky cologne.

"Oh, could we? Can we?" Joelen asked Bunny. "Please, please, please!"

After a few moments' hesitation, Bunny said, "Oh, all right. You girls can answer the door and take coats. Stay for a little while. But after that it's up to bed. Understood?" She set aside a few dresses for Deirdre to pick from, then left to check on the caterers.

Deirdre chose the pale yellow cocktail dress with a swishy tulle skirt and a lace bodice. With a borrowed bra of Joelen's, stuffed with Kleenex, the dress fit perfectly and made her feel like a fairy princess. By the time both girls were dressed and Joelen had finished fussing with her own and Deirdre's hair and makeup, Deirdre barely recognized the girls who looked back at them in the mirror. Joelen looked like Ann-Margret, the seductive redhead she'd seen singing "Bye, Bye, Birdie" on the *Ed Sullivan Show.* Deirdre looked like a complete stranger with dark, dramatic eyes, the lashes heavy with mascara, her lips strawberry red and glistening. Her hair was teased and lacquered, her face a smooth veneer of makeup that felt spackled on.

Deirdre and Joelen had made their way down as the first guests, including Arthur and Gloria, were arriving. Guests took turns playing the piano, and at one point Bunny urged Joelen to step up and sing "Let Me Entertain You."

"Sing out, Louise!" Bunny trilled near the end, before Joelen morphed from girlish coquette to sly seductress. When Joelen got to the part where she promised if they were *real good,* she'd make them *feel good,* not a single ice cube clinked as the room turned utterly silent. Joelen and Bunny sang the final crescendo together. Deirdre could still see the two of them standing side by side, flushed and beaming as the piano's chords reverberated. An awkward silence followed.

In the endless rehashing in the press of what happened that night, a photograph of Joelen and Bunny appeared in newspapers and magazines. It showed them standing, arm in arm in front of the white grand piano in their similarly low-cut, formfitting satin sheaths. Deirdre had been standing next to Joelen, also arm in arm, but her image had been cropped from the frame. The only evidence she'd been there was the corner of her tulle skirt and her arm, the wrist laden with borrowed rhinestone bracelets.

Joelen's question, "I wonder what happened to that dress?" brought Deirdre back to the present. Joelen raised her eyebrows at

Deirdre. *Ask,* she mouthed.

But before Deirdre could form a question, Bunny swept her arms like a conductor silencing the instruments. "Magic," she said, gazing out in front of her, eyes unfocused, as if watching the word hover before her. "It's all about misdirection. Make the audience attend to what *you* want them to see. What will be compelling enough to divert their attention or, in our case, make them tune out — that is the trick."

Delicately Bunny tapped her chin with long red fingernails and stared at Deirdre in the mirror. She opened one closet door, then another, and another, finally emerging with a half-dozen garments slung over her arm. None of them were cocktail dresses. "Stand up straight. And, please, would you take off that appalling top. It's making my teeth itch."

Obediently Deirdre pulled off Henry's Harley T-shirt and stood there in her bra and drawstring pants.

"Hmmm." Bunny held up what looked like a gray cotton mechanic's jumpsuit and squinted. She pursed her lips in disapproval and dropped it on the floor. A pale purple sweatshirt minidress with a hood met the same fate. A black-and-gold floor-length African dashiki joined the pile. Next she held up what looked like a stewardess uniform — navy pencil skirt and tailored jacket. "Maybe," she said, and set it aside.

Finally Bunny considered a simple shirt-waist dress, starched and pressed gray cotton with an A-line skirt, white snaps up the front, a white collar, and short white-cuffed sleeves. She held the dress under Deirdre's chin, narrowing her eyes as she gazed into the mirror. Then she broke into a smile. "Perfect, don't you think?" She didn't wait for an answer.

Fifteen minutes later Deirdre was seated at the makeup table, wearing the dress with a pair of saggy white opaque tights and orthopedic nurse's shoes. She'd stuffed the toe of one shoe with Kleenex to keep it from falling off her smaller foot. Bunny tucked Deirdre's hair into a hairnet and secured it with a hairpin. She applied a foundation much darker than Deirdre's natural skin tone and brushed powder over it, then created hollows beneath Deirdre's eyes with dark eye shadow. Finally she gave Deirdre a pair of glasses with black plastic frames.

Deirdre put the glasses on. The lenses were clear.

"Up," Bunny commanded.

Deirdre leaned on her crutch and rose to her feet.

"Stoop," Bunny said.

Deirdre hunched over.

"Not that much. Just kind of roll your shoulders and stick your head out. Think turtle."

Deirdre adjusted her stance. The mousy woman gazing back at her from the mirror looked like a Latina version of Ruth Buzzi's bag lady from *Laugh-In.* She started to laugh. "This is ridiculous. It will never work."

"Hey, what's going on?" a man's voice called from Bunny's bedroom.

"You don't think it's going to work?" Bunny said to Deirdre. "Watch this." She handed Deirdre her crutch and led her into the bedroom, then threw open the door to the hall. Out on the landing stood the young man Deirdre had seen earlier. He was barefoot and wearing jeans and a stretched-out black T-shirt.

"What's up with you?" Joelen said.

"I . . . what? Why are you two looking at me like I did something?" he said.

"It's not what you did. It's what you're not doing," Joelen said, pushing past Deirdre.

"What are you talking about?" The man looked from Joelen to Bunny.

"See?" Bunny said, turning to Deirdre.

"Not a single glance your way. It's as if you're wallpaper. I'd say the disguise is working."

"Disguise?" the man said.

Joelen took the man's hand. "Dear, meet Deirdre, my best friend all through high school. Deirdre, may I present Jackie Hutchinson. My *baby*" — her voice seemed to caress the word — "brother. Is he adorable or what?" Joelen gave him a loud wet kiss on the cheek.

"Would you cut that out?" Jackie pulled a face and made a show of wiping off the kiss. "I'm twenty-one, for God's sake."

"God help us. Just turned twenty-one," Joelen said. She chucked him under the chin and he pushed her away.

Of course Deirdre could see the resemblance. Jackie and Joelen both had Bunny's legendary electric blue eyes and heart-shaped face. But Jackie had dark curly hair, a dimpled chin, and beaky profile — not features he'd have inherited from Bunny or Bunny's late husband, Derek Hutchinson. Hutch, as he was called in the fan magazines, had a longtime starring role in a hospital-based soap opera, but he'd been much more Dr. Kildare than Ben Casey.

Recovering himself, Jackie offered Deirdre his hand. "Pleased to meet you. I'm sorry. I

158

thought you were . . ." His voice trailed off. He seemed painfully young and he made Deirdre feel painfully old.

"Go on," Bunny said. "Say it. You thought Deirdre was the new maid."

Jackie nodded sheepishly and Joelen said, "And the prize for best disguise goes to —"

"Sorry," Jackie said.

"Don't be," Bunny said. "It's very gratifying. That's just the effect I was aiming for."

Jackie smiled a perfect toothy smile. "So my sister was your best friend?"

"From sixth grade," Deirdre said, "until . . ." Her voice trailed off.

Jackie narrowed his dark eyes at Deirdre. "Was she crazy then, too?"

"Crazy?" Joelen gave him a shove. "Look who's talking."

"Not exactly crazy," Deirdre said. "I'd say fearless. She did some pretty wild things and I followed her. So I guess I was the crazy one."

Joelen snorted a laugh. "Remember thumbing a ride home from the five-and-dime?"

"Miraculously without getting abducted." Deirdre remembered the black Cadillac that had stopped. The man had leaned across the passenger seat and opened the door and they'd hopped in. Just like that. All the way to Deirdre's house the driver lectured them about the dangers of getting into cars with strangers, explaining in graphic detail just how bad things could go. Deirdre had been relieved to get out of that car.

Joelen picked up the thread. "Hey, it was raining and we'd have been soaking wet by the time we got back. So we get a ride home and Pollyanna here insists on walking all the way back to the damned store in the downpour, so she can return the stupid lipstick she pilfered."

"*I* stole it? Ha!"

"What ha? How did it end up in your pocket?" Joelen was all wide-eyed innocence.

Passionate Pink. The tube had felt as if it were burning a hole in her pocket — once she realized it was there. "I think you know the answer to that."

"Me?" Joelen turned to Jackie. "So then she gets arrested trying to put it back!"

"I did not get arrested." Deirdre felt a flush rising from her neck to her forehead. The dweeby J.J. Newberry security guard had squeezed her arm as he dragged her to the back of the store and propelled her up a smelly staircase to an office with windows that looked down over the store's vast aisles. He'd sat her down and made her give him

160

her name and phone number. Thankfully neither of her parents had been home to take his call. But before that asshole let Deirdre go, he made her sign a paper promising she'd never set foot in the store again. As if she would have. But the worst part was when he'd taken her picture and pinned her humiliated face to a bulletin board along with about a dozen other shoplifters.

"You must have been quite the pair," Jackie said.

"The original odd couple," Joelen said. "She was Miss Goody Two-Shoes."

"And you were" — Deirdre searched for the right comparison — "Bonnie Parker."

"Bonnie who?" Jackie said.

"He's such a child." Joelen pursed her lips. "What do you expect?"

They were quizzing Jackie on iconic rock singers, old TV shows, and more movie roles when the phone rang. For a moment, Deirdre's throat went dry. Joelen crossed the room to the bedside table and answered it.

"Sure. Okay, I'll tell her." She hung up and turned to Deirdre. "That was Sy. He's waiting for you. I'll get the car and meet you by the back door."

"Honey," said Bunny, squeezing Deirdre's hand, "it's showtime."

CHAPTER 17

Bunny packed Deirdre's jeans and T-shirt into her messenger bag and led her to the end of the hall, through a door, across a dimly lit passageway, and down a back stairway. *Mothballs. Floor wax.* Deirdre gagged on the smells as she grasped the wooden railing and slowly made her way down steeply raked steps. Her memory of her father spiriting her out of the house after Tito was killed clicked into place. Of course he hadn't led her out through a tunnel. It had been this narrow hallway.

They were halfway down the back stairs when Bunny stopped and turned to face her. "So you found the dress?"

Deirdre froze. She nodded.

In the half-light, Bunny looked tense and tired, her face showing her age. "Your father was supposed to take care of it."

"Take care — ?" Deirdre didn't know what to say.

"Get rid of it."

"Because?"

"Because no one needed to know that you were there."

"I was?"

"You don't remember?" Bunny asked, and when Deirdre shook her head, she sighed. "Just as well that you don't."

"But —"

"So what are you going to do?"

"Do?"

Bunny gave an exasperated sigh. "With the dress."

From outside came the sound of a car horn tooting. Deirdre automatically looked toward the noise.

Bunny grasped Deirdre's arm, bringing her attention back. "You have no idea what you're playing with here. The last thing my daughter needs is to have things stirred up again." She squeezed Deirdre's arm so hard that it hurt. "Do you understand what I'm telling you?"

In truth, Deirdre didn't, but Bunny didn't wait for an answer. When the car horn tooted again, she released Deirdre and turned away. Deirdre followed her down the stairs. At the bottom, they emerged into a laundry room.

Joelen came in to meet them. "What's the

163

holdup?"

"Just putting on the finishing touches," said Bunny. She opened a broom closet and pulled out a Ralph's shopping bag. Into it she stuffed Deirdre's messenger bag. She handed Deirdre the loaded shopping bag and then stood back, her brow furrowed. "Needs something more. Let me see —"

"She looks good. Just fine," Joelen said. "Let's go."

"Good isn't great and fine isn't finished," Bunny said. "Wait here. I'll be right back." She disappeared back up the stairs.

"*Good isn't great. Fine isn't finished,*" Joelen singsonged. "I stepped right into that. What can I tell you? She's a perfectionist."

Deirdre rubbed her arm where it was sore and reddened from Bunny's grip.

Moments later Bunny reappeared carrying a battered black vinyl purse. She hooked it over Deirdre's arm along with the shopping bag, smiled approval, then hustled her and Joelen out the back door to the car.

Deirdre threw the purse and shopping bag into the backseat and got in the front, her crutch across her lap. She wiped the sweat from her forehead. The too-tight underarms of her "uniform" were already damp with perspiration, and the fabric stuck to her back.

Joelen started driving down the long driveway. As she pulled the car out onto Sunset and turned south toward City Hall, Deirdre ran through the conversation she'd had in that dark stairway with Bunny.

You have no idea what you're playing with here. She'd been right about that.

"Are you okay?" Joelen asked.

"Sure," Deirdre lied. "Why?"

"I don't know. You seem . . . tense. Upset."

So you found the dress?

Your father was supposed to take care of it.

No one needed to know that you were there.

"You always were good at reading me," Deirdre said. "I guess I'm feeling anxious about talking to the police. And" — she looked down at her getup — "ridiculous. Conspicuous." She tugged at one of the sleeves. "Hot and uncomfortable."

Joelen turned the A/C up and adjusted one of the vents so the cool air blasted out at Deirdre. "Does that help?"

"Thanks. Yeah, it does."

"You're sure that's all?" Joelen gave her a concerned look.

"I guess it just seems weird."

"What?"

"You know, being back in the house with you and your mom after so many years."

"I hope not weird in a bad way."

165

"Your mom's the same —"

Joelen laughed. "I know. She's a tidal wave. Wouldn't want to get in her way, that's for sure. What do you think of Jackie?"

"Handsome as hell." Deirdre ran the back of her hand across her damp brow. It came away coated with dark makeup. "Sweet, actually. Is he still in school?"

"I wish." Joelen waved her hand as if she were swatting away a fly. "He barely finished high school. Not because he's not smart. He just wasn't buying what they were selling. But he's doing okay."

"Doing what?"

"Selling his favorite toys. Harleys. He's pretty good at it, too."

Deirdre remembered seeing the bike in the driveway. "Really? Where?"

"Marina del Rey. There's a dealership there that's been in business forever, and . . ."

As Joelen went on about how great the dealership was and how well Jackie was doing there, Deirdre sat in stunned silence. There was only one Harley dealership in Marina del Rey, and Henry worked there. And yet Henry claimed he hadn't heard word one about Joelen since high school?

"Sorry. I didn't mean to go on like that," Joelen said as she double-parked in front of

City Hall. She put her hand on Deirdre's arm in the same spot where Bunny's squeeze had left her red. "Relax. You'll see. No one is going to bat an eyelash at you. Look, there's Sy."

Deirdre spotted him, too, sitting beyond a news team that was broadcasting from the sidewalk at the base of broad steps that led to the main entrance. The center bell tower provided the perfect backdrop for the suited man talking animatedly at the camera.

"Go on," Joelen said. "Get out. Brazen does it! Before I get a ticket for double-parking." She reached across and opened the passenger door. Hot air flooded the car. "You're in good hands. I ought to know."

A car behind them beeped. Deirdre set her crutch on the macadam and got out. Before she reached the sidewalk Joelen had pulled away, and for a moment Deirdre felt completely exposed. The massive Spanish colonial building that housed city government as well as the police and fire departments towered before her. She adjusted her grip on her crutch and the ridiculous handbag and started past the film crew, stepping over wires that snaked back to the van. The Ralph's shopping bag banged against her side with every lurching step.

She was so close to the film crew that she

could hear the young TV news commentator, his smooth mannequin face barely moving as spoke: "Scenes from this year's number-one action movie were filmed right here. But the project that started out as a vehicle for Sylvester Stallone . . ."

"Watch where you're stepping!" said a guy she assumed was a production assistant, glaring at her, his words an angry hiss.

The commentator held the mike in front of a shaggy-haired man wearing a black T-shirt tucked into belted jeans, his silver-tinted aviator glasses reflecting the sun. He chuckled, then spoke in a raspy voice: "So Sly bails. Weeks before shooting is scheduled to begin last spring, he pulls out. And we're talking about the project with Eddie. And he says, 'Enough of this. Do you guys want to make the film or just talk about it?' "

Deirdre relaxed a notch. In this celebrity-obsessed town, how hard could it be to fly under the radar? She smoothed her dress, hoisted up the sagging panty hose, affected a slightly turtle-necked slouch, and started walking toward where Sy was perched at the edge of a raised bed of pink and purple petunias, so bright that they looked artificial. People leaving the building glanced at her, but none looked twice. The hairnet made her head itchy, but she resisted the urge to scratch.

As she got closer, Sy's gaze passed over her without a flicker of recognition. It wasn't until she was three feet away that he registered her crutch, looked her full in the face, and sprang to his feet. He eyed her up and down, then looked around. "Brava," he said in a stage whisper.

"I had help."

"I imagine you did." He picked up his briefcase and cast an anxious glance in the direction of the news team. "Come on. Let's not press our luck. There is a side entrance."

Sy led Deirdre around to the side of the building where cruisers were angle parked and a sign pointing up a narrow flight of stairs said BEVERLY HILLS POLICE DEPARTMENT. He followed Deirdre up the steps and held open one of the double doors at the top.

Deirdre passed into a cool, dark interior. An outer waiting area was lined with benches — a tired-looking woman rocking a baby in a stroller sat on one of them — and smelled of burnt coffee, stale candy, and pine cleaner. Beyond another set of glass-paned double doors, uniformed police officers milled about. When an officer pushed the door open and exited, the sound of phones ringing and loud voices pulsed out.

"Does the detective know we're coming?" Deirdre asked.

"I thought we would surprise him. When you talk to him, please remember, do not offer information. Do not speculate. Just answer his questions. This is important. Do you understand me?"

"I do. Don't offer. Don't speculate. Can I change first?"

"Go."

Deirdre ducked into the ladies' room. She ripped off the hairnet and shook out her hair. Gave her scalp a good scratch. Relief! Then she changed back into her pants and T-shirt and stuffed the baggy tights and the dress and vinyl handbag into her messenger bag. She scrubbed her face using the gloppy, bubble-gum-colored soap from the dispenser. Patted her face dry with a brown paper towel that left a residue of wet cardboard smell.

When she emerged, Sy was no longer in the lobby. He was on the other side of the glass door in the midst of what looked like a heated discussion with a visibly exasperated Detective Martinez.

CHAPTER 18

Deirdre pushed through the door to the police department in time to hear Martinez reaming out Sy. "If you people are going to start playing games —"

"No one is playing games with you. She is right here," Sy said, spotting Deirdre and motioning her over. "See? Ready and willing to answer your questions."

A vein was pounding in Martinez's forehead. He gave a tense nod in Deirdre's direction and checked his watch, then turned and led her and Sy through a busy room filled with desks, down a corridor, and through a door into a small office. The interior was Spartan — just a desk, a phone, and a half-dead ficus that Deirdre found herself wanting desperately to water. A dust-coated window overlooked a eucalyptus tree behind the building.

Martinez sat at the desk and motioned for Deirdre and Sy to sit on the other side. A half-full mug of coffee sat on the desk, white ceramic with a splash of red, the motto HOMICIDE: OUR DAY BEGINS WHEN SOME-ONE ELSE'S ENDS. A second mug, filled with pens and pencils, had SUPER DADDY on it.

Martinez took out a pad and made a few initial notations. Then he leaned back in his chair and just stared at Deirdre for what seemed like forever. Taking her measure or, more likely, trying to freak her out. "You won't mind if I record this," he said, taking a cassette recorder from the desk drawer. "Then I won't have to worry about getting everything down in my notes."

"Not a problem," Sy said. "Right, Deirdre?"

Following his lead, Deirdre nodded. Martinez snapped in a fresh cassette, turned it on, and set the recorder on the desk between them. He recorded a little preamble — time, date, and who was present. Then played it and went back to recording.

"Miss Unger, thank you very much for coming in. I'll get right to the point. I need to clarify your whereabouts late Friday night and into Saturday morning."

"I've already told you, I was in the art gallery. Xeno Art. Until late. Then I went home."

"I know." Martinez gave her a tired smile. "Like I said, just to clarify and get the details correct. So you closed the gallery? When was that?"

"We're open until eight. Then I closed up. But I stayed later, prepping a new exhibit."

"Alone?"

"With the artist's assistant."

"Do you have this artist's assistant's name? Can we contact him —"

"Her. Shoshanna."

"Shoshanna . . . what?"

"I don't know her last name. But I can get her contact information for you." The assistant had been young. Brunette. With hair that hung down to her waist and a lot of makeup. *Aspiring actress* had been Deirdre's first thought. The artist had arranged for her to come help, since he was in Israel. He said she'd be at the gallery at eight but she hadn't gotten there until after ten, complaining about heavy traffic. Two hours of heavy traffic well past rush hour? It sounded lame, but Deirdre hadn't bothered to call her on it.

"Please do. And you were at the gallery with this Shoshanna until — ?"

"After midnight." It was so late by the time they'd finished up that she'd been afraid her car would get ticketed for overnight parking. Too bad it hadn't.

"What about casual passersby? They'd have seen that the lights were on inside and the two of you in there hanging paintings. Maybe someone stopped in?"

"It was an installation. Not paintings." Shoes, actually. Avram Sigismund had shipped them hundreds of old shoes — looked like a Salvation Army resale store's entire stock of shoes that had been thrown in the mud and driven over a few times — along with some graffiti-covered canvas backdrops delivered to the gallery in crates. Shoshanna had a schematic that showed where the shoes, each of which was numbered, were to be placed — some on the floor, others climbing the walls, still others hanging from the ceiling. When all the shoes were in their appointed places, Deirdre hadn't been all that impressed. On top of that the gallery reeked of feet, something that the assistant called "texture" and insisted was an essential part of the concept. "And no," Deirdre added, "no one stopped in, and I doubt if anyone going past would have realized that we were there. We covered the windows."

"You covered the windows." Hearing Martinez repeat her in a deadpan, Deirdre realized how bizarre this sounded.

"The artist was quite definite." Paranoid, even. "He didn't want anyone to see his work until the show opened."

"Did that seem unusual to you?"

"I could understand it, really, especially with an installation of that nature."

"So this artist. What's his name?"

"Avram Sigismund." Deirdre spelled it for Martinez.

"He's well known?"

"He's Israeli. Up and coming." Deirdre avoided Martinez's gaze. In fact, she'd never worked with Avi (as he asked them to call him) before. Never even heard of him until just a week and a half ago when they'd agreed to clear their front gallery space and show his work. She could tell herself that it was Stefan who'd pressured her to break their long-standing policy and accept payment to mount a show, but that wouldn't have been fair. The gallery was struggling and they needed to pay their rent. It seemed like a gift when, out of the blue, Avi contacted Stefan with a proposal. He was desperate for gallery space for just two weeks to accommodate a curator from a major American museum who wanted to see his work firsthand. His work was represented by the prestigious (even she'd heard of it) Rosenfeld Gallery in Tel Aviv, but he'd never been shown in the United States. Stefan had gotten the strong sense that the museum interested in acquiring his work was the MOCA in L.A.

The whole deal had sounded slightly sketchy to Deirdre, because why couldn't he have found a gallery in the Los Angeles area to show his work? But what was there to lose when Avi was offering to pay expenses and then some, up front, in addition to a 40 percent commission when (not if) the museum purchased the work? Both she and Stefan held their noses and signed on. It was only for a few weeks, she'd told herself. Besides, they'd clear enough to bankroll shows for a half-dozen artists whose works they were eager to exhibit.

"So you were in the gallery until —"

"After midnight." How many times did he need for her to say it?

"And then?"

"I went home."

"Home?"

"To my house. I live in Imperial Beach. It's near —"

"I know where it is. Was anyone with you? Anyone drop by? Anyone who can vouch for your whereabouts?"

Vincent Price. By the time she got home, even Johnny Carson had gone to bed. The only thing on was the ending of *House of Wax.*

"No," Deirdre said, her tone sharper than she'd intended. She wasn't sure if she was annoyed because he kept asking the same thing, or because she was always alone in bed at night.

"Did you receive any telephone calls after you got home?"

"No."

"Are you sure?"

"Positive."

"What would you say if I told you that phone records show that calls were made to your home phone late that night?"

"Excuse me," Sy said. "You need a subpoena to examine my client's phone records."

"We haven't examined *her* phone records." Martinez placed a computer printout in front of her. Several lines were highlighted. "These calls were made to you from your father's phone."

Deirdre looked at the highlighted calls. She pointed to the first one, Friday at 3:12 P.M. "I was at the gallery then."

"Looks like you didn't answer this call, either," Martinez said, pointing to a call at 1:41 A.M. "You said you were home by then."

Deirdre swallowed and shifted in her seat. "I'd turned off the ringer."

"Why did you do that?"

Martinez just sat there waiting. "I was tired. It was late."

"Who would have called you so late?"

My father. Even though that was perfectly innocent, Deirdre felt beads of sweat prick from her upper lip.

"What is the relevance of this?" Sy said, saving her from having to answer. "Just because Miss Unger didn't answer her phone doesn't mean she was not at home."

Martinez leaned forward. "The coroner estimates the time of death at between midnight and three A.M. This" — he put his finger on the list — "would have been the last phone call your father made before he died. Unless" — he paused for a moment, like this thought was just now occurring to him — "unless it was someone else, calling you from your father's house."

Sy's warning came back to her. *Do not offer. Do not speculate.* Deirdre didn't say anything.

Martinez sat back. "So your story is that you left the gallery, drove home, turned off the ringer on your phone, and went to sleep?"

Close enough. Deirdre nodded.

Martinez pointed to the cassette recorder.

"That's right," Deirdre said.

"Alone?"

"Alone." She said it calmly but she wanted to scream *Yes! Alone! I live alone!*

"And you left the house again when?"

"The next morning. Saturday. Maybe at about nine."

"And you drove —"

"Straight to my father's house."

"Without stopping?"

"Without —" Then she remembered. "I stopped for gas and something to eat at a McDonald's somewhere around Mission Viejo."

"You used a credit card?"

Of course it would be nice if she had some evidence to support her claim. "Paid cash. But I think the cup and the wrapper are still in my car."

Martinez looked unimpressed.

"I probably kept the receipts," Deirdre added. She sounded confident but she wondered if she had in fact bothered to keep them. She saved every receipt, even small ones, when the expense was business related. But this trip had been personal. "I'll look."

"So you got to your father's house when?"

She'd answered that question already.

Several times. "At about noon. But no one answered the door and I couldn't get in. That's why I went around to the backyard."

"Who has keys to your father's house?"

"Henry, of course. He lives there. My mom, though she'd never go there. The woman who comes in once a week and cleans for my dad." Deirdre looked over at Sy to see if he had anything to add.

"Not you?" Martinez asked.

"Not me."

"Was that a problem? Not having a set of keys."

"No. I don't visit very often."

"The last time was — ?"

Was this a test? Because she'd already answered that question at the house. "January."

"Months ago. Sounds as if you and your father weren't that close."

"We got along. We just didn't spend time together."

"But you drove up to help him move."

"He asked me to. He needed help. Of course I came."

Martinez nodded and rubbed his chin. "Okay. Just a few more questions. Was your father having financial problems?"

"I don't know. He didn't talk to me about his finances and I'd never have hit him up for money."

Sy put a finger to his lips: *Just answer the question.*

"But he was putting the house up for sale."

"Right."

"Did your father have any enemies? Any ongoing disagreements with business associates or neighbors?"

"Not that I know of."

"He and your mother — ?"

"Got along fine since their divorce."

He leaned forward, as if he were about to ask another question, then thought better of it. "All right. I guess that's all."

Deirdre breathed a sigh of relief. When she started to get up from her chair, the backs of her pants were stuck to her thighs.

Martinez shook Sy's hand. He offered his hand to Deirdre and held it. "Just one more thing. There was a shovel near your father's pool. Did you notice it?" He released her hand.

"A shovel?" At first Deirdre didn't remember seeing one. And then she did, lying where Henry would have backed his car right over it. "Yes. It was in the driveway. I picked it up and moved it out of the way."

"Ah. Well, that explains why we found your fingerprints on the shaft. In fact, yours are the only prints on that shovel. And there are no traces of dirt at all. Just traces of blood. Hair. Chlorine. Like it was never actually used for gardening."

Deirdre's stomach turned over and she closed her eyes.

"The blood on the blade?" Martinez continued. "It's not a particularly common blood type. AB positive. Your father is AB positive. Shall I tell you how I think the blood got there?"

She wanted to say *No, don't tell me.* But Sy's stony look kept her from saying anything.

"Sometime after midnight, your father went for a swim. His usual thirty laps. He thought he was alone, but he wasn't. Someone else was out there, and while he was swimming, that person picked up that shovel and struck him. Right here" — Martinez indicated a spot above his own right eye — "and knocked him unconscious. It would not have taken a whole lot of strength on the part of his assailant. A woman could easily have managed it." Martinez paused, then went on, "Victims of violence usually try to protect themselves. But there's no evidence that your father did that. So either he didn't see it coming, or he knew and trusted the person who attacked him."

Martinez paused for a few moments,

watching Deirdre, his head tilted, like an osprey waiting for a fish to break the surface. "Which is it, do you think?"

CHAPTER 19

"He thinks I killed my father," Deirdre said when she and Sy were outside in his car. She felt as if she'd been punched in the stomach.

"Not necessarily. He is considering his options." Sy put the key in the ignition and turned on the engine. The A/C started to pump cool air and the clock on the dashboard lit up. It was after four. "He is poking around to see what sparks. That is his job."

Deirdre reached out to steady herself against the dashboard. "I feel sick."

"You did fine."

"The shovel. I wasn't thinking . . . I didn't know."

"You did what anyone would have done. You picked it up and moved it. If you had killed your father, more likely you would wipe it clean, yes? What concerns me more is that no one can verify where you were when your father died. It's your word —"

"I'm sure Stefan has Shoshanna's contact information. He talked to Avi. He made the arrangements. I'll get it from him."

"Good. Do it right away. Okay?"

"As soon as I get home."

"Good. Good." Sy turned to her, a concerned expression on his face. "You did not tell me about the shovel."

"I . . ." The observation rattled her. "I barely remembered it myself, and I had no idea that it was important."

"Fair enough. But think. Is there anything else? Anything that seemed unimportant at the time? Run through the timeline of what happened that night and the next morning."

Deirdre sat back. "I worked until late. I slept at home. Alone. Yes, I turned off the phone. I wanted to get a decent night's sleep. You know how he could be."

"I do."

"I left the house around nine. Stopped to get something to eat and to pee. Found him."

"Was anyone out on the street when you arrived?"

"Not that I remember."

"Any cars that you noticed parked when you got there?"

"Just Henry's in the driveway. I moved the shovel. No one answered at the front so

I went around to the back. Knocked." Deirdre closed her eyes, remembering standing on the patio as the dogs attacked the sliding glass door. "There was a glass on the table on the patio."

"One?" Sy's bushy eyebrows went up and his hairpiece shifted forward. "And then?"

"Finally Henry came to the door. Then I noticed Dad's shirt was out by the pool. That's what made me go over." She swallowed. "That's it."

Sy nodded, rubbing his chin. "You are quite sure? Deirdre, if you know anything more about your father's death, tell me." Sy returned her look with a steady gaze. "This is not the time to withhold information."

"You think I'm withholding . . . ?" Angry tears welled up. "I'm telling you everything I know. Why would I be hiding something? And you haven't asked, but no, I did not kill my father."

"Of course not." Sy put his hand on her arm. "So let me help you. I can do that."

"Like you got Joelen Nichol off?"

"Got her off?" Sy seemed taken aback for a moment. Then he gave her a wry smile. "I did not get her off. She confessed. Remember? It was the evidence supporting her confession that kept the case from going to trial, but she did not get off. She paid for

186

what she did." Sy stared out the window for a moment, then looked back at Deirdre. "Take my advice. Focus on the present. Give the police the evidence they need to eliminate you as a suspect. Find those receipts. Get in touch with the woman who was with you in the gallery."

"Sy, even if I can't convince the police that I couldn't have been here, what motive could I have for killing my father?"

"Once the police demonstrate opportunity, motive is easy to manufacture," Sy said as he released the emergency brake, switched on the turn signal, and looked over his shoulder. "Greed. Revenge. A stupid argument gets out of hand. The police find evidence and they build a story that supports it." The turn signal ticked as Sy waited for a break in the traffic. "Your friend? Now that is a case in point."

It took a moment for her to get what he was saying. "Are you saying Joelen didn't kill Tito?"

"She was only fifteen years old. Antonio Acevedo had a history of violence. He was a bully. It was no secret that he and Bunny fought. Joelen confessed. Everyone went home happy." He backed out of the parking space and pulled into traffic. "I kept you out of trouble then. Let me keep you out of trouble now."

Sy's remark left Deirdre momentarily speechless. "Me?"

"Did the police question you? Did you have to account for your whereabouts, or give a statement about what you saw or heard?"

"I . . ."

"Well, there you go."

Deirdre was still mulling that over when Sy dropped her off in the alley behind her father's house.

"Do not forget," he said, leaning across the passenger seat to talk to her through the open car door, "find those receipts and track down Susanna."

"Shoshanna. Right away. Thanks." Deirdre closed the car door and watched Sy drive away, then pushed through the back gate. If Stefan didn't have Shoshanna's contact information, he'd certainly be able to get it from Avi. But would that be enough? Because even if she could convince the police that she'd been in the gallery when she said she was, that only accounted for her whereabouts until midnight. The drive to Los Angeles was just two and a half hours. She could have driven up, killed her father, called her own phone from her father's house, then driven back and started out again the next morning as if nothing had happened. It made no sense, but it wasn't impossible.

Deirdre was at the kitchen door, digging for her keys, when she registered an acrid smell. She looked around. Despite the deepening shadows, she could see that the door in the garage leading to her father's office was ajar. Had she left it open? Or maybe Henry had gone up after she'd left. When she started back to investigate, a flock of blackbirds perched in the upper branches of a eucalyptus tree behind the garage swooped across the yard, whistling and screeching like so many squeaky hinges. For a moment she thought she saw something move across the garage's second-floor window. She squinted up at it. Maybe Henry was up there. His car wasn't in the driveway, but it could have been parked out on the street.

That's when she noticed rivulets of smoke seeping from underneath the garage's overhead doors. She moved closer and dropped her messenger bag in the driveway. Covering her mouth and nose, she peered in through a window in the door. All she could see was a dull glow on the floor between her father's car and the bay where Henry kept his motorcycles. Something was burning.

In a panic, she reached down to throw open the garage door but stopped herself. Wouldn't that feed the fire? Maybe she could drag over the garden hose. Or was there a fire extinguisher? Her mother had bought one years ago for the kitchen.

Just as Deirdre was trying to see if a fire extinguisher was hanging on the wall inside the garage, sparks exploded like messy fireworks. She heard a *whoosh* and felt a wave of heat, and stumbled backward seconds before the window she'd been peering through splintered, pieces of glass falling and shattering on the concrete threshold. Inside, flames had sprung to life and licked up toward the ceiling.

Deirdre stood frozen for what was only a second but felt like forever. "Fire!" she screamed, as loud as she could. She banged her crutch on the door and yelled at the top of her lungs, "Fire! Fire! Fire!" Inside, the blaze had doubled. She backed away, choking on smoke. Surely if Henry was upstairs in her father's office he'd smell it now.

She had to call the fire department. She hurried as fast as she could down the driveway to the house. When she finally reached the kitchen door she realized she hadn't unlocked it and her keys were still in her bag, which was lying on the ground in front of the garage. Deirdre turned and looked back. The spot where her messenger bag lay was now completely engulfed in smoke.

Weren't there alarm boxes on the street? There'd been one a few houses down. Once upon a time, Joelen had decided it would be fun to see what happened if she pulled it.

Deirdre struggled to get out to the street, wishing a police cruiser or media van were still parked out there. She focused on the tip of her crutch, feeling the vibration up her arm each time the rubber tip connected with the sidewalk, each time she took a step, dragged her leg, and moved forward again.

The alarm box was right where she remembered, three houses down. For a second Deirdre just stood before it, panting for breath, her throat burning. Then she pulled down the handle. And waited. Was something supposed to happen? A click? A whirr? She tried to remember, but was pretty sure that she and Joelen hadn't hung around to find out. They'd taken off running and hidden behind some bushes in a neighbor's yard.

Deirdre heard the *whump* of an explosion

and turned back toward the house. Another loud pop sounded. Deirdre felt paralyzed as she watched a plume of black smoke rise, thickening and hanging over the garage like a swarm of bees. Where were the sirens? Should she rouse a neighbor? Borrow a phone? Borrow a fire extinguisher?

Finally, in the distance, she heard a siren's wail. Then another joined it. *Thank God.*

Deirdre arrived back at the house at the same time that a hook and ladder truck pulled up. "It's the garage!" she cried, pointing up the driveway, though with all the smoke *where* would have been obvious to anyone. "My brother might be up there. Please, hurry!"

Another fire truck pulled up in front of the house. Neighbors on both sides had come out of their houses and were on the sidewalks watching. A police cruiser screamed up, lights flashing, and parked sideways, closing off the end of the block.

As firefighters in dark turnout gear swarmed from the trucks, Deirdre drifted up the driveway after them. She stared up at where smoke was seeping out from between the louvers in the second-floor windows, barely able to breathe. Henry was not up there, she told herself. He couldn't be. What she'd seen had to have been the shadow of a bird. He'd told her himself he never went up to Arthur's office.

"Stay clear!" a firefighter coming up behind her barked. He was carrying a fire hose. A smaller truck and a Fire Rescue van screamed up to the house. When Deirdre looked back toward the garage, the overhead doors had been flung open and the interior was engulfed in flame. Moments later, flames shot through the roof. Heat pulsed, driving Deirdre back into the street. She was sobbing. Henry could never get out of there in one piece.

At last water gushed from the fire hoses. With the water pouring on full force, the flames were quickly tamped down. A firefighter strapped on an oxygen tank, adjusted the mask over his face, picked up an ax, and waded in through the smoke, disappearing into the shrouded stairwell. Deirdre imagined him climbing the stairs to the second floor in smoky darkness. Would he have to break down the door to her father's office, or was it unlocked as the downstairs door had been? Would he find Henry laid out on the floor? Unconscious in a closet?

She felt seconds ticking by as she waited for a yell. Or a wave from the window. A signal of some kind. Any kind.

Finally the firefighter who'd gone upstairs

appeared in the doorway. He unstrapped his silver tank, shucked his coat, and wiped sweat from his face with the back of his arm. Deirdre tried to read his expression. Was he getting ready to deliver bad news?

"Deeds?" Henry's voice was loud behind her.

She whipped around. *Thank God.* "You idiot!" she screamed.

CHAPTER 20

"What happened?" Henry asked.

Deirdre gave a helpless gesture toward the garage. "It . . . I . . . And I thought you . . ." Her voice was rising.

"What did I do now?"

It was too much. Just too much. Deirdre's world kaleidoscoped and her legs buckled. Her crutch slipped away as she dropped to one knee. She felt Henry lift her and put his arms around her. She buried her face, which felt as if it were twisted into a Kabuki caricature of anguish, against his chest.

"I'm sorry," Henry said, his warm breath on her hair. "I'm sorry."

She knew it wasn't fair. What had Henry done other than not get himself killed? She pulled away and wiped her eyes with the back of her hand. The hoses had cut off, and the plume of smoke rising from the garage turned into a dark cloud that hovered overhead. Sooty water that had been cascading past them down the driveway slowed to a trickle.

"You scared the shit out of me. I didn't know where you were. And I thought I saw you —" She gestured toward the garage. Its siding had buckled. There was a blackened hole in the roof. A few window louvers hung from their frames like orphaned wind chimes. All it would take was a stiff breeze to send them crashing down.

"Why would I go up there?" He picked up her crutch and handed it to her. "It wasn't me. I would have gotten here sooner, but they made me park a block away."

"You scared me."

"You scared *me*. What in God's name happened?"

"I have no idea. When I got back, I smelled smoke. And then the fire exploded." Deirdre hiccuped. "I knew I couldn't get in and put it out. So I had to call. And then I couldn't get into the house." Her voice rose to a wail but she couldn't stop. "I couldn't get to a phone. I didn't know what to do. I . . ."

"It's okay." Henry put his arm around her shoulders. They watched in silence, enveloped in charred, steamy air, as firefighters brought in portable lighting and set up orange cones in front of the garage. One firefighter ventured into the garage. In his dark gear, he seemed to fade in the interior until all she could see was his flashlight beam. More firefighters followed.

Blackened cushions and the frames of yard furniture appeared as if by magic, hurled from the garage interior. One by one they landed in a welter in the driveway. A firefighter dragged out some cardboard packing boxes, one of which collapsed and disgorged what looked like sodden linens and curtains. A tire rolled out of the garage and spiraled lazily into the grass.

The sun had sunk below the horizon, and the last streaky pink clouds were cooling. Deirdre retrieved her messenger bag from the grass where firefighters had tossed it. Trampled and soaked, it seemed like the perfect metaphor for how she felt.

From the second floor, flashlight beams were visible through the openings where there had once been windows. Deirdre could only imagine how bad it was inside the office. Literary executor? Sort and cull? That was a laugh. She'd be sifting ashes. She hoped the yellow dress had been reduced to cinders, too, and she could forget about it — just like Bunny wanted her to.

A tall figure emerged from the garage, took off his heavy coat, laid it across his arm, and looked over his shoulder. Then he turned back and started walking toward Deirdre and Henry. He was flushed, and soot was streaked across his face like war paint. As he got nearer, Deirdre realized he seemed familiar. "Deirdre? Henry?" he said. "You don't remember me. Tyler Corrigan."

Tyler. Of course. He used to live across the street. A few years older than Deirdre, back then he'd reminded her of Opie with his freckles, straw-colored hair, and earnestness. She used to watch him ride his bike up and down the block, popping wheelies and spinning around. A few years after that he'd been out there doing tricks on a skateboard. His family had moved away when she was in high school.

"You're a firefighter?" Deirdre asked.

Tyler shucked a thick work glove and offered his hand. His grip was strong. "Arson investigator. But I work with the police and the fire marshal." He offered a hand to Henry.

"Hey, Tyler," Henry said, shaking his hand. "Arson?"

"It's routine for me to get involved when there's an unattended fire."

Routine. Unattended. Those were the words the police had used to explain why Deirdre's father had to be autopsied. Why a police detective had come to investigate.

"I didn't realize you guys were still living here," Tyler said.

"I still live here," Henry said.

"And my dad lives here —" Deirdre added, then caught herself. "Or at least he did. He died. Yesterday."

Tyler's look darkened. "I'm sorry. I didn't know that."

"He drowned," Deirdre said, swallowing the lump in her throat. "I drove up from San Diego to help him get ready to move and when I got here, I found him in the pool, and —" She clamped her mouth shut. She hadn't intended to say any of that, and now her eyes were stinging. Henry looked pained.

"And now this." Tyler shook his head. "I'm sorry. Your dad was a great guy."

A firefighter came up to him from behind and tapped him on the shoulder, drawing Tyler away. They exchanged a few words that Deirdre couldn't hear. When he returned, Tyler said, "They shouldn't be too much longer. Couple hours, max."

Deirdre edged closer to the open garage. Inside, a camera flash went off. Then another. Two men were crouched in the dark interior alongside the blackened hull that had been her father's car. Next to it, Henry's bikes were on their sides. "What are they doing?" she asked.

"It looks like that's where the fire started. They're documenting the point of ignition. At least no one was hurt." Tyler eyed Deirdre. "You told one of the first responders that someone was upstairs?"

Henry gave her a surprised look. "You did?"

"I told you. I thought it was you."

"Well, no one's up there now," Tyler said.

Deirdre could smell smoke, even from inside the house, long after the fire hoses had been reeled back and the hook and ladder truck had driven off. The street had been reopened, but a gray pall lingered in the air. Only Tyler was left, packing his equipment away in a fire department van parked on the street.

In the meantime, the mortuary had called. They expected the coroner to release Arthur's body the next day. What followed was a stream of questions to which Deirdre had no answers. When would they like to schedule a service? Did they want to reserve the Reposing Room? Open or closed coffin?

She promised to have answers for them in the morning, which was when she hoped her mother would be back. All she knew for sure was that her father had wanted to be cremated.

That led to more questions. Should they reserve a spot for Arthur's cremains in one of their lovely urn gardens? Or perhaps he'd prefer to reside in the columbarium?

The business of death had its own vocabulary, rife with comforting euphemisms, and every choice came with unstated price tags. Price tags came with guilt. Deirdre had no idea whether there was money in the estate for the kind of service to which Arthur would have felt entitled.

Deirdre went outside and stood alone on the lawn in front of the house, watching Tyler jot some final notes and load the van with bags of evidence — material to be analyzed, she assumed. He closed the van door, locked it, and looked over at her.

"Done," he said. His face looked grave. He opened the passenger door and threw his clipboard on the seat.

"Does it feel weird, being back here?" Deirdre asked.

"Kind of. It's a shame they did in our old house." He glanced across the street to where he'd once lived in a modest Spanish colonial with a walled garden. The property had always evoked *The Secret Garden* for Deirdre, with Tyler its Dickon, a character memorably described in the novel as looking like the god Pan with his rosy cheeks and rough curly hair, a charmer of wild animals and unhappy humans.

New owners had torn down the house Tyler had grown up in and replaced it with a house easily double its size. And in place of Dickon was this tall, gangly, competent human being who looked at her so intently that it felt as if he were x-raying her brain.

"My mom drives by and cries," Tyler said.

"Welcome to Beverly Hills," Deirdre said, "where anything that's just plain old is plain old embarrassing. Where is your family living now?"

"My parents moved to Silver Lake, but it's changing, too. And I've got an apartment in Culver City. Funky neighborhood that's staying funky for the foreseeable future."

"I'm guessing new owners will tear down our house, too. And maybe that's not a bad thing. It's not the great house that yours was to begin with, and my dad didn't exactly improve it."

Tyler held her gaze. "I know this isn't the best time to say this, but it's good to see you again. I've thought of you often." He looked at her crutch. "I hope you don't mind my asking, but what happened?"

"Car accident."

"I didn't know. When?"

"Sixty-three. I was fifteen."

"Sixty-three." He thought for a moment. "We'd moved away the summer before. Where did it happen?"

"I don't know exactly. It was late. My father was driving me home from my friend Joelen's house. I remember rocks and thornbushes." Thinking about it brought back the smell of creosote and sage. The air had been thick with it as she lay on the ground and later on the stretcher. That and the pain, which everyone said you forgot but she hadn't. She folded her arms to contain the tremor in them and the tightness in her chest that the memory roused.

She went on. "For a long time I was afraid to find out. Afraid to go back. Then, when I did ask, Dad said he didn't know."

"Didn't know?"

"When I pressed, he said he forgot where it was exactly."

Tyler scrunched up his face in disbelief. "Maybe he thought he was being kind."

Maybe. But if he'd thought not knowing would make her stop thinking about it, he'd been wrong. Instead she'd become obsessed.

"Do you remember anything?" Tyler asked. "The terrain? Houses?"

"No houses. They had to carry me out of a thicket of brush and up a steep embankment. Which is weird, because Joelen lived near here on Sunset. Dad said he took a back exit" — to avoid the police — "and must have taken a wrong turn. He ended up getting so disoriented that when the car went off the road, he didn't know where he was." Back then she'd bought the story.

Tyler paused, thinking. "No houses. Thick brush. This was twenty years ago?"

"Twenty-two."

"Maybe there was some undeveloped land back then, but a slope?" He shook his head. "Farther north, maybe."

"It never made any sense to me, either. When I asked an attorney if I could find the accident report, he told me it was too late. Those records had been destroyed."

"Really? Maybe he was talking about the paper copies. In the seventies they started transferring data to fiche. But it's all still there, indexed by date. So if police responded, and you know the date of the accident, it shouldn't be hard to find."

"But Sy said —" Deirdre stopped. Of course. Sy was probably trying to protect her, too.

"You're sure you want to know? Because I can look it up for you if you want."

Could it be this easy? All she had to do was say yes? Maybe her father had been right, and as a child she'd been better off not knowing. But that was no longer the case. "Would you? I know it sounds melodramatic, but it's as if a piece of me died and I need to know where it's buried."

Tyler nodded. "Okay then. I'll see what I can find out." He took his clipboard back out of the van and handed it to her with a pen. "Here. Write down the date and time and the make of your father's car."

Her hand shook as she wrote. *10/26/63.* She stared at the numbers. For so long she'd assumed she'd never find the place that marked the line between before and after. She added *Midnight? Austin-Healey convertible.*

"Okay. I'm on it." Tyler took the clipboard back and tossed it into the car. "And if there's anything more I can do to help, all you have to do is ask."

He was being so nice. She could learn to like this man. "Seriously, thank you," she said. "Is it okay to ask what you think about this fire?"

"Unofficially?"

"Whatever you feel comfortable sharing."

"Fire in an empty structure. No one injured." He ticked the points off on his fingers. "Started in a twenty-gallon bag of potting mix."

"You're telling me the fire started in a bag of dirt?"

"What they sell as potting mix for house-plants doesn't have much ordinary dirt in it. It's shredded bark and peat moss, plus fertilizer, of course. Under the right conditions, it burns."

"My mother used to grow geraniums. She might have left behind some potting mix. But wouldn't it need a source?"

"That's exactly the question the investigators will be asking. You can't just toss a match into the bag and expect it to go up in flames. And it certainly wouldn't spontaneously combust. At the very least, it would need a sustained heat source. A hot coal. A live wire. Or a cigarette. That's what it usually turns out to be, careless disposal of smoking materials."

Deirdre groaned. How many times had she seen her father mash his cigarette in one of her mother's plant pots? It was emblematic of her parents' incompatibility that he couldn't see why his doing it bothered Gloria so much, and Gloria couldn't understand why he couldn't stop doing it just because it bothered her.

Could her father possibly have started the

fire himself? "How long would it have taken to catch fire?"

"Hard to say."

"More than a day?"

Tyler frowned. "I'm not saying it's impossible, but highly unlikely. My guess? An hour; maybe as many as four. Fewer with help."

"What kind of help?"

"Accelerant. Even in charred debris, we can detect the presence of certain chemicals."

"Is there — ?"

"I won't know until I've run the tests." He grinned. "It's bizarre how life turns out. I nearly flunked chemistry at Beverly and now, when I'm not in the field, they let me use an office and what's basically a chem lab in the basement of City Hall. I get paid to produce lab reports." His wry expression turned serious. "But regardless of what started the fire, once there was an open flame it could have taken only minutes for the fire to spread. Garages are typically full of flammable liquids. Gasoline, of course. Linseed oil. Turpentine."

"Could it have been an accident?"

"Most garage fires are."

"What happens if that's what it turns out to be?"

"Accidental fire? Just property damage, no one injured or killed? Usually as far as police are concerned, case closed."

But was the fire accidental? Her father's death had turned out not to be. "And what if . . . ?"

"It was deliberately set? Insurance investigators swoop in like a flock of banshees. They'll want to know whether this fire was set with an intent to defraud. They're looking for a reason not to pay out, and they're nothing if not thorough." He paused for a few seconds. "Police get involved, too. Arson is a crime."

CHAPTER 21

Later that night, long after Tyler had driven off in the fire department van, Deirdre stood with Henry outside the garage, taking in the miserable piles of cardboard boxes and lawn furniture that had been left heaped in the driveway. At least the crime scene tape and orange cones were gone. The air pulsed with crickets, and a sliver of a crescent moon hung high in a sky that shimmered in the tepid night air.

Had the fire been deliberately set, and if so, was it a firebug who liked to watch things burn, or someone whose aim was to destroy her father's garage and office and its contents? And if so, how could it *not* be connected to her father's death?

"Promise you won't bite my head off if I ask you something," Deirdre said to Henry.

"What?"

She turned to face him. "First, promise."

"How can I promise if I don't know what

you're going to ask?"

"Did you set this fire?"

"Did I . . ." Henry's mouth fell open. "Deirdre, how could —"

"Just answer the question. Did you?"

He glared at her. "Idiot."

"That's not an answer."

Henry paused. Then said emphatically, "No."

She stared hard at him. Used to be she could tell when he was lying. Now he seemed completely opaque. "Do you know anything about how it started?" she asked.

"No. I do not. Do you?"

She entered the garage and shined a flashlight beam across the floor. Prints from the patterned soles of rubber boots tracked through the soot, and water still dripped overhead. "Here's where it started." She shined the beam on a spot on the floor.

Henry crouched over the lighted area. He ran his finger through ashes, sniffed at them, and pulled a face.

"Tyler told me that was why they were taking so many pictures right there," Deirdre said. "He said it could have been started by accident, something like careless disposal of smoking materials. Or it could have been set."

"Why would anyone set fire to Dad's

garage?" Henry said, taking the flashlight from Deirdre. "Your friend Tyler have any theories about that?"

"Why would anyone kill Dad?" she said. Henry glanced up at her, then back at the floor. "What do you have against Tyler, anyway?"

"Wasn't he the one in high school who made a big deal about there being no ROTC? He was always Mr. Straight Arrow."

"That's it? That was twenty years ago." It amazed her, the old tapes that were still running in his head. Did any of them ever outrun who they'd been in high school?

Henry walked over to where one of his motorcycles was tipped over on its side. He ran the flashlight beam across the skim of ash that now coated its twisted flank. The leather seat had been burned away, revealing bits of charred yellow foam. He shook his head. "Shit."

"That's it? Just 'shit'?"

"Hey, it's just a bike." He shrugged. "And it's insured. So's Dad's car. And the garage, too, for that matter. They're just things. Not like it got one of us or the dogs."

Someone would have to call the insurance company — and as usual that someone would end up being her. Deirdre stared up at the ceiling where the fire had burned through. A huge cleanup lay ahead of them. Any records that her father had kept up there, like their homeowner's insurance policy, had probably gone up in flames along with financial records and whatever "literary estate" he'd left for her to execute. *Execute* seemed the apt term, since that was pretty much what the fire had already done to it.

"Don't even think about going up there now," Henry said.

"I want to know how bad it is." What she really wanted to know was whether anyone had been messing around with her father's papers after she'd left and before the fire started.

"It's late," Henry went on, "and besides, there's no electricity. You don't know if it's even safe to walk around. The insurance adjuster is coming over first thing in the morning. At least wait until after the inspection —"

"You actually called the insurance company?" Deirdre said, astonished.

"You know, you're completely batshit," Henry said. "Believe it or not, I do plenty of things without you or Mom telling me I'm supposed to and then pecking me to death until they're done."

Deirdre yawned. She could feel the

adrenaline that had been fueling her drain away. "I think you enjoy being pecked at. I just never thought you'd figure out where to call. Especially when most of Dad's records are probably up there." She kissed Henry lightly on the cheek. He reeked of smoke. She realized she did, too. Her clothing. Her hair. Even her skin smelled charred. "Seriously, thank you," she said. "The truth is, I'm exhausted. What I need more than anything right now is a hot shower and my pillow. Maybe a drink to help me pass out."

"Take your shower. I'll uncork some wine," Henry said.

Ten minutes later Deirdre was in her bathroom. When the water was hot enough, she peeled off her shirt and pants and underwear and stepped into the shower, holding on to the grab bar that her parents had had installed after her accident. Smoke-scented steam filled the air as she shampooed her hair and soaped her body, then closed her eyes, letting the water pulse against her back. She couldn't help thinking about what she'd find when she went up to her father's office in the light of day and took in the destruction.

She stepped out of the shower, dried off, and put on clean underpants — her last pair — and one of her father's soft chambray shirts, the tail of which grazed the backs of her knees. Then she scooped her clothing from the floor and carried it out to the little back room off the kitchen. She was about to stuff her pants into the washing machine when she noticed a piece of paper sticking out of the pocket. She eased it out. Staring back at her from the faded snapshot was the ghost image of Joelen Nichol, on her knees in front of the window in Deirdre's father's office. The other Polaroid snapshots of young aspiring actresses had probably gone up in smoke.

Henry was right. Joelen did not look unhappy. Far from it. The corners of her mouth were curled in a bemused Mona Lisa smile, as if she were taking the photographer's measure every bit as much as he was taking hers.

■ ■ ■ ■

MONDAY,
MAY 26, 1985

■ ■ ■ ■

CHAPTER 22

Before dawn, the heat broke with a crash of thunder. Deirdre had fallen asleep nearly the instant her head hit the pillow, leaving the glass of wine Henry poured for her untouched on the bedside table.

She lay awake, the quilt pulled up to her chin, listening to the steady thrum of rain. Her stomach turned queasy as she imagined water pouring into her father's office through the damaged roof and windows. Hope grew fainter by the minute that any of her father's papers could be salvaged.

When the rain let up and the sky lightened to gunmetal gray, she got out of bed. It was barely six. She pulled on her extra pair of dark leggings. In the closet she found a pair of once soft, now stiff fringed suede boots that she'd worn in college. She put them on and looked in the mirror. With her father's long work shirt, now wrinkled; her wild hair; and those boots, all she needed was a flower painted on her cheek and love beads.

In the living room, she found the flashlight that she'd used the night before and let herself out through the sliding glass door. The tip of her crutch left the lawn punctuated with a trail of tiny puddles of standing water.

The door to the garage was open, and the base of the staircase up to her father's office was dark. Even though Deirdre knew the electricity wasn't working, she tried the switch. When nothing happened, she turned on the flashlight and climbed the steps, pushing off with her crutch from each riser and taking shallow breaths of rank, smoky air.

She couldn't remember whether she'd locked the door to her father's office when she'd stormed off yesterday, her anger boiling over at the pictures her father had taken. It was ajar when she reached the top of the stairs. Swelled with moisture, the door creaked when she pushed it open. At least the firefighters hadn't had to break it down.

Her father's office was a monochromatic, ash-coated gray as daylight seeped in through empty window frames that would soon have to be boarded over. A section of ceiling had collapsed, and the floor was blackened where the fire had burned through from beneath. Several file cabinet drawers hung open, their contents strewn across the floor in a sodden mess.

But not everything had been damaged. The cover on the electric typewriter was barely singed, and the pullout couch was soaked but not burned at all. For the next hour, Deirdre worked her way around the room, sticking to the edges for safety's sake, taking a mental inventory of what had survived and what had not, prioritizing what she'd deal with after the insurance adjuster had assessed the damage. Everything on the bookshelves on one wall had been burned, and the shelves themselves had come down. But the shelves on the opposite wall were still in place. The first book she pulled down from one of those shelves was wet but probably salvageable.

Anything left in the middle of the floor had been reduced to cinders. Deirdre poked her crutch into the floorboards, carefully testing, before she shifted her weight and moved closer. The spines of the Players Directories had survived, but the pages were curled into ashes, oddly beautiful, like petals of a fragile, slate gray rose. One of the cigar boxes had survived, as had Arthur's Chasen's ashtray.

Deirdre crouched and reached across with

her crutch to nudge the ashtray closer. Several marbles, disturbed by the crutch, rolled over as well. She examined them closely: they weren't marbles at all, but equal-sized turquoise beads, all of them blackened on one side. Poking around, she found more. Eight in all. She dropped them into her pocket.

Finally, Deirdre circled around to the closet door. It hung open a few inches, and Deirdre suspected that the firefighters had looked in the closet for a victim. The wood had swelled so much that she could barely wrench it the rest of the way open. Moisture and smoky stink seemed to have settled in the interior. There was the plastic bag, sitting where she'd left it.

She took out the bag, shaking off the moisture that had pooled on top. Opening it, she shined the light inside. The dress that was bundled around the knife was unscathed.

It was only later, when she'd left her father's office and was feeling her way down the dark stairway, carrying away with her the plastic bag, that she started to wonder: Why would firefighters have taken it upon themselves to open and empty out file drawers? Because, as far as she knew, she'd been the last person to set foot in her father's office before the fire, and she was certain that she'd left every one of the file drawers closed with its files intact.

CHAPTER 23

Baby and Bear greeted Deirdre as she crossed the yard. Henry opened the sliding glass door for her. It was just eight o'clock.

"What are you doing up?" Deirdre asked. She smelled coffee.

Henry held his finger to his lips and whispered, "What were you doing up in Dad's office?"

"Why are we whispering?" she whispered back.

"Mom's here."

"Mom?" Deirdre followed his gaze toward the kitchen. So she'd finally shown up.

"What were you doing up there?" Henry grabbed her arm. "You couldn't wait until after the insurance adjuster —"

She wrenched free. "Henry, I needed to see. Turns out Dad's file cabinets are open and papers are all over the floor. Someone's been up there."

"The firefighters were up there."

"Throwing around his files? How likely is that?"

"And what's that?" He was looking at the plastic bag that held the yellow dress and the knife.

Deirdre ignored the question and headed for her bedroom. She dumped the bag in the back of her closet, then closed herself in the bathroom and washed her hands and face, trying to erase the smell of smoke that clung to her like a second skin.

When she emerged, she recognized a new smell. Bacon? That seemed impossible; her mother had long ago given up eating meat. Deirdre's stomach rumbled anyway. She was starving. She headed for the kitchen.

From the back Deirdre recognized the slender figure standing at the stove, wearing a saffron-colored turban, loose-fitting cotton pants, and a linen top. "Hi, Mom."

Her mother turned around, fork in her hand. The turban framed her pale, shiny face, the skin stretched taut. She tilted her head and gave a sympathetic smile. "Hello, darling." Crow's-feet fanned at the corners of her eyes.

Deirdre said, "I'm glad you came."

"Of course I came. I'm sorry it took so long. I had car trouble. And then . . ." Her mother put down the fork and turned off the burner. She approached Deirdre and placed a warm hand on the side of her face. "Well, never mind my woes. It's nothing compared to what's been going on around here." She fingered the collar of the chambray shirt that had been Arthur's and her eyes filled with tears. "I'm so sorry about Daddy. I know you must be very sad, too."

Sadness was just one of the emotions in the mix, Deirdre thought, blinking back her own tears. She'd barely begun to sort out the other feelings.

Her mother kissed her on the forehead. "Isn't it just like him? Couldn't die like a normal person. Had to make a production out of it." She wrapped her arms around Deirdre and rocked her, not something Deirdre could remember her mother ever having done. She'd never been one for kissing boo-boos. Instead she'd clap her hands and assure Deirdre she was fine, even when it was obvious that she was not.

Gloria held her at arm's length and gently tucked a lock of hair behind Deirdre's ear. "And yet life goes on, doesn't it?" There. That was more like it. "Act four. Act five. Your father always insisted that a really good story makes you care about what's going to happen to the characters after the movie ends."

"He was full of good advice," Deirdre said. "For everyone but himself."

The doorbell rang. Henry went to answer it.

"I hope that's not another reporter," Deirdre said. "They were camped outside yesterday, and the police have been —"

She was interrupted by Henry's return. Following him was a woman about Deirdre's age with a mane of shoulder-length, lion-colored, perfectly layered hair. She had on brown work boots and a raincoat and carried a hard hat and a clipboard, a sturdy canvas bag, and a walking stick.

"Mom? Deirdre?" Henry said. "This is the insurance adjuster."

"Sondra Dray," the woman said. Her canvas satchel thunked on the floor when she set it down to shake hands with Gloria and then Deirdre. The thick belt on her coat was hung with tools — a heavy-duty flashlight, a tape measure, a pry bar. "I was just telling Mr. Unger" — *Mr. Unger?* Deirdre's stomach turned over, and it was a moment before she realized Sondra meant Henry, not Arthur — "that I'll need at least a few hours to complete my inventory. The sooner I get started, the sooner I'll be done."

"Here, I'll take that." Henry picked up the satchel and led her out through the kitchen door.

"Your brother can be a gentleman when he feels like it," Gloria said.

"He can also be a jerk."

"That," her mother said, "is not news." She returned to the stove and turned the burner back on.

"You're cooking?"

"Now don't you start with me," Gloria said, shaking a fork at Deirdre. "Your brother's already been there. I may not be a gourmet chef, but I've always been able to put together a perfectly serviceable breakfast. I could have been a short-order cook."

Deirdre snorted a laugh. "I'm not questioning your competence. But bacon? You once told me it has more carcinogens, ounce for ounce, than tobacco."

"Not this bacon. This" — Gloria lifted a strip of what looked like pink-and-white rubber — "is soy based. Nothing toxic in it. And it doesn't taste bad as long as you forget that it's supposed to be bacon." She glanced sideways at Deirdre. "Don't look at me like that. I do remember what bacon tastes like. And yes, I do miss it."

The truth was, whatever it was that her mother was cooking, it smelled yummy. Deirdre's mouth watered.

Gloria went on, "I also brought organic

eggs and whole-grain bread. Or I have granola, too. Would you rather have that?"

"Just bread." Her mother's granola was so healthy it tasted like wood chips. Deirdre opened the bag of bread and put two slices in the toaster.

"Your brother told me what happened. About your finding him." Gloria shuddered. "About the police."

"Someone killed him. And the police actually think it could have been me."

"That's ridiculous." Gloria looked out toward the pool. "Whatever else you can say about the police, they are not complete fools. Why would they think you killed him? It's absurd. You got along. Unlike plenty of other folks who might have wanted to kill your father at one time or another. Myself included."

Her mother was always so definite, regardless of whether her opinion was informed or not. For once Deirdre found that reassuring. "You weren't here," Deirdre said. "You have an alibi."

Her mother lifted a strip and checked the underside. Then she removed strip after strip of soy bacon from the pan and laid them on a paper towel. "I'm glad you called Sy."

"He talked to you?" Deirdre asked.

"Henry told me."

"Sy went with me to talk to the police."

"He's the real deal. Defended Timothy Leary. Emily Harris. Patty Hearst."

"Joelen Nichol."

"Joelen Nichol." Her mother broke an egg into the pan. It sizzled and spat. She lowered the heat. "I hear she's turned up again."

"Mom, Sy said something to me that I didn't understand. He said he helped me stay out of trouble then. And I got the impression he was talking about the night Joelen's mother's boyfriend was killed."

Her mother's hand froze in midair above the egg carton. "One egg or two?"

"Two."

"So what is she doing?"

"Joelen? She's living with Bunny — again or still, I don't know which. Selling real estate. Dad had an appointment to talk to her about putting the house on the market."

"He did, did he?" Gloria broke the second egg into the pan.

"Sounds like you're surprised that he'd hire her."

"With all the Realtors to choose from? Yes."

"I thought you were friends with her mother."

Gloria tucked a wisp of hair into her

turban. "Friends? Me and Elenor Nichol? Whatever gave you that idea?"

Deirdre took in her mother's makeup-free face, baggy clothing, and battered leather sandals with rubber-tire soles. The only hint of vanity was the turban hiding her shorn hair. The idea that her mother and Elenor Nichol had been bosom buddies was preposterous.

"Something she said. When reporters and police showed up here, Joelen drove me over there and Bunny helped me dress up so I wouldn't be recognized. She said you were chorus girls together at Warner Brothers."

Gloria gave a shrug, allowing that it was true. "We worked at the same studio, along with a lot of other people."

"You and Daddy went to her parties."

"Us and half of Hollywood." Gloria bit her lip and poked at the eggs, breaking one of the yolks. "Poor thing. After the scandal, she had quite a lot to deal with. I think your father helped her out where he could. Got her a cameo in *Towering Inferno*. He was one of her many admirers." She stated that last part as if it were just a fact. "It was a mistake, letting you stay over there whenever you wanted to. I was . . . distracted."

It struck Deirdre, not for the first time, that her mother's transformation — from wisecracking broad who took her scotch straight on the rocks and bought tailored suits from the same exclusive designer as Pat Nixon, to New Age acolyte in sackcloth — had always felt like some kind of penance. But neither the old chic-but-prickly Gloria Unger nor this new dowdy-but-outwardly-serene version had even the slightest bit in common with Bunny Nichol. And Bunny was shrewd enough to know that. So why pretend otherwise?

Gloria shook the pan, loosening the eggs, and with a practiced gesture flipped them. Smiled. She reached into the overhead cupboard and pulled down a plate. Deirdre got out some silverware and a napkin and sat at the kitchen table while her mother slid the eggs onto the plate along with strips of soy bacon and the toast, which had popped. "Bon appétit!"

Deirdre picked up a piece of the soy bacon and nibbled on it. Salty. Sweet. Crisp, not greasy. Not awful at all, just odd. She stuffed the entire piece into her mouth and chased it with a bite of egg. "Did you know that Dad named me his literary executor?"

"I did." Her mother went to the sink and ran the water. "He asked if I thought it was a good idea." She shot Deirdre a quick glance as she scrubbed the pan. "I know.

Not something you'd have volunteered for. Don't panic. I'm here to help. We can take a quick first pass through his papers — shouldn't take more than a day or two if we put our minds to it. With the fire, there's less to deal with."

That was an understatement. Deirdre dragged a piece of wheat toast through the yolk and put it in her mouth.

Gloria picked up a dish towel. Leaning with her back against the sink, she started drying the pan. "Have you and Henry made plans for the funeral?"

"I talked to the mortuary, but I didn't know what to say about a service. The coroner is supposed to release Dad's body today."

"Right," her mother said, drying her hands, snapping the dish towel and folding it smartly. "Finish your breakfast. Then get me the phone number of the funeral home and find me your father's Rolodex. We'll schedule a service for day after tomorrow. Keep it simple. Tasteful. I'll get some of his friends to say a few words. I'll have food delivered to the house for after. And after it's all over, how about the three of us drive out to Paradise Cove? Scatter your father's ashes in the sea. He always said he was part fish. Then I'll take you and Henry to Holiday House. I haven't been back there in ages. We can order cracked crab and champagne and sit out on the patio and toast your father's memory."

Gratitude pulsed through Deirdre. Henry had called the insurance company. Her mother was offering to organize the funeral and help sort through Arthur's papers. At least she wasn't going to be on her own acting out the role of the dutiful daughter, something she'd never been very good at anyway.

"Holiday House. That sounds perfect," she said. And it did. Her father would have loved to see them toasting him, the consummate celebrity wannabe, at the storied celebrity hangout. It was where JFK and Marilyn, Liz and Eddie, Frankie and Ava had supposedly shared intimate tête-à-têtes and then slipped off to the attached no-tell motel. Its ultramodern design of glass and steel and stone and spectacular view would have made it a tourist attraction if the maître d' hadn't courteously but firmly barred anyone who smacked of tourist or, even worse, paparazzi. Deirdre had a soft spot for it as well. She'd once handled the sale of a photograph by Man Ray of a weather-beaten shipwreck washed up on a stretch of beach that could only be viewed from the Holiday House patio.

"That's it then. Decided," Gloria said with a wry smile. She sat at the kitchen table opposite Deirdre, took a deep breath, and bowed her head. Her lips moved in a whisper as she rubbed together the thumb and fingers of her left hand. This was Gloria's way of maintaining her cherished tranquility, reciting a mantra and fingering the string of prayer beads that for years she'd worn wrapped around her wrist. Portable valium, Arthur used to call them. One hundred and eight beads, four lapis lazuli and the rest turquoise.

Only now there was no string of beads wrapped around Gloria's wrist.

Chapter 24

"Missing something?" Deirdre reached across the kitchen table for her mother's hand and dropped two of the beads she'd found among the ashes on the floor of her father's garage office into Gloria's upturned palm. "Three guesses where I found them."

Her mother's eyes snapped open, but she didn't say anything.

"You weren't late because you had car trouble. You were here yesterday. It was you I saw up there in the window before the fire, wasn't it?"

Gloria pursed her lips and rubbed her fingers together. "Along the road to truth, there are only two mistakes you can make. Not starting. And not going all the way."

Serenity could be so irritating. "Did you set the fire?"

Gloria reared back as if she'd been slapped. "Of course I did not set the god-damn fire. Do you think I'd have been up in your father's office if I had?"

That, at least, made some sense. "Then what were you doing up there? And why didn't you come in? You could have at least —" What? Shown up? Said hello? Been there for Deirdre and Henry?

"I'm sorry. I'm so sorry. I —" Gloria moved to embrace her.

"Sorry?" Deirdre sobbed and pushed her away. "You never think of anyone but yourself."

Her mother held up her hands and backed off. "Okay. Fair enough. You have every right to be angry. Let me try to explain. I got back yesterday." She swallowed. "And actually I did call. I called because I wanted to be sure you and Henry weren't going to be here when I arrived."

Deirdre felt her jaw drop. "Because?"

"Because . . ." Tension drained from her mother's face. "Deirdre, I knew you'd be going through your father's papers. I was trying to protect you and your brother from what you might find."

"I don't need protecting. And Henry certainly doesn't. And why now? How long's it been since I've seen you? Months? And then only because I drove to Twenty-nine Palms." Her mother flinched, but Deirdre kept going. "Besides, if you were trying

235

to protect us, that train left the station a good long time ago."

"Deirdre, Deirdre. Don't." Her mother gave her a long, mournful look. "Holding on to anger is like holding on to a hot coal."

"Spare me the bumper stickers. Why were you up in his office?"

"Deirdre, your father never meant to hurt you."

"What were you looking for? His creepy snapshots?"

Gloria blinked. "Snapshots?"

"You didn't know? He was bringing young women, some of them just teenagers, up to his office and taking their pictures. And I can only imagine what else."

"Teenagers?" Creases deepened between her mother's eyes. "I don't believe it."

"The photographs got destroyed in the fire, but I saved one of them." Deirdre went into the laundry room and got the Polaroid she'd left on the shelf. She slammed it down on the kitchen table.

Her mother recoiled. "Oh my." She stared at the photograph for a moment, then across at Deirdre. "Joelen Nichol."

"She's the only one I recognized." Deirdre turned the picture over to show her the asterisks written on the back. "He even rated them. See?"

"And you think your father would . . . with your best friend? You can't seriously believe that." Gloria took the picture from Deirdre and held Joelen's face under the light. "She was a beautiful girl, wasn't she? And I don't doubt that she was" — she paused for a moment — "precocious, in some respects. Frankly, I wasn't thrilled that you and she were such close friends. But I had no idea that anything like this was going on." She put the picture down on the table and looked hard at Deirdre. "I don't know everything that your father was getting up to. I didn't want to know because I was leaving him, and it would have been just one more thing to be furious about, and I knew enough already. It would have been like drinking poison and wanting *him* to die." Realizing what she'd said, Gloria shook her head. "I don't mean that literally, of course. I'd never have wanted him to . . . I mean . . . I just meant that metaphorically. But here's the thing. Joelen was still a teenager when this picture was taken. And whatever else Arthur may have been, he was not a pedophile."

CHAPTER 25

"I'm back." At the sound of Henry's voice, Gloria shot up from the kitchen table. The dogs tumbled into the room and swarmed at her feet. She reached over to the counter for two pieces of raw soy bacon. They'd barely hit the floor before the dogs had scarfed them up.

"Is the insurance adjuster done out there?" Gloria asked Henry.

"She's done with the garage downstairs. Other than the bikes and the car, there wasn't a whole lot more to claim. Now she's upstairs, working on the office." Henry helped himself to a piece of fake bacon. Sniffed. Took a bite. Chewed. Pulled a face. "What *is* this?"

"It's healthy," Deirdre said. "Mom brought it."

"It's weird," he said, snagging a second piece.

"When your brother was a toddler, he ate

carpet backing," Gloria said. "A real connoisseur of kapok."

"Ah! So *that's* what this tastes like," Henry said, popping the last piece into his mouth. "Sondra says they won't be able to begin processing the claim without a copy of the official incident report. One of us has to go to City Hall and request it. Even with that, the bureaucracy can take weeks to spit out the report . . . *unless* it's goosed along by someone on the inside." Henry eyed Deirdre. "Know anyone who might be able to help?"

"I do not *know*" — Deirdre drew quote marks in the air — "Tyler Corrigan."

"Tyler?" Gloria said. "The boy who lived across the street?"

"Used to show off for Deirdre," Henry said. "He was kind of a prick."

"He was a nice boy," her mother said. "Delivered our newspaper for a while."

"He's the city's lead arson investigator," Henry said, "and Sondra says he's the one who signs off on cases."

"So now we're a case?" Deirdre said. Henry's fixation on Tyler was starting to annoy her. "How is *Sondra* doing?"

"She's up there," Henry said, "literally picking the place apart. Talking into a cassette recorder and making an inventory of everything that got damaged, from the carpet to the toilet paper dispenser. It's like watching an autopsy. Slow. Painstaking. Messy."

"I'll bet," Deirdre said, sniffing at her own fingers. She didn't know if that was the soy bacon or barbecued prayer beads that she smelled.

"She's got rubber gloves and baggies that go over her boots. The smell and the heat got to me right away, but she's oblivious. Girl knows how to travel — she's got water in her backpack and a very long straw." Henry poured himself a cup of coffee and sat at the table. "So what were you two talking about?"

"Those photographs that were stuck in the Players Directories that Dad wanted you to throw away? There's only one that didn't get incinerated." Deirdre turned it over so he could see Joelen's face.

For a few moments, the only sounds in the room were Baby's claws clicking across the floor and a chuffing as she sniffed, ever hopeful, at the floor where bacon had landed. Deirdre waited until she couldn't any longer. "Recognize her?"

Henry raised his eyebrows and smirked, allowing that he did.

Deirdre turned the picture over to show

him the asterisks. "Mom says Dad didn't write those."

Henry picked up the snapshot. "Really?" He and Gloria exchanged a look.

"What?" Deirdre said.

"*What* what?" Henry said.

"Don't give me that. I'm not blind. What's up with you two?"

Gloria said, "Henry, your sister thinks your father was responsible for that." She pointed to the photograph.

"And the others like it," Deirdre said.

"He was responsible." Henry stared impassively at Gloria. "A regular trailblazer."

"Henry —" Gloria started.

"And what do you know about it?" Henry said, cutting her off. "You were on *the path.*" *The path* was the term that their mother used for her cleansing journey to what she called self-awakening. It had started long before she left Arthur, and even though Deirdre knew Gloria had needed to do something to preserve her own sanity, like Henry she resented the way Gloria had spun herself a protective cocoon.

Gloria reared back. "And look what you were on your way to, Henry." She spread her arms and looked around. "Still living with your father in a house that's literally falling down around you."

"It wasn't my fault that I got thrown out of school. My roommate —"

"Right. He's the one who made you stop going to classes. Did he make you give up music and wreck your car, too?"

"Oh, remind me again, how much did you pay for that car?"

Deirdre knew from experience that they were just getting warmed up. "Stop it!" she said, standing so fast that her chair tipped over backward. She snatched the photograph from Henry, nabbed her crutch, walked her plate to the sink, and dropped it in with a clatter. Across the room, her messenger bag hung from a hook by the back door. She grabbed it. It was still damp and weighed almost nothing. All that was in it was her keys and wallet. She slipped the photograph in, too, and headed for the door.

"Where are you going?" Gloria asked.

"Out."

"Go to City Hall, why don't you," Henry said, "and file the request for the form we need."

The last thing Deirdre felt like doing at that moment was agreeing with Henry, but it was actually a good suggestion. She paused, the door open. "What's it called?"

"An incident report," Henry said. "And remember to charm Tyler, won't you?"

Deirdre stepped outside and slammed the door behind her. She clumped down the back steps, out the driveway, and into the street to her car. She'd started the engine when she realized a ticket was stuck to her windshield. She got out and snagged it. *Overnight parking* was checked. There was an envelope for remitting her twenty-five-dollar fine. *Damn.* She got back into the car, jammed the ticket in her glove compartment, and took off.

Charm Tyler. She glanced at her reflection in her rearview mirror. Eyes wild. Skin blotchy. Hair a rat's nest. On top of that, her outfit — those ridiculous boots and her father's shirt — made her look as if she were on her way to a Halloween party. She needed to pull herself together if she was going to get anywhere in the charm department.

It had been many years since Deirdre had shopped for clothes or gotten her hair cut in Beverly Hills. She parked in the lot behind the stores on Little Santa Monica near Beverly Drive and fed some coins into the meter. Across the street was the park where she used to stand and wave at trains that rode through. If she was lucky, someone hanging out of the last car, a real red caboose, would wave back at her. That was even better than getting a semi on the freeway to toot its air horn at you.

Walking along Little Santa Monica, feeling as if she were throwing a dart at a map, she stopped in front of Latour's Hair Salon. A small WALK-INS WELCOME sign was in the window. She pushed open the heavy wood door and stepped inside.

A spectrally thin young woman in a black turtleneck and fringed leather vest stood at the front desk, talking on the phone. Her gaze flickered over Deirdre and then away. It was the same dismissive look the clerk at Jax had given her when she was in high school and ventured into the elegant store where the popular girls at school bought their straight skirts and shells and matching Geistex sweaters. Back then, Deirdre had turned tail and fled. Didn't matter that she had saved up enough from babysitting to pay for any of their outfits.

Now she held her ground. Behind the counter, stations on facing walls were half-full of customers and the air was laden with the sewer-gas smell of perms.

Finally the receptionist got off the phone. She gave Deirdre a brittle smile. "Do you have an appointment?"

"Do I need one? I'd like to get my hair

cut." Quite deliberately Deirdre laid her crutch on the desk.

The woman looked startled for a moment, then turned and buried her nose in an appointment ledger. "Cut? Blow-dry?"

"Please."

An hour later, Deirdre emerged from the salon, her hair cut short and layered, just framing her face, the bangs poufy and saucily blown to the side. She caught glimpses of her new self reflected in store windows as she continued to Rodeo Drive. For so many years she'd cursed her curls and now they were in style. The chambray shirt and boots, on the other hand, had to go.

She entered a new shopping complex with a glass atrium. She couldn't remember what had been at that address when she was growing up — maybe Uncle Bernie's, the toy store with a lemonade tree in the back. Now it was home to Gucci, Giorgio, and Chanel. They made Jax look like J.J. Newberry.

Farther down the street Deirdre passed boutique after boutique. Finally she entered a dancewear store and bought a dark purple scoop-necked leotard, black leggings, and a flowy white silk shirt that grazed her knees. She passed on the slouchy pink leg warmers the Jennifer Beals–look-alike salesgirl tried to foist on her.

Next door, among Indian bedspreads, Moroccan leather handbags, and feathered earrings, she found a suede belt with a brightly enameled buckle and a long Indian scarf in reds and pinks. A few doors down was a consignment shop with a GOING OUT OF BUSINESS, LOST OUR LEASE sign. There Deirdre found a whole row of what looked like brand-new Keds. She bought two pairs in white — she always had to buy two pairs of shoes because one foot was now two sizes smaller than the other.

She ducked into the consignment shop's makeshift dressing room — sheets hung from a clothesline in a back corner of the store — and stripped off her clothes, then assembled her new outfit. She fluffed her newly shorn hair with her fingers, cocked her hip, and examined her reflection in the mirror. *Locked and loaded.*

She was ready to find Tyler Corrigan.

CHAPTER 26

City Hall was nearby, but just a little too far for Deirdre to walk there and back with her bad leg. So she drove the few blocks over and parked in a handicapped spot in front. This time no news crews were there filming.

She climbed the long, broad front staircase, though there was probably a handicapped entrance at ground level. She caught her reflection in the glass of the door just before she pushed it open. The hair was cute and bouncy, the shirt elegant and casual, the sneakers a hint that she wasn't taking herself too seriously.

Cool air oozed out as she stepped into the lobby, a magnificent Spanish Renaissance two-story entryway with terrazzo floors, white marble walls, and a coffered ceiling. The vast space hummed with a steady flow of uniformed officers, men and the occasional woman in business suits carrying thick briefcases, and lost-looking citizens who were probably there to file for tax abatements, report for jury duty, or, like her, request a copy of an official document.

It was past noon, and the soy bacon and eggs seemed a long time ago. Deirdre bought a granola bar from a newsstand tucked incongruously in the corner under a massive California state flag and wolfed it down. She chased it with a stick of Dentyne, hoping to dispel the miasma of perfumed conditioner and hair gel that felt as if it were floating in a thick cloud around her head.

She had no desire to run into Detective Martinez, so she made her way quickly down the hall, following the signs to Public Records. The room had linoleum, not terrazzo, on the floor, and its walls were painted mustard yellow. Six rows of folding chairs took up half the space, most of the seats taken. A man wearing a bright green golf shirt and sunglasses on top of his bald head brushed past her on his way to the door. "Good luck," he said. "Effing incompetence. An hour and a half wasted."

The number 110 flashed over a counter with a bank of clerk's stations. Deirdre took a number from the feeder — *142*. She found the Request for Records form on one of the shelves, stood in the back, and started to fill it out. Her name. Address. She checked the box beside "Incident Report," then wrote in the date and time of the fire, the address, and a description. When she finished, the number counter had crept up to 112. Two harried clerks seemed to be actually serving customers. Several others were on phones, another hunched over his desk, all of them studiously avoiding eye contact with the thirty-plus impatient citizens sitting and standing beyond the safe barrier of the counter.

Clearly, she had plenty of time to kill. Tyler had said his office was next to some kind of lab in the basement. Deirdre left the waiting area and wandered back through the hall to the atrium lobby. There she found the elevators, their outer sliding doors elaborate wrought-iron grillwork. She stepped inside one and pressed B. The elevator descended two floors and slid open to reveal a basement hallway.

Paint the color of wet sand peeled on the walls. Two rows of Wanted posters — all men — hung on the bulletin board across the hall. The air was cooler and clammier than on the main floor, and Deirdre wondered if that was a whiff of formaldehyde under a layer of Pine-Sol. Signs pointed one way to Maintenance and the elevator, the other way to the restrooms, Arson Investigation, Crime Lab, and Records Storage.

Deirdre followed the sign pointing toward Arson Investigation, continuing to a door with a pebbled glass inset stenciled with the words ARSON UNIT. She was about to reach for the knob when the door opened. A man she didn't recognize came out. He held the door for her.

The Arson Unit was a single room, mostly bare with a half-dozen desks crowded in, surrounded by shelves and file cabinets. A folding table against a wall was loaded with pamphlets. On the side wall was pinned a massive gray-and-green topographic map with colored pushpins stuck in it.

Tyler was sitting at a desk under a high window by the back wall. He was engrossed in some typewritten pages, switching between writing in pen and highlighting with a yellow marker. Deirdre headed his way. When she was within reaching distance, she said, "Tyler?"

He looked up. "Deirdre!" He shoved the papers he'd been working on into a file folder and stood, grazing his head on one of the pipes that ran overhead. "Hey. I was just thinking about you." His eyes widened. "You look . . . different."

Deirdre felt a flush creep up her neck. "I hope it's an okay different."

"Very okay. I was" — he shot a guilty look at the closed file folder — "just working on your case. Report's almost finished."

"I thought it takes weeks."

"Who told you that?"

"Our claims adjuster."

"I guess it can take that long to get processed once I file it. But the analysis — well, we know pretty much what we're dealing with. Most of the time, anyway."

"As in now?"

He nodded.

"So? Tell me. You can tell me, can't you? What started the fire?"

Tyler sat. Deirdre could feel herself trembling as she waited for his answer.

"I can tell you what we know," he said. "The fire started right where we originally thought it did. In a bag of potting mix."

"Right. Probably left over from years ago when Mom was still living there."

Tyler gave her an uneasy look. "You said your mother grew geraniums?"

"Scented geraniums," Deirdre said, wondering where this was going.

"The thing is, the concentration of ammonium nitrate in that potting mix is much too high. It would have burned the roots of

251

her plants. Even amateur horticulturists know that. Maybe your father bought it?"

"Not likely," Deirdre said. There was only one way her father messed around with potting mix. "Were there any cigarette butts in it?"

"There were. But they're not what started the fire."

Deirdre took a deep breath. "So what are you saying?"

"It looks like someone tried to make it appear as if the fire was caused by careless disposal of smoking materials. So we'd find the cigarette butts and stop looking for what really fueled the fire."

"Which was?"

"Good old-fashioned kerosene." Tyler gave her a long, somber look.

Arson. Deirdre dropped into the chair opposite his desk. It wasn't unexpected, but still the certainty of the verdict knocked the air out of her. Someone had set fire to her father's garage. Someone had killed her father. "Who? Why?"

"Those are questions for the police."

Deirdre tried to put it together. Cigarette butts stuck into kerosene-laced potting mix that her mother never would have purchased. Whoever did that knew her father was a smoker who stubbed out his cigarettes wherever happened to be convenient. "Could it have been set up in advance?" she asked.

"Probably was. It would be simple. Lace the mix with kerosene. Wait till there's no one around, sneak in, and put the bag in the garage. Poke a few burning cigarettes into it and let nature take its course. Might have taken a few minutes or a few hours to really get going, but it was a pretty sure bet that eventually it would."

Only whoever it was had miscalculated. The house might have been empty, but their mother was in the garage's second-floor office. While Deirdre was pulling the alarm, Gloria must have bolted and then tried to hide the fact that she'd been there. Deirdre never would have known if she hadn't found the prayer beads.

"So there's no way it could have been an accident?" Deirdre said. She knew she was grasping at straws.

"An accidental kerosene spill at just the right moment? How likely is that?" Tyler paused. "You can be sure that the insurance company will bring in a professional investigator to see if the fire was set for financial gain."

Deirdre groaned. "Here we go. They'll think one of us did it."

"Maybe. But fire damage doesn't add value to a property you're about to sell. So what would you have stood to gain?"

Deirdre thought about it. If the fire wasn't set for financial gain, then why? Pure malice? Why target just the garage? Unless that was the point, maybe to destroy what was in the garage, including whatever her mother was up there trying to keep Deirdre and Henry from finding.

"Well, thank you for telling me," Deirdre said. She started to get up.

"Deirdre, there's more. I found your accident report." Tyler's solemn tone and grave expression dropped her back into the chair. She swallowed hard and waited for him to go on.

"The records from 1963 are all on microfiche, so it should have been easy to find. And it would have been . . . if the accident had been in Beverly Hills. But it wasn't."

Not in Beverly Hills. That meant that her father hadn't been driving her home from Joelen's house. He'd been driving . . . where? Deirdre sat back and took a deep, shuddering breath.

"Once I was sure the report wasn't in our records, I called a buddy over at the LAPD. They've got a huge repository. Good thing there's not many Austin-Healey convertibles

254

out there to get into traffic accidents. He found it and sent me a copy." He opened his desk drawer, drew out two grainy faxes, and laid them on the desk in front of Deirdre.

She leaned forward. Across the top in capital letters were the words *POLICE INCIDENT REPORT.* Below that:

```
Crash investigator: TROOPER
          MITCHELL

Vehicle # [1] Year [1957] Make
[AUHE] Model [CV]
```

Deirdre ran her fingers across the letters. This was the footprint she'd been sure she'd never find.

Then she read the next line.

```
Driver [DEIRDRE UNGER] [F] [15]
of [BEVERLY HILLS, CA]
```

It felt as if the floor had opened up under her and she was in free fall. There had to be some mistake. "This has my name as the driver." When Tyler just nodded, she said, "But how could that be? I remember riding in the *passenger* seat. The top was down. I was thrown from the car. It was cold. I . . .

I can remember all kinds of details."

"You thought you were in Beverly Hills."

"I did . . . and I didn't. I wanted to believe that, but it never made any sense. Even with a detour in the wrong direction, it just wasn't right. But this? This is completely insane."

"I'm sorry. I know it's not what you expected."

Deirdre gripped the arm of the chair. *She'd driven the car off the road. Not her father.* "I'm just trying to understand."

For a minute, Tyler didn't say anything, giving her time to absorb the shock. Then he said, "You wanted to know where it happened." He turned to the second stapled sheet and pointed to a paragraph in the middle of the page.

Deirdre pulled the faxed sheets closer and read.

Narrative: V1 DRIVER WAS DRIVING EAST ON MULHOLLAND. V1 CRASHED INTO A GUARDRAIL LOCATED AT APPROXIMATELY 10536 MULHOLLAND DRIVE. DRIVER EJECTED FROM THE CAR. DRIVER TRANSPORTED TO NORTHRIDGE HOSPITAL. THE CRASH REMAINS UNDER INVESTIGATION AND CHARGES ARE PENDING.

Deirdre shook her head, and then shook it again. *Mulholland Drive?* It was at least five miles from the Nichols' house, and in the opposite direction from home.

Tyler went over to the map on the wall. He stuck a white pushpin at a curve on a road highlighted in yellow, a road that snaked along the crest of the finely drawn, crenellated landscape that was the Santa Monica Mountains. "You're not the only one who's wiped out there. There's a reason they call that spot Suicide Bend."

Deirdre read aloud the final line of the report. " 'The crash remains under investigation and charges are pending.' What does that mean?"

"You were never charged?"

"I don't remembering being charged. But I don't remember driving, either." Maybe this was what Sy had meant when he said he'd kept her out of trouble *then.* No charges.

She walked up to the map and stared at the white pushpin. She hadn't driven that stretch in many years, but she knew it well. After she'd mastered driving in the flats between Santa Monica and Sunset, her father had taken her into the canyons for serious driving lessons. There, she'd learned to start from a dead stop on a steep incline without rolling backward. To take curves, downshifting first, judging how well the road was banked to determine how much to decelerate going in and how fast she could accelerate coming out. Always, always, her father reminded her, *stay in control and stay in your goddamned lane.*

Driving Mulholland was the ultimate test. In her mind's eye Deirdre could run the curves and straightaways of the infamous road that was known as "the snake," catching glimpses of the vast and usually smog-skimmed San Fernando Valley unfurling to the northwest.

With her finger she traced the yellow-highlighted road. She tried to envision the spot, right at a sharp elbow. Was this where her father had always cautioned her to respect the signage and slow the hell down? Where he'd once made her pull over and hike twenty minutes down a steep embankment until they reached a Dodge Dart lying in the scrub, its blue paint nearly rusted away? Nearby, in a dry streambed, a red Porsche had lain on its back, looking like the empty carapace of a stranded beetle. Deirdre had peered into the car through the broken windshield, fully expecting to find a skeleton sitting at the wheel. But the car's interior had been stripped, filled only with a tangle of vines and what she later realized was poison oak. Surely her father had been trying to convey a lesson about the dire consequences of reckless driving, but what stayed with Deirdre, even now, was the brutal beauty of the landscape and the power of time.

Maybe she'd been going too fast that night. Maybe she'd been blinded by oncoming headlights. Swerved to avoid another driver? Skidded on a gravel spill?

But why had she been there at all, and where on earth had she thought she was going?

CHAPTER 27

Deirdre left Tyler's office feeling numb. She barely registered his parting words: "Call me if there's anything more I can do." He added, "Anytime." *Really?* And then, as if he'd read her mind, he'd written his home and office phone numbers on the accident report and repeated, "Anytime."

She sleepwalked from City Hall out to her car, nearly missing a step off the curb. When she settled into her car, she gripped the steering wheel tightly, holding on to the present as if it were a life preserver as piece by piece her memories bumped up, at last, against facts. She'd gone for so many years assuming she'd never know exactly where the car had crashed, and now, just like that, she had the answer.

So much for the fantasy that her father had taken a wrong turn leaving the Nichols' estate. One thing was clear. She hadn't been taken to Northridge Hospital because of their trauma unit. She'd been taken there because it was the closest hospital.

So where had it come from, her vivid memory of her father helping her down the Nichols' dark back stairs and out to the car? Of curling up on the passenger seat, shivering with cold because the top was down and she was wearing only her pajamas? Of her father's voice telling her to "sleep tight," followed by a kiss on her forehead? Of feeling so sick and dizzy when the car started to move that she'd had to close her eyes? Had she simply imagined her father's silhouette at the wheel?

She closed her eyes now. Were her memories of what came next as tainted? The sound of metal on metal at the moment of collision. She didn't remember being airborne, only the bone-jarring impact as she landed. The horrifying sound of her femur cracking. And then pain. Pain so intense she was afraid to move. Afraid to look.

She'd heard a groan in the dark, and her name: "Deirdre?" If it hadn't been her father's voice, then whose was it?

She must have passed out because the next thing she remembered was pebbles and grit hitting her face. Footsteps scrabbling. Hands reaching for her. She'd tried to reach back.

"It's a girl," a man's voice had called out. "She's hurt bad. Better call an ambulance, quick. I'm afraid to move her."

A motorcycle revved in the distance, somewhere above her, and roared off. Then quiet enveloped her. Crickets. The rustling of a breeze through tree branches. And pain, still so much pain.

The voice that called to her from somewhere in the dark as she lay on the embankment, trying not to lose consciousness as she waited for help, could not have been her father's. The labored breathing must have been her own.

She'd heard the first siren, a cry, deep in the night. She imagined pulling it toward her, reeling it in like a hawk caught on a fishing line. Finally, bright lights. Voices. The crunch of feet on unstable hillside. A reassuring hand on her shoulder. Gentle pressure. Antiseptic smell. Then pain like lightning seared through her as she was jostled and lifted, brush pulling at her clothing and snagging in her hair. That was her own voice that she heard, screaming into the night.

"It's going to be all right." A woman's voice. "We have to get you out of here. I know you're hurt. This should help. Hold still. Just a pinch." She'd felt a prick on her arm and slowly, gradually, she disconnected. The pain took shape and pulsed in front of her as the stretcher was lifted, more like heat lightning than jagged spikes, a phantom that grew ever more transparent with each step closer to the light. To the street.

"Deirdre . . ." A man's voice. She'd strained to see behind her, but her head was too heavy and it hurt too much to move. Finally she floated into the ambulance, from noise to stillness, from shadow to bright. The slam of the doors was muffled, and she was in another world of whiteness and stainless steel and blood.

The next morning Deirdre had woken up heavily sedated and still in pain. Her head ached and dark circles under her bloodshot eyes made it look as if she'd been punched in the face. Her father sat grim-faced by her bed. He'd emerged from the accident unscathed. He'd been belted in — that's what he told her. She hadn't.

At the knock on the window, Deirdre jolted out of the past. A woman in a dark uniform was peering in at her through the windshield. A meter maid.

The last thing she needed was another parking ticket. Deirdre rolled down the window and called out, "Thank you! I was just leaving." As she backed out, she realized she still had the accident report clutched in her hand, along with her number 142 from the Records Office.

The night Tito was killed she might have gotten into her father's car and, upset and disoriented, ended up on Mulholland. Now she drove there deliberately. It was all she could do to keep from blowing through stop sign after stop sign as she crossed the empty intersections between residential blocks, driving north on Beverly.

Could her fifteen-year-old self have driven off in her father's car? Her gut said *no way.* Drive without a driver's license? Not the good girl who'd detour a half block to avoid jaywalking. Who'd never been tardy to school, never ventured into the school hallway without a pass, never borrowed a library book she hadn't returned. Not the girl who'd walked all the way back to J.J. Newberry in the rain to return a tube of Passionate Pink lipstick that her best friend had slipped into her pocket.

No. She'd never have taken off in her father's car, not unless she'd been running from the devil himself. And no matter how drunk she'd been, she'd have remembered that.

By the time Deirdre was above Sunset her grip on the wheel had loosened. The mystique of Mulholland Drive had spawned urban legends: tales of a headless hitchhiker, of a depraved sex maniac with a hook for an arm who stalked couples necking in their cars at the overlooks, of a phantom Ferrari that led motorists off cliffs. As if the road's twists and turns weren't hairy enough, many a driver saw bodies hanging among the dangling boughs of willow trees that lined Mulholland's edges. It didn't help that the Mafia really had used the road's steep banks to dispose of corpses.

It would take some of the fun out of it, driving an automatic. But with only one good leg, operating a stick shift was impossible. It was like trying to hitchhike without a thumb. She passed a grassy park and kept on going. There was the gate that her father told her led to what had once been Jimmy Cagney's estate. A driveway that disappeared into the bushes led to the home of Mel Torme. Arborvitae lined the driveway to Charlton Heston's estate.

By the time Deirdre reached the turn onto Mulholland she was calm. In the zone. She waited at the stop sign as a motorcycle flew past. Then another. Mulholland was dangerous for motorcycles, and yet this was where they all came to be challenged.

She flipped on the radio. As if summoned

from the underworld, there was Mötley Crüe. *Shout! Shout! Shout!* The pounding beat filled the car. Deirdre's heart kicked into gear as she turned and accelerated, her tires spitting gravel. She pictured the overlook where she was headed. Grasping the wheel with two hands, she eased into the first curve, the Valley rising before her. She accelerated past the entrance to Coldwater Canyon Park, then took the next curve a bit too fast and felt the rear wheels start to slide toward a rock face.

Adrenaline pulsed in her ears along with the Crüe's sinister chant. She amped the volume until she could feel the bass drums and snares vibrating through the steering column. Under her, the road undulated and straightened, tilting and righting itself. Mentally she tracked her path as she beat the steering wheel with the heel of her hand. She sped past one overlook, then another. She knew she was getting near where Tyler had stuck the white pushpin in the map.

Belatedly, she registered the 10 mph hard right arrow and skid marks all over the road. She was already into the turn before she realized what was happening. The car slew sideways. *Turn into it, turn into it!* Her father's voice rang in her head. *Steer in the direction of the skid!*

It was too late for a tidy recovery. The car slid backward, toward a cluster of motorcycles parked at the overlook. Deirdre pumped the brakes, praying that the tires would gain traction. In her rearview mirror, she watched the bikers leap out of the way, like fleas off a dog's back, as the car fishtailed to a halt, a cloud of dust blooming around her.

CHAPTER 28

Thank God Deirdre had missed the bikers. Missed the bikes. Not to mention missed smashing into the guardrail and going over the edge. Heart hammering, she peeled her fingers off the steering wheel for the second time that day, bashed the radio into silence, and killed the engine. A green-and-white sign at the edge of the parking area read SUICIDE BEND OVERLOOK.

This was the spot where she'd crashed twenty-two years ago.

Emerging from the dust in front of her was a guy with a blue bandanna tied Indian style over his forehead. He had on a black leather jacket that might, in another lifetime, possibly have zipped over his paunch. He stomped over to her car until his presence filled the windshield, flicked a cigarette on the ground, and crushed it with the sole of a tooled black cowboy boot, then folded his arms across his chest and glared at her.

Deirdre reached for her crutch, opened the door, and got out. "Sorry, sorry!" She held up a hand in surrender. "Is everyone okay?"

The big biker took off his mirrored aviator glasses. His hair was nearly all gray and pulled back into a long, thin ponytail. "You act as if you want to get killed," he said, his voice a gravelly John Wayne imitation.

Deirdre relaxed a notch. It was a line from *Gunfight at the O.K. Corral,* a movie John Wayne wasn't in. She even knew Doc Holliday's deadpan response: *Maybe I do.* But now was not the time to show off.

"Nice wheels," the big biker went on, stepping over to her Mercedes and stroking its fender. "Can it do any other tricks?"

The other dudes who'd gathered around cracked up. Deirdre's face burned.

"Hey, you okay?" one of them asked. "Maybe you'd better sit a spell."

"Thanks," she said. "I'm fine. Just stupid."

That earned nods all around. Then, one by one, they got on their bikes and took off. Last to leave was the guy who'd greeted her, revving a whole lot louder than he needed to and shooting a cloud of soot out the tailpipe. "Let's be careful out there," he shouted to her over the din. *Hill Street Blues.* "I wouldn't want to find your pretty little bumper hanging from one of these trees." Sounded like that line he'd written all by himself. He put his glasses back on and roared off. *Into the sunset,* only it was well past high noon.

A skim of fine dust had settled over Deirdre's car. With her finger, she wrote on the front fender: JERK. What she should have scrawled there was DAMNED LUCKY THIS TIME. Her rear wheels were just a few feet from a forty-five-degree drop. She leaned against the guardrail, waiting for her heart to stop pounding. Her mother's string of prayer beads would have come in handy. Her white sneakers were streaked with dust and she felt ridiculous in her new outfit with her perfect hair.

Two cars sped past. Then a bike. The sweat coating Deirdre's face cooled as she turned and gazed out past trees and scrub and into the omnipresent haze that settled over Sherman Oaks, turning landmarks, if there'd been any, into smudges.

A sharp smell wafted from the surrounding chaparral. For a moment it took her back to when she'd been carried from the underbrush. She remembered staring up at a moon that seemed to be caught in tree branches.

But she didn't remember hearing the

sounds that she heard now, thunks and clangs like dull wind chimes, from beyond the edge of the overlook. She stood and turned to get a better look. There really was a car bumper hanging from a branch of one of the trees growing on the embankment. Sunlight reflected off its dull chrome. The remnants of a bumper sticker, REAGAN in blue block letters under a wave of stars and stripes, came in and out of view as the bumper twisted in the breeze. Other branches were hung with hubcaps and license plates. One sagged under the weight of a car's dented front grille with a Volkswagen W in the middle.

At the tree's base, maybe fifteen feet down a scrubby incline, lay bouquets of flowers, one merely wilted, the rest virtually mummified, along with framed photographs and stuffed toys, including a teddy bear that looked like her Ollie. But not Ollie, of course.

As Tyler had said, there was a reason this spot was called Suicide Bend. Nailed to the tree's thick trunk was a plank of wood hand-lettered in red paint: SLOW DOWN OR REST IN PEACE.

All the way back to the house, Deirdre seethed. She scolded herself for driving so

271

stupidly and putting her own and others' lives at risk. She was no longer fifteen years old. She was also furious that all these years she'd allowed herself to be convinced that there was no way to find out where she'd crashed. That she'd been blind to the fact that she'd been driving. What else didn't she know?

She parked the car in front of the house and went inside, slamming the door behind her. "Mom? Henry?" she called out.

"Hello, dear! In here." Her mother's reedy voice came from the den.

Deirdre stomped in. "Did you know?" she said.

"Oh good. You're back." Gloria looked up from the legal pad on which she'd been writing. Scattered about at her feet were videocassettes of the movies she and Arthur had written. The VCR was going — Fred Astaire in top hat and tails danced his way across the tabletops of a French sidewalk café.

Gloria paused the video and put the pad on the desk. "Just in time to help us put together a list of clips for a montage to show at the memorial service."

Deirdre put her hands on her hips. "Did you know?"

Her mother blinked. Then frowned.

272

"Goodness. What did you do to your hair?"

Immediately Deirdre felt twelve years old. She could just barely stop herself from shooting back, *And what did you do to your hair? Since when is shaving your head a fashion statement?* It was so aggravating that her mother still had the power to push her buttons.

Deirdre leaned forward on her crutch. "I just found out that everything I thought I knew about what happened to me the night of the car accident that did this to me" — she lifted the crutch — "is a lie."

Her mother's jaw dropped but she didn't say anything.

"Deirdre? What is this all about?" Deirdre jerked around, recognizing the deep, gravelly voice with just a hint of an Eastern European accent. Sy Sterling rose from the wing chair.

"What about you? Did you know, too?" Deirdre threw the words at him. "Because you're the one who kept telling me there was no way to find out where the accident happened. Turns out it's ridiculously easy."

"I did try to find out for you," Sy said. "The record wasn't there."

"It was there. In the Los Angeles Police Department records."

Gloria turned to Sy. "What on earth is

273

she talking about?"

"See for yourself." Deirdre tossed the report on the desk. "Since when is Mulholland Drive on the way from the Nichols' house to ours? And who made up the fiction that it was Daddy driving —"

"Whoa, whoa, whoa." Sy held up his hands. "Slow down. Sit."

Deirdre didn't want to sit but she did, perched on the edge of the chair opposite her father's desk. Sy came around behind the desk and put his hand on her mother's shoulder. "Okay, then. Let me see what you have here." He slipped on reading glasses and picked up the report. As he read, his scowl darkened. At last he handed it to Gloria.

"See," Deirdre said. "That's the official report of my accident. One person in the car. Not two. I was driving, on Mulholland Drive. And all this time —"

"You were not driving that car." Her mother's hand trembled as she stared at the report. "I don't care what this says." She tossed the paper back on the desk.

"Then what happened? Dad drove up to Mulholland for a joyride? Crashed the car and then abandoned me?"

Gloria and Sy looked at each other, but neither of them spoke.

"The police thought I was driving. I didn't have a driver's license, I got into an accident, but charges against me were never filed. Was that your magic?" Deirdre stared at Sy. "Was that the trouble you said you kept me out of?"

Sy didn't answer, just raised his eyebrows, allowing that there might be some truth to that.

"And there's more," Deirdre went on. "Yesterday, very early in the morning, around two A.M. or so, before you came over to read us the will, I woke up and found Henry dragging a bag out of my father's bedroom. A bag of things that he said Dad would have wanted him to get rid of. There were snapshots of young women in there. Lots of them. One of the girls" — she stared hard at Sy — "and she *was* just a girl, was Joelen Nichol."

"Christ," Sy said. He seemed dismayed but not particularly surprised.

"Know what else I found in that bag?" The words came tumbling out. Now that she'd started, she couldn't stop herself. "A dress. The dress I was wearing at the party earlier that night. The night Tito was killed. So here's what I want to know: How did the dress get covered in blood? And how did my father end up with it?"

Sy hesitated, gazing out into space, his face blank. "This is news to me." Deirdre remembered that her father always said Sy was a brilliant poker player, but a moment's hesitation was his tell.

Well, if Sy wasn't going to spill, Deirdre would. "I also found a knife." Sy's eyes widened. "A carving knife with a bone handle. Something else that Henry said Dad wanted him to get rid of."

"And you think —" Sy started. Now he looked genuinely bewildered.

"I don't know what to think." Tears welled up behind Deirdre's eyes. She clenched her jaw to keep them from spilling over. "But I'm starting to wonder. What if the police don't have the real knife that killed Tito, and what if my father did? And what if I wasn't asleep when it happened?" She looked from her mother to Sy and back again. "Why won't anyone tell me the truth?"

"No one is trying to torture you," Sy said. "We would all like to know exactly what happened. Maybe if your father had written about it, we would know." He paused for a moment, looking directly at Deirdre, so intently that she wondered if he knew about her father's memoir.

Gloria got up from the desk and came

around to Deirdre. She took her hand and held it between hers. "I'm so sorry that you've had to go through so much pain and confusion. And it's so unfair that it's all getting dredged up again."

"I didn't kill Tito," Deirdre said in a small voice.

Her mother stood back. "Of course you didn't."

"Did I?" Deirdre asked Sy.

This time there was no hesitation. "You did not. Of that you can be absolutely certain."

"How do you know?" Deirdre said.

"Because I was there," Sy said.

CHAPTER 29

Sy returned to the wing chair and sank into it, his face receding into shadows. He closed his eyes for a moment and tented his fingers over his belt buckle. Then his eyes opened and he glanced across at Gloria, who was still standing behind Deirdre with her arms around her. Some kind of message seemed to pass between them.

"All right," Sy said. "Well then. I was hoping it would never come to this, but here we are and so it is. As you know, I have for a very long time been Elenor Nichol's personal attorney. I am also her friend. She called me that night. Very late. She called and asked me" — he gave a tired smile and shook his head — "make that *commanded* me to come over right away. She said something terrible had happened to Tito.

"I told her to call an ambulance. She said it was too late for that. She needed me to be there when she called the police. So of

278

course I dressed and went right over. As I was driving up the driveway to the house, I passed a car pulling out. It was dark, and I could not see who was driving. But it was a sports car with the top down. Naturally I assumed it was your father. And when I learned what had happened, and that you had been in the house, I further assumed that he had come to get you out of there before all hell broke loose. That is what I thought until just now when you showed me the accident report. I still find it difficult to believe that you were driving that car."

"The dress? The knife? Why did my father have them?"

"I'm afraid that is something I do not know. This is what I do know. When I got there, Bunny took me up to her bedroom. Tito was on the floor. Dead, of course. Bunny said they had had a terrible fight. Worse than usual. Trying to placate him, she had told him that she was pregnant. She thought that would make him happy. Instead, he exploded. Punched her in the stomach. Tried to choke her. Tito knew it could not be his child. He was sterile."

"Elenor Nichol killed Tito?" Deirdre asked.

"That is what she told me. And right away

I thought, 'self-defense.' I did not doubt it for a moment, and I am sure I could have persuaded a jury. Police had been called to the house before. Newspapers had printed photographs of them fighting in a nightclub. On top of that, Antonio Acevedo had a long, well-documented history of violence. If Bunny had been charged, I would have tried to make the jury aware of the rumors that he had his last girlfriend disposed of. Elenor Nichol would have come across as a sympathetic victim. Desperate. And —"

Gloria said, "And an accomplished actress." The bitterness in her tone took Deirdre aback.

"Of course she is," Sy said. "But this did not seem like an act. She was agitated. In acute distress, emotionally and physically. Her neck was red and her vocal cords were so badly bruised that she could barely speak."

A chill ran down Deirdre's back. Why on earth had she and Joelen been allowed to hang out all those long afternoons with just Tito in the house?

"I placed the call to the police," Sy went on. "While we waited for them to get there, I prepared Bunny for the questions they would ask. I told her that I had seen your father's car pulling out when I arrived. She said she had called Arthur to come get you. That you had been sound asleep and knew nothing about what happened. We agreed, the police didn't need to know that you'd been there.

"The police came. Examined the body. They were about to start questioning Bunny when Joelen made a rather dramatic appearance. She staggered into the room, unsteady on her feet, slurring her words. Bunny told me later that she had given Joelen a sedative, but apparently it had not knocked her out. Slurred speech or not, there was no question about what she said. 'I did not mean to kill him.' The police took it as a confession."

"Bunny didn't contradict her?" Deirdre said.

Sy shook his head and pressed his lips together. "After that, things moved quickly. One of the officers read Joelen her rights. They tried to cuff her but Bunny broke down, sobbing and screaming at them to stop. After all, Joelen was just a child.

"Finally Bunny calmed down and the police let her find a coat for Joelen to put on. And that was classic Bunny — always thinking about how things would look, and she was absolutely right. Photographers were already assembled outside the house, of course, just waiting for her to come out. God knows how they knew." Sy stood, stepped to the window, and looked out. He pulled a handkerchief from his pocket and blew his nose. "Very next day, first thing Bunny did was get a security gate. Too bad she had not installed it earlier."

"What did you think?" Gloria asked. "They can't both have killed him."

"What I thought? *Pffft.* What difference did it make? The police heard Joelen's confession. I did my job. I told them both to stop talking." He gave a world-weary grimace. "That is about the best an attorney can do in a situation like that."

"Why would Arthur have ended up with the knife that killed Tito?" Gloria asked.

Sy pondered for a moment, working his lips in and out. "We don't know that it's the same knife." He turned to Deirdre. "Where is it now?"

"I threw it away." The lie popped out without a moment's hesitation.

"You did, did you?" Sy said. Deirdre could see the skepticism in his eyes.

"Day before yesterday. I tossed it into a neighbor's garbage can."

"Hmm. And what about the dress?"

"Destroyed in the fire."

"And —" The sound of the front door

opening stopped him.

"Henry?" her mother called out. To Deirdre, she said in a quiet voice, "Let's discuss this some other time. All right?"

A moment later Henry walked into the den, his motorcycle helmet hanging from his hand. He looked from Gloria to Sy to Deirdre. "Who died now?"

"Just your father," Gloria said. She and Sy exchanged a look, and they both eyed Deirdre. *Later.* She'd already gotten the message. "Henry, you're back in time to help us call around and let people know about the memorial service."

Henry looked Deirdre up and down. "Wow. So you pulled out all the stops. How'd it go at City Hall? Did you get Tyler to spill?"

Deirdre felt exhausted and drained. She took a breath. They were all watching her. "He says it was arson."

"Arson? But that's absurd," Gloria said.

"The fire started in a big bag of potting mix, but it was the wrong kind. Too much nitrate, or something like that. He said you'd never have used it for growing geraniums. There were cigarette butts in it. And kerosene."

Henry's gaze shifted toward the garage. "So does this mean the insurance claim gets tied up?"

"It means somebody deliberately set fire to the garage," Deirdre said.

"Henry's right," Sy said. "This will surely tie up any kind of settlement. The insurance company will send in an investigator, and the police will be back, too, asking the obvious question: Was the fire connected to your father's death?"

The logic was inescapable. A death that turned out to be murder. Two days later, a fire that turned out to be arson. How could they not think there was a connection?

"What should we do?" Gloria asked.

"There's nothing to do," Sy said. He crossed to the television and unpaused the VCR. A jazz trumpet blared and on the screen, Fred Astaire twirled, scooped up a silver tray with demitasse cups on it, and gracefully leaped off the table without losing a cup. "Just sit tight and try to give Arthur a proper send-off."

CHAPTER 30

It's only a movie. It's only a movie. That was what Deirdre used to whisper to herself as she tried to drown out the sound of her parents arguing. She'd repeated those same words to get her through round after round of torturous physical therapy.

It's only a movie, she told herself now, as she made phone call after phone call, working her way through a list of Arthur's friends and associates, telling everyone that Arthur's memorial service had been scheduled for Wednesday, day after tomorrow. *I hope you'll be able to make it. We'll have sandwiches at the house after if you can drop by.* She tried not to think about when the police and insurance investigators would descend next.

Henry worked the other phone line while Gloria cleaned the house. After about an hour, Gloria put out a platter of tuna fish sandwiches and the three of them took a break to eat. Deirdre tossed her leftover crusts to the dogs and then went back to making calls.

Meanwhile, Sy went out for a case of Arthur's favorite scotch and bags of ice. When he came back, he stood beside Deirdre and leaned close. "I noticed," he said under his breath. "You did not seem worried about what the police might find out in the alley when they come back." It smelled as if he'd helped himself to a nip of the liquor he'd purchased.

Deirdre had forgotten her lie, so it took her a moment to realize that he was talking about the knife. Flustered, she started to dig herself in deeper. "I took it up the alley and buried it in a bag of grass clippings."

"Grass clippings? You're sure about that?" When she mustered a weak response, he held up his hands. "No. It's better that I am ignorant. But try not to forget, I am much better at sussing out lies than you are at telling them."

Deirdre's face grew hot. Henry, who was standing in the doorway, must have overheard that because he guffawed.

"Henry," Sy said, "that goes for you, too."

The smirk wiped itself off Henry's face. Abruptly, he turned and walked away.

Sy turned back to Deirdre. "And you really do need to find that person who helped you with the exhibit Friday night in the gallery. If she verifies your account, the police will back off. If you do not . . ."

Sy's tone shook Deirdre into action. She called Stefan at the gallery. "Did you talk to Avram?"

"I've tried, believe me. But . . ."

"But?"

"When I call the number he gave us, I get a recorded message that isn't in English. At first I thought it was just a problem with international connections, but —"

"There has to be a way to reach him. Stefan, this is serious. His assistant is the only person who can vouch for where I was that night."

"I get that. But listen, I think we have a problem. I tried calling some other galleries, thinking maybe one of the other dealers might know how to reach him. Not one of them has ever heard of Avram Sigismund."

Deirdre felt like a stone sank in the pit of her stomach. "I thought you checked him out."

"I did. His portfolio seemed solid. His sales records in Europe looked good. But it was all a sham. On top of everything else, the last check he wrote us bounced."

"I don't understand. Why — ?"

"And you know what else? Turns out I

could have stayed at the gallery that night and worked on the exhibit with you after all. That journalist I was supposed to meet? She stood me up."

"Stood you up?" Deirdre felt numb.

"Didn't even call to apologize. Can you believe it? I drove all the way down to Coronado, waited at the bar at the golf course for over an hour."

It didn't require much paranoia to wonder if someone had gone to a lot of trouble to ensure that no one could vouch for Deirdre's whereabouts that night. Then she herself had sealed the deal by picking up that shovel from the driveway and leaving her fingerprints on the shaft.

By the time Deirdre hung up the phone, her hands were sweaty. When Detective Martinez returned, she'd have to explain to him that she had no idea how to reach the person who was in the gallery with her until late Friday night. That the artist whose show Deirdre had been preparing to open could not be reached and might not, in fact, exist. That she and Stefan had been conned by cartons of smelly old shoes and the promise of payment up front.

CHAPTER 31

That night, Deirdre had dinner with her mother and Henry at Hamburger Hamlet. Then they drove to Hollywood Boulevard for sundaes at C.C. Brown's, where the booths were like church pews and they served mammoth scoops of ice cream in chilled tin cups with thick hot fudge and crispy whole almonds, a pitcher of extra fudge sauce on the side. Deirdre would have preferred the small, elegant sundaes served with a single amaretto cookie at Wil Wright's, but Brown's had been her father's favorite and Wil Wright's had closed.

Later, when Deirdre got in bed, she thought about how readily Sy had seen through her lies. Knew full well that she hadn't gotten rid of the knife. She wondered if he knew that Arthur had been working on a memoir. It seemed so unlikely that Arthur would have kept that from his oldest friend and closest confidant.

Deirdre pulled the manuscript out of the drawer in her bedside table. *One Damned Thing After Another* — not only was it the perfect title for Arthur's memoir, but it also described precisely what her life had turned into since the moment she'd agreed to help him get his house ready to go on the market. She paged through the beginning, skimming past what she'd already read. In the next section, Arthur wrote about arriving in Hollywood and rapidly blowing through his savings. Broke, he'd holed up on a friend's couch. Crashed some cocktail parties. Made connections and bullshitted his way into some low-level jobs, working with other talented newcomers. Met and fallen in love with a chorus girl. Born Gertrude Wolkind, she'd changed her name to Gloria Walker. The truth was, she was a whole lot smarter than she was sprightly, and soon she'd quit dancing and started to work with Arthur. *Helping him write* was how Arthur saw it.

From the moment Arthur started collaborating with Gloria, his luck changed. Deirdre had intended to skim the pages — after all, she'd heard most of the stories many times over. But she found herself caught up in her father's storytelling.

In one chapter he told how he and Gloria talked their way into getting assigned their first movie script. Gloria stole a copy of the Academy Award–winning screenplay for *Casablanca* from the studio library and they cribbed shamelessly from it for story structure and formatting. When their script passed muster, they had their first movie credit and their career took off.

From there on, Arthur's memoir read like a movie with Hollywood's greats in supporting roles and a bit player holding the camera. In one scene Spyros Skouras, the head of Fox, rose from his breakfast in a rage, jowls quivering, spewing incomprehensible English and crumbs of half-chewed toast at Arthur. A few chapters later, Arthur was in the dressing room with a half-dressed Marilyn Monroe, resisting her advances while coaxing her into costume and out onto the soundstage to deliver a knockout performance of "Heatwave." He claimed to have held Marilyn's hand and offered this advice:

Keep trying. Hold on, baby. And always, always, always believe in yourself, because if you don't, who will? Head up, chin high. Most of all keep smiling, because life's a beautiful thing and there's so much to smile about.

Could that have been Arthur? Sensitive, supportive? It sounded more like lines he'd written. Or was Deirdre's view of her father tainted, warped by the angry adolescent girl she still had snarking away inside her?

As she read on, what came across was how much her father adored everything about the movie business. And despite the prism through which Arthur saw the past — selective memory colored by an oversized ego — it was clear that he and Gloria were much in demand in those heady early years when they churned out hit after hit.

Every so often, Arthur would mention Deirdre or Henry, and when he did it was with blind affection and pure delight. In the bitterness that had built up over the last twenty-plus years, Deirdre had forgotten how unabashedly gaga he'd been about his kids. Forgotten the many times he'd taken her to the studio to show her around but also to show her off. First they'd have lunch, sitting at a corner table in the cavernous studio commissary, surrounded by actors and actresses in full makeup and extraordinary getups. Then they'd walk over to one of the vast soundstages where invariably a movie was being shot. Deirdre had to be careful not to trip on the cables that crisscrossed the floor, and she got goose bumps remembering how absolutely still and silent she had to be the moment a voice boomed, "Quiet on set!" The painted backdrops that looked so phony in person were somehow rendered utterly believable through the magic of filming.

She was near the end of the manuscript, tired and ready to turn out the light when she read these words: *There are parties and there are parties, but the shindigs at Elenor Nichol's house were legendary. Why did it have to be that night of all nights that our attorney finagled an invite there for us to mingle with the crème de la crème of Hollywood's most glamorous?*

A chill passed through Deirdre as she read on.

The setting was out of a movie script. Liveried attendants valet-parked the Jaguars and Mercedes that pulled up at the end of the driveway. Gloria and I got out of my six-year-old Austin-Healey feeling like pikers. We waited for a golf cart to ferry us up to the house.

Tuxedoed waiters, most of them out-of-work actors, glided about with silver trays bearing champagne flutes of Dom Pérignon and shots of Chivas and Glenlivet. The crowd included stars and studio executives, a heady mix of staggering beauty — men and women both — and arrogant power. The men swaggered about, bravado masquerading as brains. Oscar Levant seemed permanently ensconced at the piano, completely brilliant and completely soused, per usual. Needless to say, writers like Gloria and me, a dime a dozen in Hollywood, were in short supply. Most of the folks there were under the illusion that actors and directors made up lines as they went along, so who needed writers, anyway?

Bunny, as Elenor Nichol was known, though there was nothing remotely soft or cuddly about her, reigned over all. Queen of wanton amorous fire, that night she wore a crimson dress with a plunging neckline and ropes of pearls that couldn't hold a candle to the luminescence of her skin. With her swelling bosom and round bottom, her sultry voice somewhere between a purr and a snarl, she had every man in that house salivating, including yours truly. But no one dared to make a pass at her — not with Tito Acevedo watching her every move like a dyspeptic guard dog.

Thug. Bully. Gigolo. Goon. Those were just a few of the labels hung on Tito —

never to his face, of course. Supposedly he used to be errand boy for Mafia boss "Sam the Cigar" Giancana in Vegas before shifting his base of operations to Hollywood. Here, rumor had it, he threatened to castrate the director of Bunny's last film when he got what Tito deemed a bit too chummy. On top of that, he fancied himself a player and took meetings, reading scripts and throwing around wads of cash. A crass charmer, he'd have made a great character in a B-movie. In real life, he was a black hole of pure nastiness. Everyone gave him a wide berth.

That night, Tito glowered silently from the shadows beside a massive potted palm in the corner of Bunny's palatial living room. He was doing a second-rate Humphrey Bogart imitation, his eyes half-closed, pinching the end of his cigarette between his thumb and forefinger behind a cupped hand.

Like the cigarette he was smoking, it turned out Tito Acevedo was on a slow burn.

Deirdre paged ahead, looking for but failing to find any mention of her or Joelen at the party. Like Oscar Levant, Arthur would have been plenty "soused" himself with all that high-class booze floating around, more than a few rungs up from his usual Dewar's. Finally she found her own name.

Gloria and I had long ago bailed and were home sleeping it off when the phone rang. I was thinking, Christ almighty, who calls at two in the morning? I almost didn't pick up. But then I did.

"Arthur? It's Bunny." Her voice didn't sound soft or sultry — more midway between outraged and petrified. "Get Deirdre."

Get Deirdre? For a crazy moment I was thinking: great title. Then I realized my daughter was sleeping over at Bunny's house. I'd seen her at the party, she and Bunny's daughter all dressed up and parading around like grown-ups.

I sat bolt upright, wide awake. "What's wrong?"

"Something's happened," she said.

"To Deirdre? Is she all right?"

"She's fine. But you've got to get her away from here before they come." Before I could ask who "they" were, she hung up. Talk about your cliffhanger ending.

I slapped some water on my face, threw on some clothes, and drove over there as fast as I could. Up Bunny's long driveway to the big white house that had been lit up like a stage set hours earlier but now had just a single light on in an upstairs window.

Before I could knock, Bunny pulled open the front door. It was dark, but I could see she looked pale, her face puffy and teary-eyed. She had a nasty bruise under one eye and her lip was split. She wore a flowing peignoir that, it only occurred to me later, looked like a leftover costume from her movie *Black Lace.*

I followed her up the stairs into what I realized right away was her daughter's bedroom. Pink walls. Twin beds. One of the beds was empty. Lying facedown on the other was Tito Acevedo.

I could smell the blood that had soaked into the quilt under Tito. The soundtrack, high-pitched squeals, turned out to be a pair of thoroughly spooked guinea pigs. Bunny's daughter, Joelen, was huddled in a corner by their cage. She was hugging a pillow and leaning against the wall. Her eyes were shut tight. At first I thought she was asleep.

I looked around for Deirdre. Thank God she wasn't there.

When I reached for Tito's wrist to feel for a pulse, Bunny stopped me. "He's dead,

297

for Chrissake. Can't you see that? Help me move him." Imperious as ever.

Deirdre read on. Her father had helped Bunny wrap Tito in the quilt. They'd pulled him off the bed and dragged him down the hall to the master bedroom, where they'd rolled him over onto the floor. That must have been where the news photographers later snapped pictures of what was supposedly the crime scene. Deirdre clearly remembered a shot of a cop sitting at the edge of Bunny's satin-covered bed, staring down at the dead man.

What happened? Who killed him? When I asked Bunny Nichol, she showed me a knife. "Recognize this?" she wanted to know.

Of course I recognized it. The last time I'd seen it was in a drawer in the buffet in my own dining room. It had been a wedding present. So what was it doing here?

I was desperate to take the knife from her. At the same time, I was afraid to touch it. The thought of how it had been used made me sick to my stomach. I know I've seen too many cop shows, but I was worried about leaving my fingerprints on top of those of the killer. At the same time, I realized it was too late to worry about fine points like that. The arms of my jacket and my trousers were already stained with Tito's blood.

Bunny said not to worry. She'd get rid of the quilt from her daughter's bedroom that we'd just dragged Tito in on. And she'd "take care" of the knife. Then she showed me a dress she said my daughter had worn to the party earlier that night. It was covered in blood too. I stared at it, too stunned and frankly afraid to ask the obvious question. Bunny promised me she'd take care of the dress, too. That the police would never know.

Know what? I wanted to ask.

If I didn't tell, she said, she wouldn't tell, and she'd keep these items somewhere safe. She called them her "little insurance policy."

I asked her what in God's name she meant by that. She blew up. What happened was my fault as much as it was hers. If I'd been a better father, and so on and so on. I had no idea what she was going on about.

Finally she calmed down and said, "If you know what's good for you, you'll forget we had this little talk."

Even at the time it sounded like a line of

dialogue from one of her movies. But then, the whole situation felt like it was out of a movie. Everything except for Tito Acevedo, who was not pretending to be dead. And my daughter, who was somewhere in the house, needing me to get her out of there.

I asked Bunny where Deirdre was. Her answer stunned me to my core: "Shouldn't you be asking, where's Henry?"

Deirdre felt her jaw drop. What on earth had Henry had to do with what happened that night?

Apparently Arthur had had the same reaction.

I was about to ask what my son had to do with any of this when I heard a car outside on the gravel. I looked out the window. Headlights. Taillights. Then I realized I was looking at my own car driving away.

Bunny was beside me, looking out, too. "If you want to protect our children," she said, coming down hard on *our,* "you'll go home and never breathe a word of this to anyone."

I thought about that as I walked home, hoping the police wouldn't stop me for loitering even though I was moving as fast as I could. I was praying that when I got

300

back to the house I'd find Deirdre safe and sound, asleep in bed.

Fortunately, it was not very far. Unfortunately, my daughter was not there. Neither was Henry.

That was the end, the very last typed line. Below it were handwritten notes, scrawled at the bottom of the manuscript's final text and on the back of the page.

Gloria New Age. Deirdre knew what that would be about.

Talk That Talk. Deirdre recognized the title of the movie that had been her father's one and only attempt at directing.

Baby boy. She had no idea what that referred to.

Sy trust. That was underlined twice.

Jack Nicholson, Robert De Niro, Harrison Ford, Maximilian Schell.

The list made Deirdre smile. Arthur was considering A-list actors to play himself.

Deirdre gathered up the manuscript pages and was about to slide them back into the folder when she realized something was stuck in one of its pockets. A small envelope. She slipped from it a greeting card. The front was printed with a ring of flowers circling a baby-carrying stork. Inside was a handwritten message:

Congratulations! It's a baby.

That's all. No name. No date. No six pounds eleven ounces. No return address on the envelope. Just a postmark: Beverly Hills, May 11, 1964. Six months after Deirdre's accident. Six months after Antonio Acevedo was killed.

■ ■ ■ ■

TUESDAY,
MAY 27, 1985

■ ■ ■ ■

CHAPTER 32

At four thirty in the morning, Deirdre lay awake in the dark, mulling over what her father had written. There was some comfort in knowing that she had not, after all, been at the wheel of her father's car when it crashed. But her father hadn't been driving either. It was Henry who'd led her from the house. Henry who'd driven her up to Mulholland and crashed the car into the guardrail. For some reason he'd been at the Nichols' house, too, the night Tito was killed.

And what about the dress and the knife? What kind of "insurance" was Bunny buying for herself by holding on to them, and how did her father end up getting them back?

Deirdre got out of bed, pulled out the torn plastic bag she'd stashed in the closet, and took out the dress. Unwrapped the knife. Examined the flourishy· initial engraved in the silver cap at the end of the bone handle. Was it *n* for *Nichol*? Or — she rotated the knife 180 degrees — *u* for *Unger*?

And what about the dress? As she smoothed it out on the floor, brittle bits of netting broke away. Were the brownish stains on it blood? They could as easily be cocktail sauce or red wine. She and Joelen had gorged on both after the party, then thrown up.

Deirdre sniffed at the stains, but after all these years the only smell was of dust and decay. There was no telling what had made them. Or was there? Would Tyler, with his chemistry lab, be able to identify the stains? He'd offered to help. Urged her to call on him "anytime." Did that mean it was okay to call at five in the morning? Would he write her off as a crazy nut job? She hoped not.

She crept into the kitchen, where she'd left her bag by the back door. In it was the report of her accident on which Tyler had written his phone numbers. She dialed the one marked "Home" and held her breath.

"Corrigan," Tyler said, picking up on the third ring. His voice was thick.

"Tyler? I'm sorry, it's —"

Before she could give her name, he said, "Deirdre! Hang on." She heard muffled sounds on the other end, then he came back on the line. "Are you okay? Is everything all right?"

It didn't sound as if he was writing her off. "I'm sorry to call at this ridiculous time, but you did say that if I needed anything it was okay to call anytime."

He yawned. "Said it and meant it."

"The thing is, I'm not sure this is something you're allowed to do. I found a very old dress and was hoping that you might examine it and tell me whether the stains on it are blood. Off the record, of course. Just as a favor."

"So you think the stains could be blood?" He said it in what sounded like a cop voice: *Just the facts, ma'am.*

Had she been right to trust him? After all, she hadn't seen him in more than twenty years and they'd hardly had what you'd call a relationship. Why *was* he so eager to help her, anyway? And why was she so ready to trust a virtual stranger when she couldn't trust her own mother, whose prayer beads she'd found in her father's office? Or her brother, who'd never admitted that he was responsible for the accident that crippled her and who seemed to have a vested interest in burying her father's secrets? Even Sy made her feel apprehensive, though she couldn't put her finger on why.

Any of them could have purchased a shovel and used it to bash her father in the head during his midnight swim. Even if Arthur had seen one of them in the yard, he'd never have expected to be attacked. Any of them could have arranged for a mythical Israeli artist and a no-show news reporter to ensure that Deirdre didn't have an alibi.

"Sorry, Deirdre," Tyler said, "but I have to ask. Does this have anything to do with the fire?" It was a fair question, and he sounded like a real person asking it. She relaxed a notch.

"The stain is old. Really old. From twenty years ago. So I can't imagine how it could be connected to the fire," she said with a twinge of guilt. Because it was just possible that the fire had been set in order to destroy items in Arthur's office, that dress among them.

"Okay then. Sure. It's not complicated. I'll bring over my own test kit and you can do the test yourself."

"That would be great," Deirdre said, feeling as if a heavy weight had lifted.

"How about later this morning? I could come to your house —"

"No," Deirdre said, louder than she'd intended. She heard the dogs stirring in

Henry's bedroom. "Sorry. My family is already stressed out, and I'd rather they not know about this."

"Then how about I meet you somewhere and we can do it right now?"

"Now? Really?"

"Sure. I'm awake." He yawned again.

"Sorry."

"No need to apologize. I'm glad you called. Where do you want to meet?"

Where? She hadn't gotten that far. Somewhere nearby. "You know the fountain on the corner of Santa Monica and Wilshire, across from Trader Vic's? Will that work?"

"We should be able to find a spot there that's dark enough to see the reaction. Assuming you don't mind crawling around a bit under some bushes."

It wouldn't be the first time she'd crawled around under those bushes. She and Henry used to play hide-and-seek in that park, but never at five in the morning.

"Meet you there in thirty minutes," Tyler said.

"Thirty minutes." Deirdre couldn't believe how easy this was turning out to be. "Thank you so much."

"If you want to thank me, let me take you out to breakfast after."

He was being so nice it scared her. "Okay.

But my treat."

"We can argue about that later."

Deirdre rummaged through the dresser in her room and found a white T-shirt to wear with her leggings. She ran a brush through her hair, and scrawled a note for Henry and her mother in case they got up and found her missing. Carefully she folded the dress around the knife again and tucked them in her messenger bag. At the last minute, she stuffed the folder with her father's manuscript in the bag, too.

When she drove off, it was still dark. It took only ten minutes to drive to the little park that was home to the fountain. She parked around the corner and made her way across the hard-packed dirt path leading to the tiled piazza. The moon was a substantial crescent that hung right over the head of the kneeling Indian on the plinth in the center of the circular fountain. As always, his head was bent and he held his hands out in front of him as if to capture the water playing around him. Or perhaps he was offering thanks to the gods for finding him, among all his compatriots, such a cushy permanent home.

Even at this odd hour the plaza wasn't deserted. A young couple was entwined, necking on one of the benches. Deirdre picked a spot upwind from the fountain's spray, feeling first to be sure the bench was dry. The parade of colored lights in the fountain was still going, but as the sky was starting to lighten, the jets of water looked pale rather than vibrant — powder blue, then seafoam green, then pink, cycling through color after color until the grand finale, all the colors at once. When she was little, her father would occasionally bring her there after getting ice cream at Baskin-Robbins. Even as they faded, the lights still seemed magical.

Traffic was sparse in the usually busy intersection of Santa Monica and Wilshire. Deirdre remembered when there'd been a vast empty field across the street where the Hilton Hotel now stood. Trader Vic's, attached to the hotel's near end, stuck its palm-tree-lined, Tiki-bedecked entrance into the intersection. More and more, Los Angeles and Disneyland were merging into a single entity with reality at a far remove.

Tyler loped across the plaza in jeans and a black T-shirt that showed off a muscular chest and powerful shoulders and upper arms. "Hey, sorry. I got held up," he said. He held a black backpack with white letters stenciled on: ARSON.

"It's been ages since I was down here

when the lights were going," Deirdre said. "I forgot how cool it is."

"Me too. I feel personally responsible for that," Tyler said, pointing to a sign that read NO SKATEBOARDING ALLOWED. "We used to come down here when they were doing repairs and the fountain was empty. We'd race around in circles inside the fountain. Jump in and out. Popped more than a few tiles, I'm ashamed to say."

Deirdre said, "My brother claimed he and some friends put a box of Tide in the fountain once. Supposedly the suds spread all the way out onto the street and stopped traffic. He was very proud of that accomplishment."

"Adolescent boys are all idiots." Tyler sat next to her on the bench. Deirdre could smell his aftershave. "So what you want tested is in there?" He indicated the bag in her lap. "Let's have a look, see what you've got."

"It's a dress," Deirdre said, opening the bag. "It's probably nothing." Leaving the knife in the bag, she pulled out the dress and handed it to him.

Tyler turned his back to the fountain and took the dress from her, holding it gingerly away from him. "Like I said, we need to take this somewhere dark enough to see the reaction." Just then the lights in the fountain went out and the fountain's jets turned off. Deirdre looked back at Wilshire. The streetlights had gone off, too.

"We should do this now, before it gets much lighter. Behind there." He pointed to the tall wall that formed the back of a long bench at the rear of the plaza.

Deirdre followed him out and around to where tall bushes lined the back of the wall. It smelled just like it had years and years ago when she'd hunkered down, waiting for Henry to find her. Pee and rotten eggs.

Tyler turned on a penlight, crouched in the shadow between the bushes, and crept in closer to the wall. Taking shallow breaths and steadying herself with her hands, Deirdre followed him, frog walking in close to the base of the wall where it was darkest.

Tyler waited until she was right there in position, too. Then he opened his pack and pulled out a plastic spray bottle. "Okay. You ready?"

"Ready." She hoped she really was.

"Let's see what we have here." Tyler turned off the flashlight and waited. In moments, Deirdre's eyes adjusted to the dark. Tyler held the dress in front of them and gave her the spray bottle. "Just give it a spritz or two." Deirdre aimed the nozzle and gave it two squeezes. An instant later, bluish-green puddles of light glowed on the underskirt and the netting lit up like a star-sprinkled fisherman's net.

"Probably blood," Tyler said.

CHAPTER 33

After the blue glow faded, Deirdre returned with Tyler to the park. The air felt laden with moisture even though the fountain was off. The sky had turned pale gray and traffic was coming to life.

"Why *probably* blood?" Deirdre asked.

"It's called a presumptive test. Luminol occasionally gives a false positive."

"It glows like that when it hits something other than blood?"

"Like bleach. That's why people use bleach to clean up a blood spill. It camouflages the stains. Animal blood would luminesce, too. And horseradish. I know, more than you need to know."

Horseradish? How weird was that? Because the cocktail sauce that she'd gorged on at the party and then thrown up all over herself had been spicy. It could have been that. Maybe. But if that's all it was, why would Bunny and then her father have held on to it for all these years?

Deirdre said, "I'm amazed at how bright the reaction is, given how old the stain is."

"The older the stain, the stronger the glow. But like I say, it's not proof positive. If you want to know for sure if it's human blood, I'd need to take a sample to the lab and run more tests."

Knowing whether the stains were blood wouldn't bring her any closer to understanding how they'd gotten there or how her father had ended up with the dress. But it would be another piece of information about what happened that night. Eventually, all of it had to fit together.

"Could you?" she said.

"Sure. I'll take a sample."

While he was digging in his backpack, she considered whether to show him the knife and ask him to test it, too. But he'd said luminol glowed when it came in contact with animal blood, and surely the knife had been used to carve meat.

Tyler used scissors to cut a small square of stained fabric from the dress and tucked it into a plastic bag. He gave her back the dress and she stuffed it into her bag.

"Sorry," he said. "Forensics is not an exact science. Sometimes the more you know, the less you're sure of. Do I still get to take you to breakfast?"

A little while later, Deirdre was sitting next to him on a stool at the counter at Canter's on Fairfax, inhaling the aroma of pastrami and garlic pickles. The waitress, wearing a shirtwaist with white trim almost exactly like the one Bunny had dressed Deirdre up in for her visit to City Hall, brought them coffee and took their orders. Even as early as it was, the restaurant hummed with customers.

Deirdre sipped her coffee. When she looked across at the mirrored wall opposite them, she caught Tyler staring at her reflection. "Twenty-year-old bloodstains," he said. "So does this have to do with your car accident?"

Deirdre felt her face flush. She looked away. She was ready to call him for help at five in the morning but not ready to spill her guts.

"Okay, don't tell me," Tyler said. "But I might even be able to help with whatever it is that's got you so stuck."

"I'm not stuck."

"Yeah, you are. You can't even look me in the eye and talk about it."

The waitress brought over their plates and topped off their coffees. Deirdre poked at her egg. Took a bite. The potatoes in the corned beef hash were crisp and the eggs were done exactly right.

"I'm sorry." She shook her head. "These last few days have been a bit much. Between my father and the fire and the mess, it's a lot to deal with."

Tyler tucked into his pancakes. "I can't even imagine. Though I do know cleanup is brutal after a fire, even when you're not grieving. You know, there are companies who will come in and do it for you."

"I need to do it myself. At least a first pass. My father named me executor of his literary estate, and a lot of what should have been preserved was up in his office on the second floor of the garage."

"Have you started? Because water can be just as damaging as fire, especially to paper."

"So far, the only thing I've managed to save is a sleazy photograph."

"A photograph?"

Deirdre found it in the bottom of her bag and showed it to Tyler. "How's this for legacy?"

"Joelen Nichol," Tyler murmured. He took the photo from Deirdre. "You two were always together."

Of course Tyler remembered Joelen — he and the rest of the male population of Beverly Hills.

Tyler raised the photograph to the light. "You think that's your dad?" he asked, pointing to the photographer reflected in the mirror over Joelen's head.

"Isn't it?" she said.

He slipped a key ring from his pocket. Hanging on the ring along with keys was a small magnifying glass. Tyler examined the photograph through it. "Have a close look, why don't you?" He handed Deirdre the magnifier.

Deirdre positioned the lens and looked through it. The photographer's face was hidden behind the camera's viewfinder, the lens accordioned from its box. The man had her father's hair. Same general build. Same stance. But that wasn't what sent a shiver down Deirdre's back as she leaned closer to the magnifying glass. On the arm of the photographer's leather jacket was a Harley-Davidson double-winged eagle patch.

Her father wasn't a biker. Her brother was.

CHAPTER 34

Staring at the Harley eagle patch, Deirdre tried to remember when Henry had gotten into muscle bikes. Seemed like it hadn't been until after he dropped out of college with only a collection of electric guitars and a few demo tapes to show for his dreams of becoming a serious musician.

"What are you thinking?" Tyler asked. He pushed away his empty plate and signaled the waitress to top off their coffees.

"I'm thinking it's a shame that my brother never finished college."

"He was cool. I remember in high school, he had that swagger. And girls —" Tyler whistled.

"Yeah. Girls were all over him. I think he had a great time in high school. Not me. I was so glad when it was over."

"Me too."

They talked for a while longer, comparing notes on what Beverly had been like if you didn't cheerlead or play football or drive a Ferrari. Deirdre could easily have stayed and talked longer, but at half past eight Tyler said he had to get to work. He told her that first thing in the morning was the best time to file a request for the record that the insurance adjuster needed. The Records Office at City Hall opened at nine. Deirdre stopped on her way home, pulled the number 12 from the number dispenser, and was out of there twenty minutes later.

As she drove home, she thought about Henry. He'd tacitly deflected the blame to Arthur for photographs that he'd taken. He'd also let her father take the blame for the car accident that left her crippled. Which reminded her of something Arthur had mentioned in his memoir — Bunny's comment that Arthur was as much to blame for what had happened as she was.

When Deirdre got home, she would question her mother and Henry, both of them. Together. She wanted to know exactly what each of them knew about what happened that night. No more sidestepping, shading the truth, or lying to protect anyone, including herself.

But when she neared her father's house, she realized a dark sedan was parked in front. She pulled over to watch from a distance as a pair of uniformed police officers got out of the car and started up the front walk.

Any plan she'd had of confronting Henry and Gloria evaporated. The police must have obtained another search warrant, as Sy had predicted. If they looked in her bag, she didn't have a good explanation, even for herself, for what was in it.

She drove slowly past the front of the house. Caught a glimpse of the front door opening. Just then, a motorcycle came roaring out of the driveway and sped past her, up the block. Deirdre recognized Henry's red-and-gold helmet. He'd probably seen the police arriving and decided to disappear. She made a quick U-turn and took off after him.

Henry slowed at a stop sign a few blocks later. Deirdre tooted her horn and flashed her lights. But he barely glanced over his shoulder. Just flipped her the bird before peeling out and roaring up the street.

So it's like that, is it? She accelerated, peeling out after him. Thirty miles an hour. Forty. Henry slowed but didn't stop to turn left onto Sunset. Deirdre had to screech to a halt at the corner as a stream of cross traffic held her back. Taking advantage of a minuscule gap between cars, she nipped out onto Sunset, earning herself a horn blast and her second expressive middle finger of the morning. Ahead of her, she could see Henry on his bike slowing. Turning into the driveway of the Nichols' estate. Why was he going there?

Without thinking, Deirdre turned in behind him, making it through the gate just before it closed. By then, Henry and his motorcycle had vanished up the driveway.

Deirdre stopped the car. Now what? Should she drive up to the front door, march up the steps . . . and then what? Throw pebbles at Joelen's window? What Henry was up to was his own business. At least it would have been if he hadn't been lying to her, insisting that he had no ongoing relationship with Joelen Nichol. Maybe she could figure out what was going on without embarrassing him.

She drove slowly up the driveway. When she got to the pool, she backed into the carport that was camouflaged by a bank of bougainvillea, then killed the engine, grabbed her crutch, and started to walk up the drive toward the house. Bunny was obviously not addicted to thirty laps a day. Close up, the pool not only looked gross, it smelled scummy, like sour milk and rotting leaves.

Deirdre continued up the hill, moving as quickly as she could. By the time she rounded the final bend she was out of breath. Henry had parked his bike in front and was crouched behind it, looking at the engine or the tires, she couldn't tell which. His fancy, custom-made helmet hung from one of the handlebars.

The minute he stood, Deirdre realized her mistake. The man by the bike wasn't Henry; it was Jackie Hutchinson. He started walking toward the front door, wobbling a little on the chunky heels of a pair of black cowboy boots that, like his helmet, could have been Henry's.

"Looking for someone?" The voice from behind her startled Deirdre. She whipped around to see Bunny Nichol wearing a pink satin quilted bathrobe, a chiffon scarf wrapped around her head and tied over her forehead. She was in full makeup, of course. "You're here a little early for a visit."

"I thought —" Deirdre started. But before she could come up with a plausible excuse for being there, Bunny hooked her arm and called out, "Jackie!"

Jackie turned around as Bunny propelled Deirdre forward toward the house. "You remember Deirdre?" Bunny said. "She was at the house a few days ago?"

"Sure. You were up there." Jackie pointed vaguely in the direction of Bunny's bedroom. "You look . . . different. I'd never have recognized you."

"I didn't recognize you in that helmet," Deirdre said.

Jackie looked down at the helmet hanging from his hand. "Pretty cool, isn't it?"

"I've only seen one other like it."

"You must know Henry Unger."

"He's my brother."

Jackie narrowed his eyes at Deirdre. "You and Henry? Really. I was just over there. Small world."

Maybe not that small. "You work with him?" Deirdre said.

"Not with him. *For* him. He's an old friend of Bunny's."

"Deirdre," Bunny said, "I know you need to be on your way. I'll walk you back to your car." She started escorting Deirdre down the driveway.

Deirdre didn't mind being given the bum's rush, as her father used to call it. She was as anxious to get out of there as Bunny was to be rid of her. But as they walked away from the house, she picked up her head. Was that the *woop-woop* of a siren?

"Shit," Bunny said under her breath. "You parked at the pool?"

325

Deirdre nodded.

"You must have triggered the alarm." Bunny gripped Deirdre's arm tighter. "You really should have telephoned first."

As they approached the carport by the pool, the alarm fell silent. A black-and-white car with a row of stars and SECURITY stenciled on the door was parked behind Deirdre's car, blocking it in. A uniformed guard with a brushy salt-and-pepper mustache emerged from under the overhanging bougainvillea. "Der-dra Unger?" he said, mispronouncing Deirdre's name. He had her wallet open in his hand and was holding her messenger bag. "That your Mercedes parked in there?"

"Yes. And that's my bag."

"She's all right, Martin," Bunny said. "False alarm. I'll take those."

Martin the security guard reached into Deirdre's bag and pulled out the knife. "You sure she's all right, ma'am?"

"She's just returning that to me," Bunny said, and held out her hand. Martin gave her the knife, hilt first.

Bunny turned the knife over. The blade flashed in the sun. "Did you know," she said, giving Martin a coy smile, "that I once worked with quite a famous magician? In the early days, of course. Before I became a star." She rotated the knife so she had the blade between her fingertips. "Can you imagine this? I'm dressed" — she poked a bent knee through the opening in her robe — "scantily." She gave Martin a wink. "Strapped to a board. Then Jasper sets me spinning. Backs away. Looks out at the audience as if to say *Dare me.* Pretends he's about to throw the knife but doesn't. Not yet. Suspense builds. Tension thick. You can hear a pin drop." Bunny reared back, holding the knife aloft. "Then suddenly Jasper throws the knife. The audience gasps. The board slowly stops spinning and everyone can see where it's landed, right between my legs." She drew her leg demurely back into the folds of her robe.

Martin exhaled audibly.

"Pure skill," Bunny said. "Not an illusion, as so many magic tricks are." She lowered the knife, moving it to her other hand and grasping it by the handle. "It was simply quite amazing that he could throw as accurately as he could. Frankly, I was terrified. I needed a stiff drink before each performance and kept my eyes shut from the moment he set that board spinning until it stopped."

Bunny's gaze softened, focused in midair. "He also used to make the knife vanish."

She blinked. "Now that's a trick I can show you. I store some of our props — mementos, really — in the pool house. Of course, I'm not a master like the Great Jasper, but I've always been a quick study, and I saw him do the trick often enough."

Bunny handed Martin the knife and let herself in through the gate to the pool. Moments later, she emerged holding a painted box. "Here we are." She blew on it, raising a cloud of dust, and rubbed it with her sleeve. "Covered in cobwebs. Like we'll all be ourselves one day." The box was red lacquer, decorated with gold stars and crescent moons.

Magic. It's all about misdirection. That was what Bunny had said when she contemplated how to costume Deirdre so she'd be invisible for her visit to City Hall.

With a practiced gesture, Bunny tapped the surface of the box with delicately tapered nails. "Tricks are so much fun when you don't know their secrets." She rotated the box, then twirled it corner to corner until the stars and moons painted on its shiny enamel surface were a blur. Then she held the box perfectly still. She glanced in Deirdre's direction, then lifted the lid and opened a door in the side. Lowered her hand in through the top. Her fingers waggled, visible through the open side door against a black-and-white-striped interior. "See? Nothing whatsoever inside." She pulled her hand from the box, closed the side door, and held out her hand to Martin. He gave her back the knife. With a flourish, Bunny dropped it into the box. It made a thump when it landed.

Bunny snapped the lid shut. Frowned and looked at the box as if she wasn't sure what to do next. Smiled, like a lightbulb had gone off in her head, then twirled the box again. Once, twice, three times. Waved her hand over it. Murmured, "Magic words, magic words, magic words."

Anyone who'd ever seen a magic act knew that the knife would disappear. Even so, Deirdre gasped when Bunny opened a side panel to reveal that it had. She closed that panel and opened the lid, peered in, and gave a momentary look of surprise. Then she reached in and began pulling out a shiny red silk scarf. Knotted to the end of it was a green scarf. Then a yellow one. Scarf after scarf streamed from the box until there were no more.

"*Et voilà!*" Bunny said with a wave of her arm, sending the string of scarves flying in a zigzag overhead before stuffing them back into the box.

Martin applauded. Deirdre applauded. Bunny tucked the magic box under her arm and took a little bow. "I'm sorry, Martin, that you had to bother coming all the way up here for nothing," she said.

"Not a bother," Martin said. "Never a bother, Miss Nichol. Wouldn't have missed this for anything." He dropped Deirdre's wallet into her messenger bag and transferred it into Bunny's arms. "You're sure there's nothing more I can do?"

"I'm sure. Thank you. Thank you so much," Bunny said. She rose on tiptoe and planted a kiss on his cheek. Martin flushed so red that for a moment the lipstick smear she'd left on his cheek seemed to disappear.

A minute later Deirdre stood alone with Bunny, watching the security car disappear down the driveway.

Bunny turned to face Deirdre, hands on her hips. "So."

Deirdre's first instinct was to apologize, but she was through apologizing. She was tired of being treated like a child who had to be lied to. "I thought you might recognize that knife."

"Should I?" Bunny opened the messenger bag and, to Deirdre's astonishment, pulled the knife from within it. Then she peered into the open bag. Lifting the edge of the yellow dress, she added, "I see you still have this. Where did you find it?"

"Among some things Henry says Dad told him to get rid of. I think that's the same dress and knife that you showed my father the night Tito was killed. You told him you were keeping it for insurance. Insurance against what?"

Bunny's eyes turned watchful. "How do you know that?"

"I . . . he told me."

"He told you?"

Deirdre stared hard at Bunny, determined not to let her gaze drop to the bag Bunny was holding. The manuscript was in it, underneath the yellow dress.

"I asked, how do you know that?" Bunny repeated with a cold, hard look.

"He wrote about it in his memoir," Deirdre said defiantly.

Bunny reared back, clearly shaken. "Where did you find this memoir?"

"Does it matter?"

"Where is it?"

"I gave it to Sy," Deirdre said without missing a beat.

"You gave it to Sy?" Bunny narrowed her eyes and stared into Deirdre's.

"He said he'd take it to his office. He thinks publishers will be all over it, given the content."

"Your father wrote musicals and romantic comedies. He got paid to make things up."

And you get paid to act, Deirdre thought.

"Don't you think it's time people knew the truth?" Deirdre said, the words coming out strong and sharp even as her eyes filled with tears. "My father was here. He helped you move Tito's body from Joelen's bedroom. When he asked you where I was, you said he should be asking where Henry was."

Henry. Bunny mouthed the word as her eyes widened. "What else did he write about Henry?"

Deirdre tried to swallow the lump in her throat. "What I want to know is how did the dress I was wearing that night get like this?" She pulled it from the bag. "And how" — Deirdre waved her crutch — "did I get like this?"

Bunny's look softened. "I understand why you feel you need to know. And I'm sorry you've ended up with so many . . . questions." She gave Deirdre a long look, stripped of artifice. "But I'm telling you, as clearly as I possibly can, that it would be much better all around if you simply stopped asking them." She lifted the dress out of the bag and bundled it around the knife. Then she gave Deirdre back her messenger bag, opened the gate to the pool, and went through it. A moment later Deirdre heard a splash.

When Bunny came back through the gate, her arms were empty.

CHAPTER 35

Deirdre waited until she was off the Nichols' estate to pull over and check that her father's manuscript was still in her bag. It was. In an odd way, it was a relief to be rid of the dress and the knife.

When she got back to her father's house, the police car was gone. Henry's car was gone, too. The dogs greeted her at the door. She gave each of them a desultory pat on the head. One glance past the front hall told her that the place had been thoroughly searched. She made her way through the living room and into the den. Rugs were pushed back. Shelves cleared, with books and videocassettes dumped on the floor.

Deirdre continued to her bedroom. She leaned against the doorjamb and took in the disarray. The mattress had been stripped, the bedding piled on the floor. Her duffel bag had been taken out of the closet, unzipped, and its contents emptied out. The hollow-eyed, kitten-holding orphan was staring from the closet at her. Cardboard boxes that she'd piled in front of the orphan had been pulled out and opened, their contents strewn about. High school yearbooks. Scrapbooks. Spiral notebooks from college classes.

Deirdre wondered what on earth the police were looking for. It would take hours to straighten the mess.

She sank down onto the bare mattress, pulled the pillow off the floor, and hugged it to her chest. She wanted nothing more than to tip over, curl up, and shut down.

"Deirdre? Is that you?" her mother's plaintive voice called.

Deirdre squeezed her eyes shut and pulled the pillow over her head.

"Deirdre?"

Deirdre threw the pillow aside and stood, steadying herself with her crutch. She followed her mother's voice into her father's bedroom. On the way past Henry's room she looked in. His prized electric guitars were piled in a corner instead of lined up against the wall. The contents of his bureau had been dumped on the floor, his closet emptied out too.

Gloria was sitting up in Arthur's bed, her turban askew and her eyes red from crying.

Spent tissues were crumpled on the bed covers. This room had also been tossed.

"I see the police came back," Deirdre said.

"Twice."

"Twice?"

"First, two of them showed up and took Henry in for questioning."

"They arrested him?"

"I don't think so. Henry said to call Sy." Gloria's voice rose. "But before I could, another police officer arrived to search the house. I couldn't stop him. He tore through the place while I tried to call Sy. I called his office, and I tried him at home. I tried over and over, but I couldn't reach him."

"Did the police officer say what he was looking for?"

"Looking for?"

"Didn't he show you a warrant?"

Gloria hung her feet off the side of the bed, put her hands on her hips, and worked her thumbs into her back. She looked exhausted. "All he did was show me a badge and tell me to keep out of his way."

"And I'll bet he didn't leave behind a list of what he took, either."

"He didn't leave anything and he didn't take anything, either."

One officer. No warrant. Nothing taken. Sounded like a pretty sketchy police search.

Gloria went on. "Look what a disaste r he left the place. The funeral is tomorrow. People will be here." Her voice dropped to a whimper. "It's too much. It's just too much."

"And Henry's still not back? He hasn't called?"

"I haven't heard a word from him." Gloria's face crumpled, and she pulled out another tissue. "I'm so glad you're here, at least."

Deirdre imagined Henry being questioned by Detective Martinez in that little room for hours on end, his words captured on a tape recorder without Sy's reassuring presence to guide him. She tried phoning Sy but, like Gloria, got no answer. She hung up and stared at the phone, willing it to ring. But of course it didn't.

"Come on," she said to Gloria. "At least we can start straightening up."

For the next hour, Deirdre and her mother worked their way from room to room, putting the house back together. They were finishing up in the den when the phone rang. Gloria raced to answer it in the kitchen. Deirdre listened, praying it was Henry.

"Vera?" Deirdre heard her mother say. A long pause. "Oh my God, no!" Deirdre rushed into the kitchen. Gloria was ashen, a trembling hand over her mouth as she listened. "Right. Right." A pause. She shook her head. "How awful."

"What is it?" Deirdre whispered.

"Give me a piece of paper, quick."

Deirdre pulled open one kitchen drawer after another until she found a cash register receipt and a pen.

"Okay. Right." Gloria listened. Then wrote on the back of the receipt. Then listened some more. She just stood there for a few moments, staring at the receiver. At last she found her voice. "That was Vera. It's Sy." She waved the receiver. "He was mugged in the parking garage on his way in to his office this morning. That's why we couldn't reach him. He's in the hospital."

"Is he going to be okay?" Deirdre could barely get the words out.

"All Vera could tell me was that he got robbed and beaten up. They've admitted him." Gloria dabbed at her eyes with a fresh tissue. "Vera's been calling people, canceling his appointments. Meanwhile, Sy is all alone. If it were one of us, he'd be there. Like when you were hurt, he was the first one to show up at the hospital to help your father."

He was? Until that moment, Deirdre

hadn't remembered that there'd been some-
one else there. Now it came back to her.
She'd woken up strapped to a gurney.
Bright fluorescent lights streamed overhead.
Unfamiliar smells. She'd been shivering
from what was probably shock, not cold.
Her leg throbbing with pain.

If she'd been alone, helpless panic would
have overwhelmed her. Only she hadn't
been alone. Her father had been there, pale
and clearly shaken, and beside him was Sy,
a calm, comforting presence. Sy had taken
charge, demanding blankets from a passing
nurse and piling them over her. Rubbing
her hands until she stopped quaking. Asking what she remembered. Explaining to her
what had happened, how the car had gone
off the road. Staying with her and Arthur
until she was rolled into the operating room.
Promising not to leave until the doctors
were finished putting her back together and
she was safely in the recovery room.

Henry had abandoned her, broken on the
hillside. Sy had been there with her father
at the hospital.

Gloria looked down at the handset she
was still holding and hung up the phone.
"I'm going over there."

"No. I'll go," Deirdre said. She held out
her hand for the notes her mother had writ-

ten. "You're right. He's been there for me."

"Thank you." Gloria gave her the piece of paper and kissed her on the cheek. "You always were my good girl."

CHAPTER 36

Before Deirdre left the house, she stopped in the bathroom and washed her face and hands. Then she soaked the washcloth in hot water and sat on the toilet seat with the cloth pressed to her face. When it had cooled, she dunked it again, wrung it out, and pressed it to the back of her neck. She was so tired it hurt.

As she made her way out to the car, her messenger bag felt heavy even though all it contained was her wallet, her keys, and her father's manuscript. Gloria had written down *Urgent care – Beverly Medical Center,* and an address on San Vicente in Brentwood. Deirdre had never heard of the place. It wasn't all that far away, just the other side of the San Diego Freeway. But even though it wasn't yet rush hour, traffic and roadwork made the trip slow going.

The medical center was tucked in the back of a half-block-long shopping plaza. A small red-and-white sign directed her to underground parking, where she left the car.

Deirdre leaned on her crutch, hitching her bad leg along behind her, her messenger bag bumping against her hip as she followed the signs to an elevator that deposited her in a bright, plant-filled atrium. The medical center was down a corridor, past a dental office, a law office, and a tae kwon do studio. The door was marked BEVERLY MEDICAL CENTER. Underneath that, in smaller print it said COSMETIC SURGERY, and beneath that in still smaller print it said URGENT CARE. Any other time, the irony of that juxtaposition would have cracked her up.

The waiting area was small, only a half-dozen chairs. One patient was waiting, a woman with a bandage over her nose and her face buried in a *Cosmopolitan.* Deirdre made her way over to a counter topped with a sliding glass window. Behind the glass were desks and a wall lined with a bank of vertical file cabinets with multicolored tabs. A poster of a cocker spaniel with a white bandanna and a stethoscope around its neck hung on the wall.

A woman wearing blue scrubs emerged from a door at the back of the inner office.

She slid the window open. "Can I help you?"

"I'm here to see Seymour Sterling," Deirdre said.

"Are you a relative?"

"I'm his daughter," Deirdre said without blinking.

"You are?" The woman looked surprised.

Deirdre started to cry. She couldn't help it. She was worn down from sheer exhaustion. But it also made the lie more convincing.

The woman offered her a tissue. "Let me just check in on him. Make sure he's feeling up to visitors."

She disappeared and a few moments later returned, beckoning Deirdre through a doorway. Deirdre followed her down a corridor lined with examining rooms and through double glass doors. At the threshold of an antiseptic-smelling room, Deirdre stopped for a moment. The smells and the sounds of what looked to be a miniature emergency room were terrifyingly familiar. She had to fight the urge to buck and run.

There were just four hospital beds in the room. The attendant eased past her and disappeared behind curtains that were pulled around one of the beds. When she reappeared, she held the drapes open for

Deirdre. "I'll leave you. Don't stay too long. Your father needs his rest."

Deirdre thanked her and turned to Sy. She tried to hide her shock. He looked as pale as the sheets he was lying on. The top of his head was bandaged and black stitches tracked down the side of his face. There was a massive bruise on his forehead, and his right eye was filled with blood. She pulled the folding chair by his bed closer and sat.

"I did not realize that I had a daughter. Lucky me," Sy said with a weak smile.

"Surprised the hell out of me, too." Deirdre took his hand. Her lower lip began to quiver as she stared at the back of Sy's hand, livid around the spot where a needle was taped to a tube that was attached to an IV bag hanging by the bed.

"*Sh, sh, sh,*" Sy said, though Deirdre hadn't spoken. "The only reason I am not home? Doctor is afraid I will have another heart attack. Do not worry. This looks worse than it is." He chuckled. Winced. "Ouch. Cracked rib."

Heart. That explained the tubes attached to suction cups that snaked off his bare chest. A monitor by the bed beeped, a repeating fluorescent green wave pattern tracing out on the screen. Deirdre hated that beeping sound.

"Coming here brings it all back?" Sy said.

"Yeah. The sounds. The smell." Deirdre glanced around the room with its three empty beds. "Why did they bring you here? It's so small." And it was less than a mile from UCLA, with its world-class hospital.

"I am just here for monitoring. Besides, I am not good at waiting in line," Sy said. He coughed and winced again. "Plus my doctor is here in the building. No reason to get stuck in a big emergency room for bumps and bruises."

It looked like a whole lot more than bumps and bruises, but Deirdre didn't push it. "What happened?"

"I got —" Sy licked his lips and pointed to a cup with a straw on the metal table by the bed. Deirdre held it to his mouth while he sipped. Then he settled himself again. "I got out of my car in the parking garage this morning. Guy must have come up behind me while I was walking to the lobby. One minute I am thinking about my appointments for the day. Next thing I know I am on the ground, my head hurts like hell, and a cop and a lot of strangers are staring down at me."

"Did anyone see what happened?"

"No one came forward. No surprise there. The parking lot is quiet by the time I get in.

After the morning rush. And like I say, seemed like the guy came out of nowhere."

"It was a man?"

Sy's brows drew together. "You know, I am not sure. But I think so."

"Did he get your wallet?"

"Oddly enough, he did not. Or my Rolex. Or my ring." He raised his hand with the diamond pinkie ring. "And I still had my keys out, so he could have driven off with my car, for Chrissake. All he takes is my old briefcase. I have had that since law school. What did he think was in it?" Sy stared up at the ceiling for a few moments, his eyes squinting into the fluorescent light. "If you ask me, whatever he was hoping to find? He was disappointed."

Hoping to find? It took Deirdre a moment to register what Sy was saying. "You think you were targeted because of something he thought you were carrying? But what?"

"I have been asking myself that very question."

Deirdre swallowed hard as one possible answer occurred to her. "This could be my fault. This morning I told Bunny I'd given you Dad's memoir."

CHAPTER 37

"So Arthur *was* writing a memoir." Sy reached down the side of the bed and pulled a lever. With a hum, the head of the bed raised him to a sitting position. "I accepted as much."

Accepted when he meant *expected* — the occasional slip like that was a reminder that Sy's native language wasn't English. "You didn't know?" Deirdre said. "I thought for sure he'd have talked to you about it. Asked you to read it."

"He did not. I can only assume that he had his reasons."

"Earlier today I told Bunny that I'd found it. That I'd given it to you, and you were going to try to find a publisher."

"Which is what I would have done, if you had given it to me."

Deirdre winced at the tacit rebuke. "I'm sorry. I even told her that you thought it would be an easy sell."

"Did you tell her why I thought that?"

"Because he wrote about the night Tito was killed."

"Did he now?"

Deirdre shifted uncomfortably under his gaze. "He wrote about the party. How Bunny called him late that night and he came back and helped move Tito's body from Joelen's bedroom. That must have been before she called you."

Sy let his head drop back against the pillow. The bruise on his forehead was an angry purple against his ashen skin.

Deirdre went on, "He wrote about Bunny showing him the dress that I'd been wearing and a knife that belonged to us. She warned him that if he wanted to protect me and Henry he'd keep his mouth shut about what happened."

"You and *Henry*?" Sy tilted his head, considering. "Henry was there?"

"That's who you saw driving away from the house. Not Dad. Henry crashed the car."

"I always knew your father was hiding something, but I never guessed that. And Bunny thinks that you have given this manuscript to me? At least this is starting to make sense. You still have it. Someplace secure?"

"For now." It was all Deirdre could do to keep herself from looking down at the messenger bag she'd dropped on the floor and where the manuscript was safe, at least for the moment. "Of course, it's unfinished. There are just some notes at the end."

"Notes about what?"

"Stuff he was going to write about, I think." Deirdre tried to remember those scrawls on the final pages that had seemed like random thoughts. "Something about you and Mom and trust."

"Ah, the trust."

"*The* trust?"

"It is one reason why the estate is as small as it is. Years ago your father had me draw up a trust. Every month he paid a set amount into it. Elenor Nichol was empowered to draw money out. The trust expired a few weeks ago."

Her father had been paying Elenor Nichol? That made no sense. Unless . . . "Starting right after Tito was killed?"

Sy's expression told her she'd guessed right. "Some months after."

"She must have been blackmailing him. He was paying her for her silence." Deirdre looked at Sy but saw no reaction. "Sy, it's got to be connected. My father stops paying into the trust. He starts to write about what he knows, but before he can finish, he's killed. His office is burned to destroy the manuscript, only it's not in his office. Today a fake police search of my father's house fails to find it. Then you get mugged because —"

"What fake police search?"

"Two cops came and took Henry in for questioning, and right after that another one showed and ransacked the place."

Sy's eyebrows raised in surprise, then his brow furrowed. "I suppose it makes sense that the police would come back and also take your brother in for questioning."

"Maybe. But the way they executed the search sounded sketchy. Mom said a single officer got out of an unmarked car, came to the door, flashed a badge, and bulled his way into the house. She just assumed he was legit. After all, he was in uniform, and when someone's in uniform you don't really see him, do you? You told us yourself they're supposed to give you a copy of the search warrant and leave behind a list of what's taken. This guy failed on both counts."

"Not every police search goes by the book. Maybe he left the paperwork but your mother was so upset she —"

"Now I know she can be a little out to lunch, but Mom is not a complete idiot.

Whoever she let in to search the house was not operating like a cop. I'm wondering if he's the same person who mugged you because I told Bunny I'd given you the manuscript."

"But —"

"In fact —" Deirdre cut Sy off, talking as fast as she was thinking, "That police officer who was there in your office building when you came to? Are you sure he arrived *after* you got mugged?"

"I . . . he . . . well of course I assumed after."

"But you didn't see who mugged you, did you?"

It took Sy a moment to get what she was suggesting. "You are saying I got mugged by a pretend cop?"

"Could have been. The first passerby would think the cop was there to help." Deirdre remembered what Bunny Nichol had said about magic. *Make the audience attend to what* you *want them to see.*

"I guess it is possible," Sy said, "but it seems so unlikely —"

"We should be able to figure it out. If a real officer responded, there will be a record of it, won't there?"

"But how —"

"I know someone who can find out."

"A fake cop." Sy shook his head. "Suppose that's what it turns out he was. Then what? Call the police? Deirdre, are you sure that is what you want? Why, they will ask, would anyone go to all that trouble just to keep an old movie hack's memoir from being published?"

"He wasn't a hack."

"I know. I am just telling you what they will say. Before you know it, you find yourself having to speculate about what your father knew that was so" — he paused, searching for the word — "toxic. Do you want the world to know that you and Henry were there the night Tito was killed? Because you have no idea how quickly things can escalate from there."

Sy was silent for a few moments, his eyes focused on the middle distance between them. "Remember those pictures that ran in the paper the morning after Tito was killed?" He shook his head. "Headlines that ran way beyond the facts? It was horrifying. And who do you think allowed photographers to go up to Bunny Nichol's bedroom? Who gave them entrée and permission to photograph a fifteen-year-old girl, still distraught over what happened that night? Joelen hadn't been charged with a crime." His voice shook with rage. "Shameful. But it happened all the time. If you want to find out whether it still does, go ahead and call in the police. Just don't be surprised at what happens next. You saw what it did to your friend."

That stopped Deirdre. The events of that night had derailed both Joelen's and Deirdre's lives, but at least for Deirdre the aftermath had been a private affair.

"Maybe your father's memoir is publishable. Hell, maybe it has the makings of a bestseller. I would need to read it in order to form an opinion on any of that. But for the moment at least, one thing is clear: that manuscript could get someone killed —"

"Someone already did get killed," Deirdre said. "My dad."

Sy gazed at the machine beside his bed, which was tracing out a regular wave pattern. "I'm not going to disagree with you. But if you have it, or maybe you are carrying it around with you" — she squirmed under his intense gaze, even though there was no way he could know that it was right there in her messenger bag — "you are putting yourself in danger. Hide it in the house and the arsonist might burn the house down next time. Carry it around and you could be the next person who gets mugged. My advice? Before anyone else gets hurt, get rid

353

of it and make it widely known that you have done so. Leave it somewhere safe. The only question is: Where?"

When Deirdre got back into her car, she took out the manuscript. Was this what it was all about? Her father's murder. The garage fire. A fake police search. Now Sy's attack. All because someone desperately wanted to keep this from being published?

Deirdre riffled through the pages. What was in it that was so, as Sy put it, toxic? What Arthur had to say about the night of Tito's murder hadn't seemed, to Deirdre at least, to be that much of a game changer. Maybe the murderer was afraid of something Arthur hadn't yet gotten around to putting on the page? But what secret could he reveal about Tito's murder? And if there was something he'd kept secret for all these years, then why had *Arthur* been paying Bunny for her silence? Wouldn't she have been paying him?

Sy was right. Deirdre needed to put it somewhere safe, and then get out the word that she'd done so. After going back and forth with Sy on where, they had agreed on Sy's office. Neither Sy nor Vera would be in there for the next few days, and he had an alarm system that went straight to the police if someone tried to break in.

But looking at the manuscript, a thought occurred to her. What she had in her hands was a carbon copy. Which meant that somewhere out there was the original, and possibly even more carbon copies. Placing the manuscript in Sy's safe only took care of the problem in the short term. On the other hand, announcing where she'd put it might tempt whoever wanted it to reveal himself. Or *herself*. The more she thought about it, the more she liked it.

Deirdre picked up takeout from a Japanese restaurant on the way home. Vegetarian maki rolls for her mother; spicy tuna, yellow fin, and salmon maki for her and Henry. Then she stopped to make a Xerox copy of the manuscript. The first few sheets of onionskin jammed the copier, so she had to feed them in a sheet at a time. That gave her plenty of time to think through exactly what she intended to do. The plan she came up with required the help of a man and a woman. She knew who to ask.

She slipped the Xerox copy into a FedEx envelope, addressed it to herself in San Diego, and left it in the copy store's drop box. Then she bought a ream of paper, got some extra change, and used the pay phone to make two calls before heading home.

■ ■ ■ ■

Deirdre was relieved to find Henry was back, talking to Gloria in the kitchen when she returned. He looked exhausted and he smelled like he needed a shower.

"How was it — ?" Deirdre started, intending to ask Henry how it had gone with the police, when Gloria interrupted with "How's Sy?"

"Concussion and a cracked rib. He's shaken and hurt, but he seemed okay. And he claims the only reason they're keeping him there is to monitor his heart. But he looks ragged. He's going to miss the funeral."

"Miss the . . ." Gloria's face fell. "It won't feel right, burying Arthur without Sy there. And he was going to speak." She reached across for Henry's arm. "Henry, you'll say a few words? Deirdre, maybe you'd like to get up and —"

"No," Deirdre said. "I'm sorry, but no. I couldn't. I'd be too emotional."

"I suppose we do have the film clips. And we can ask people to share their memories," Gloria said as she unwrapped and plated the maki rolls. "That's what they do at a Quaker funeral. Silent meditation and the sharing of memories."

Silent meditation? Good luck with that in a room full of movie people.

"I've got a limousine coming at noon tomorrow to drive us to the chapel," Deirdre said.

"A limo?" Gloria asked. She peeled away the rice paper wrapping and sniffed at a piece of cucumber maki before eating it. "Isn't that a bit extravagant?"

"It's what people do," Deirdre said.

"Did they catch the attacker?" Henry asked. He'd already polished off a piece of spicy tuna roll.

"No. And Sy was hit from behind and knocked out, so he didn't see who it was. For all that, the only thing that got taken was his briefcase."

"That's lucky," Gloria said.

"Maybe it was luck. Or maybe that's what the person was after."

"His briefcase?" Gloria said.

"Sy thinks the person wanted Dad's memoir," Deirdre said, even though she'd been the one who came up with the theory.

"*Our* dad?" Henry said.

"Arthur wrote a memoir?" Gloria said.

"Why would anyone care?" Henry said.

"Sy thinks publishers will care," Deirdre said.

"Really?" Henry gave a dismissive snort.

"Of course they will," Gloria said. She ate another cucumber roll. "Your father was a born storyteller. A true raconteur."

"Right," Henry said. "Now he can tell his stories to people who haven't already heard them a million times. But why would someone mug Sy to get Dad's memoir?"

"Maybe because he wrote about what happened the night Tito Acevedo was killed," Deirdre said, watching Gloria and Henry for their reactions.

Gloria winced. Henry, reaching for the last piece of spicy tuna roll, paused.

"Dad was there." Deirdre leaned close to Henry and stage-whispered to him, "And according to his memoir, you were, too."

Henry's eyes widened and he looked momentarily stunned.

"Henry?" Gloria said.

"That's crazy," Henry said, not very convincingly.

"That's what I thought," Deirdre said. "But hey, why would he write it if it wasn't true?"

"Do you have the manuscript?" Gloria asked.

"I do. Sy wants me to take it over to his office and leave it there on the way to the funeral." With each word, as Deirdre felt as if a burden lightened, Henry looked more and more uncomfortable. He pushed away from the table.

"Do you think that's —" Gloria started.

"So do you want to know what happened with me and the police?" Henry said, interrupting her. He didn't wait for an answer. "I expected it to be a lot worse. He took me —"

"He who?" Deirdre asked.

"Martinez. Took me to a room and asked a lot of questions. Most of them I'd already answered. What happened the night Dad died? Where was I? What did I know about a shovel? Then he started in on the fire in the garage. I told him I don't know anything about that, either, and besides, I was at work."

"Did he seem satisfied?" Gloria asked.

"I couldn't read him. I did my best, but I really wish Sy had been there. Because after that he started asking about you." He looked at Deirdre. "Where you were that night. How you and Dad got along. When I last called you from the house." He paused. "He even wanted to know how your gallery was doing."

"And you said?"

"I said I didn't know."

Of course Henry didn't know. God forbid

he'd take the time to pay her a visit and see for himself. .

"Which made me think," Henry continued, "I should come down one weekend. See the gallery. Meet your business partner. See your house. Would you have room if I wanted to stay over?"

Shocked, it took Deirdre a moment to come up with an answer. "Of course there's room. I'll make room. You can even bring Baby and Bear."

The dogs, sleeping next to each other in the corner, picked up their heads. They seemed as surprised as Deirdre.

CHAPTER 38

Later that night, Deirdre heard a canned laugh track rumbling from her father's bedroom. Sounded as if her mother, who'd lived for the last ten years without television, was catching up on the latest sitcoms. Deirdre crept out into the hall and knocked lightly on Henry's bedroom door. When there was no answer, she knocked again. "Henry?" she whispered.

"Go away. I'm sleeping."

"Henry," Deirdre said through the closed door, "I was there at the house the night Tito was killed, and I know you were there, too."

No response.

"Are you listening to me? I know you were the one who was driving Daddy's car. You may not want to talk about it, but —"

The door opened. Henry had a pair of earphones loose around his neck. "Shh," he said. He let her into his room and pressed the door shut behind her.

"Don't you think it's time you told me what happened?" Deirdre said.

Henry sat down on the edge of the bed, his shoulders slumped. "I had to get us both out of there. I'm sorry."

I'm sorry? Those were two words she never thought she'd hear coming out of her brother's mouth, and certainly not with the kind of genuine contrition that seemed to fuel them now. "I thought Dad came to get me out of there."

"I had no idea she'd even called him. I found you passed out on the floor in one of the upstairs bathrooms. I had to practically carry you down the back stairs and I was afraid I'd have to carry you all the way home. But when I got outside, Dad's car was right there, with the keys in the ignition. The answer to a prayer. Or that's what I thought at the time." He gave a tired smile and shook his head. "I put you in the car. You were so out of it. I reclined the seat and you curled over on your side."

"You said, 'Night night, sleep tight' and kissed me on the forehead. I thought you were Daddy."

Henry blushed. "What I should have done is belted you in. Believe me, I wish to hell I had. And I wish to hell that I'd stopped long

362

enough to put up the convertible top and calm down. But I was so angry and so —" He broke off, a guarded look crossing his face. "Anyway, I got behind the wheel and started the car."

"Why did you drive up into the canyon?"

"I just drove. I wasn't even thinking about where I was going. Before I knew it, I'd turned onto Mulholland. I was cranking, pushing the car, taking those turns just as fast as I could."

Speed. Deirdre understood how it focused the senses. Obliterated second thoughts.

"I lost control. The car crashed into the guardrail. It was so weird, the car came to a dead stop but the engine just kept screaming. I thought I had my foot on the brake but I was practically standing on the gas pedal. The steering wheel was bent and my chest hurt so badly I could barely breathe. When I looked across to see if you were okay, your seat was empty. I'll never forget that moment."

"Then what? You thought you could just walk away and leave me there?"

"No! God, no. I was frantic. I heard you crying. I crawled through the underbrush and found you. Then I scrambled back and flagged down some bikers. Told them I'd been hitchhiking and witnessed a crash. I begged them to go call for help. All I could think was that you were going to die and it would be my fault. But then, when the ambulance got there, I hid."

"You hid? Why?"

"They'd have —" Henry mumbled something.

"They'd have what?"

"Taken away my driver's license."

"Taken your . . . ? I'm lying there, I could have been dying for all you knew, and you were worried about losing your damned driver's license?"

Henry looked down at the floor and swallowed. The years seemed to fall away and Deirdre could see the vulnerable sixteen-year-old he'd been: tall and charming, goofy and sweet. "I know. I was a coward. I was a jerk." He looked mortified. "You should hate me."

But Deirdre didn't hate him. All she felt at that moment was sadness. "You were a kid. Kids do incredibly stupid things."

"That was beyond stupid and then some. And it wasn't just about losing my license. The truth is, I was afraid they'd find out where I'd been and what I'd been up to." Agitated, Henry got up and crossed the room, then crossed back. He stopped and looked at Deirdre. "Did he write about me and her? Did he?" Before she could answer, he went back to pacing the room. "I knew I should stop seeing her. Tito threatened to kill me if he caught me there again. But she'd whistle and back I'd come. Like some kind of trained puppy. Sit up. Roll over. Sit in my lap. Give us a kiss."

Deirdre tried to put together what Henry was saying. "You came to see her after the party?"

Henry stood still. "I did. She'd told me to meet her at the pool. I rode over on my bicycle. On my *bike*, for Chrissake. At the last minute, I grabbed a knife, thinking I'd flash it at Tito if he showed up. I got to the pool and waited and waited. She never came."

After the party. That was when Deirdre and Joelen were making themselves sick gorging on leftovers, finishing off drinks, and smoking cigarette butts. "She didn't come because we'd gotten smashed. Threw up. Passed out."

"You and Joelen?" Henry blinked. Then he barked a laugh. "You thought I had a thing for Joelen?"

"Didn't you?"

"I . . . I guess I did. Sort of. But not like that."

Not like that? Then she got it. Of course it

365

hadn't been Joelen. A wave of pity and disgust came along with the realization. "You were meeting Bunny Nichol?"

Henry put his hands to his face and closed his eyes. An image of him came back to her. Onstage with his guitar and a microphone in front of him, an ambitious kid swaggering with unearned experience. And Bunny, twenty years older. *Queen of wanton amorous fire,* as her father had described her in his memoir. "What a sleazy —" She couldn't finish.

"I guess that's how it looks now. At the time, it was amazing. I thought I was such a big deal. Supersuave. In charge."

"Oh, Henry. She seduced you. She was glamorous. A famous movie star, for God's sake." Deirdre could only imagine what would have happened if people had found out. Bunny Nichol, involved with a younger man — that might have made a few waves. But that she was sleeping with a sixteen-year-old kid? A tsunami of bad press and ill will, and probably the end of her career. "Did you come up to the house looking for her?"

Henry looked sick. "I did. Even from outside the house I could hear them arguing. She was shouting. Tito bellowing. Then just her, screaming and screaming.

"I ran into the house. I don't know what I thought I was going to do, but I ran inside. I can remember standing at the base of the stairs, looking up. They weren't arguing anymore. Now there was complete silence, so quiet I could hear my own heart pounding.

"Then Bunny was there, like she'd just materialized on the upstairs landing, cold as ice. She came down and took away the knife. I didn't even realize I was holding it. She told me to get the hell out of there, to take you with me, and not to even think about coming back. Ever. So that's what I did. Except the not thinking part. It took me a long time to stop doing that."

Deirdre felt ashamed that for all these years she'd just assumed Henry was Teflon, holding every girlfriend who came along at arm's length emotionally. They came and then they went at his whim, or so it had seemed. This, at least, explained why.

"Did you know why they were fighting? That she'd told him she was pregnant?"

Henry narrowed his eyes. "How do you know that?"

"Sy told me."

"And he knew because . . . ?"

"Bunny told him. He came over later and she had him call the police."

"No. I didn't know that." Henry shook his head.

"But you did know she was pregnant."

"I didn't find out until later, when the baby was born and she came to Dad to negotiate terms and Sy set up the trust. She said the baby was mine. All you have to do is look at Jackie to know that's true."

Of course. She'd seen the resemblance too. She'd felt that frisson of recognition when she first saw Jackie Hutchinson standing on the stairs. There had been something about him. The way he carried himself, his sardonic smile, his hair — all of them echoes of Henry.

"Jackie knows you're his dad?"

"He thinks I'm a friend of the family, and that's what I've tried to be. It's the one good thing that came out of that mess. He's a great kid, even if he is a little lost right now."

That made two lost boys, Deirdre thought as she looked around the room. Henry's prized electric guitars were once again lined up against the wall. Above them on the shelf stood the Battle of the Bands trophies he'd won. Best Band. Best Guitar. He and his buddies had taken top prizes. Henry had had real talent. Looks and charm, too. And he'd been on his way.

But by his senior year of high school, his

grades had slipped. He'd stopped playing in the band. Never applied for summer jobs, just hung around, got high, and slept. Gloria and Arthur, distracted by their own unhappiness and Deirdre's surgeries, had barely noticed. After a few months of college, he dropped out and moved home. And he was still there, lost on the way to a real life.

Now Deirdre understood why her father had kept the mysterious baby announcement that she'd found tucked in with his manuscript. Jackie Hutchinson had been the unnamed baby whose arrival was heralded in the card mailed in an envelope postmarked twenty-one years ago. Of course her father had saved it. He was the baby's grandfather.

She also understood one of the notes that her father had jotted on the last page of the manuscript: *Sy trust.* Her father hadn't been paying Bunny hush money. It had been child support. And Arthur had been bound and determined to write about it. He was going to blow the story wide open, and blow away Bunny's reputation in the process.

■ ■ ■ ■

WEDNESDAY,
MAY 28, 1985

■ ■ ■ ■

CHAPTER 39

The next morning, the dull roar of a vacuum cleaner reached down and hauled Deirdre from a deep sleep. She lay in bed, listening to the nozzle bang against the baseboards in the hallway outside her bedroom. Sounded as if her mother still hated housekeeping and was taking it out on the house.

Deirdre propped herself up on her elbows. It was half past nine already. Rain beat steadily on the window. After her talk with Henry, she'd gone for a drive to clear her head and to find an all-night drugstore where she could buy a disposable camera. Even though she hadn't gotten to sleep until well past midnight, it was the best night's sleep she'd had since she found her father's body floating in the pool.

All these years she'd blamed her father for crippling her when it was Henry who'd been driving. In the end, Henry had been crippled, too, in his own way. The two of them had more in common than she'd ever have imagined.

She got out of bed and took a quick shower. Toweled her hair dry and ran her fingers through it. Her new cut didn't need more than that.

Beyond her trench coat, she hadn't thought about what she had to wear to the funeral service. She couldn't go swanning about the chapel in leggings and a long silk shirt. Her Xeno Art T-shirt was out, too. Ditto her father's chambray shirt. Which left . . . she poked through the old clothes hanging in the closet and pulled out the navy blue, swingy tent dress that she'd worn in college before abandoning dresses for long paisley skirts or hip-hugging bell-bottoms with embroidered peasant blouses.

She slipped the dress on. It was a little tight on top but it would do. She draped her new scarf loosely around her neck and checked herself out in the full-length mirror. Innocuous. Unremarkable. Perhaps even a little retro chic. The skirt length was the only problem — it was ridiculous how short hems had been back then. But she could live with it. Besides, she'd be wearing a coat over it, so it hardly mattered.

She got her crutch and made her way out into the hall. Gloria was dusting the living room. She was wearing a dark straight skirt and matching shell she'd taken from Deirdre's closet. Too small for Deirdre, they fit her mother with room to spare.

"Would you stop!" Deirdre said. "No one's going to expect a perfectly clean house."

Gloria gave Deirdre an appraising look. "We bought that dress at Robinsons. I like it with that scarf, but —" She came over and removed the scarf from around Deirdre's neck, then redraped and tied it. "Better."

Deirdre smiled. There was the shadow of the old Gloria Unger, the woman who had a subscription to *Vogue* and bought her shoes at Delman's.

"Why don't you go wake up your brother," Gloria said.

Henry's bedroom door was closed. Deirdre rapped on it. "Henry? Henry, wake up!"

"Go away." Henry's voice was a barely audible croak.

"The car is coming for us in an hour."

"I'll drive myself over."

"You will not. Now get up!" She waited. Didn't hear anything. "Henry, are you getting up?" She pushed the door open and looked in.

The covers heaved and she heard the bed

creak. "All right, all right. I'm up. Now go away."

"I'm not going until you're *up* up."

Henry picked up his head and glared at her. "I'm not getting up until you get out."

By the time a dark limousine pulled up, Henry looked sober and handsome in a dark shirt and tie and pressed jeans. Gloria looked oddly chic, certainly striking. Her growing-in hair framed her face like a dark shadow, and she wore her turban unraveled and tied loosely like a cowl around her neck. A pair of Deirdre's thick, red enameled hoop earrings gave her an exotic, Caribbean look. Her shoes were the only off note — battered black Birkenstock sandals.

Gloria stepped out into the rain, raising the cowl to loosely cover her head as she walked quickly to the car. Henry followed. Deirdre locked the door and carried a large envelope out to the black Cadillac limousine.

The driver in dark livery, the brim of his cap pulled low over a pair of wraparound sunglasses, held the door open for them. The dark interior of the car was cool and smelled of leather and Old Spice. As the car pulled away from the curb, Deirdre leaned forward and gave the driver Sy's office address.

"I see you're going incognito," Henry cracked, a comment on Deirdre's belted trench coat, head scarf, and dark glasses. Deirdre ignored him. Henry ignored her ignoring, instead practicing the informal tribute he planned to give, using notecards and talking about what Arthur had taught him to do. Play guitar, drive a car, mix drinks, pick up girls, and take all the fun out of TV movies by providing a running critique of the dialogue. By the time the limo turned into Westwood Village and pulled up in front of the three-story, pink stucco office building that housed Sy's office, Deirdre was wiping away tears.

"That was perfect," she told Henry. She was glad she'd had a chance to hear his speech.

"I don't know why you have to take care of this right now," Gloria said.

"Sy made me promise I'd leave Dad's manuscript in his office this morning. It'll just take me a minute."

Deirdre got out and speed-walked — as fast as she could with her crutch — out of the rain and in through the arched doorway marked PUBLIC PARKING. The interior, with its gated entry and ramp to upper parking levels, smelled of rubber tires and warm, moist pavement. She wondered if this had been the spot where Sy was attacked.

She pushed through a door to the building's lobby and made her way up a flight of tile-covered stairs, holding on to the wrought-iron railing. Sy's office was halfway along a shadowy, second-floor corridor that was lit by metal sconces with orangey, flame-shaped glass shades. She took off her sunglasses and unlocked the door with the key Sy had given her.

The moment Deirdre pushed open the door and set her crutch in the dark room, an alarm started to beep. She'd known it would, but still the piercing sound rattled her. She turned on the overhead light and hurried over to the wall where Sy told her she'd find the security panel, though with its flashing lights, she'd have easily found it on her own. She punched in the code and the alarm fell silent.

Deirdre turned on the lights and looked around. On a corner table, a copper lamp with a golden mica shade gave off an eerie glow. This outer room where Vera presided — Arthur used to say she was like a lioness guarding the gate — seemed smaller without Vera in it.

On the wall behind Vera's desk were two doors. One connected to Sy's office. The other was a louvered door to a walk-through supply closet. When Deirdre was little, before she started kindergarten even, she often came here with her father. While Sy talked with Arthur, he'd leave both supply closet doors and the connecting office door open so Deirdre could ride her tricycle from Vera's office to Sy's and around through the supply closet on her own miniature speedway.

Deirdre stepped into the supply closet, letting the door click shut behind her. Lines of light shined through between the slats in the door on the opposite side. Through the openings she could see Sy's massive desk, large enough for a pair of law partners to work facing each other. Behind it a pair of casement windows overlooked the street. No coats hung from a coat stand made of deer antlers, the perfect foreground for a large oil painting of a Hollywood western landscape, complete with a cowboy astride a stallion that reared against the sunrise.

At the funeral, Deirdre would let everyone she talked to know exactly where she'd left the memoir. She hoped that the person who'd been looking for it would hear. The closet would be the perfect vantage point from which to watch and see who took the bait. Deirdre slipped the disposable camera that she'd picked up the night before from her pocket, held it up to her face, and aimed the lens through an opening between the louvers. Through the viewfinder she had a perfect view of Sy's desk. She pressed the shutter. *Click. Whirr.* The film wound itself.

Deirdre left the camera within reaching distance on a shelf and pushed her way through the door at the back of the closet into Sy's office. A glass bowl filled with cellophane-wrapped peppermints was on the desk. She put her hand into it and felt around for the desk key. It was there, right where Sy said it would be. Then she unlocked the desk's wide center drawer and placed in it the envelope she'd brought with her. The words, written on the front in dark marker, would be hard to miss: *One Damned Thing After Another by Arthur Unger.*

With that, Deirdre locked the desk, just in case someone got there before she got back. She took the key with her and left, rearming the alarm on her way out. When she got down to the lobby, she put her sunglasses back on and tightened her head scarf. Then she exited through the parking garage and out into the drizzling rain. The limo was waiting at the curb.

The driver got out and opened the door for her. "All set?" he whispered.

Even she wouldn't have recognized Tyler in that uniform and sunglasses.

CHAPTER 40

The cemetery and funeral chapel were just minutes away. The limousine turned in through a driveway between buildings. Hidden behind them was an oasis of green lawn and flowers, a true secret garden that was Westwood Memorial Park. The limo pulled up in front of the path to the chapel. Its sides were lined with benches, tidy flower beds, and shrubs clipped into perfect circles and domes. It struck Deirdre how much effort had gone into controlling the outdoor space — ironic, given that death was so not something that humans could control.

The three of them got out of the car. Deirdre hooked her arm in Henry's, held her crutch in her free hand, and started up the path, through the misty rain, thick with cigarette smoke and crowded with umbrellas.

Arthur would have been pleased by the size of the crowd that overflowed the narrow A-framed chapel. Gloria embraced a man in a dark suit who greeted her and drew her over into a group. Among them, Deirdre recognized Vera, Sy's secretary. Deirdre waved, but she didn't follow. She had a mission, to get out the word that her father had written a memoir, that it had survived the fire, and that it was in Sy Sterling's office even as Sy was in the hospital recovering from being attacked.

It felt awkward at first, approaching people she recognized from the parties her parents had thrown, people who'd come over to dinner. "Yes, it's very sad. And so unexpected," she said, trying her story out first on Milton Breen and his wife, Anne. He'd been a screenwriter, now a director, who had a house with a pool up in the canyon. Arthur and Gloria had taken Deirdre and Henry there to swim before they built a pool of their own. "And then on top of everything else," Deirdre added, "the garage caught fire and we lost all the papers Dad had up in his office. Fortunately we were able to save his memoir. In it, he sets the record straight." She added, even though it sounded a bit lame, "I left the manuscript in Sy's office for safekeeping."

The Breens didn't ask which record got set straight. When she ran the same tape by

Lee Golden and a man Lee introduced as another set designer, the reaction was more one of surprise. A little glee, perhaps, at whose secrets might be revealed.

As Deirdre worked her way through the crowd, she noted how each of Arthur's friends reacted to her announcement that Arthur had written a memoir. To one and all, she added that Sy would be handling its publication as soon as he was released from the hospital.

A blond woman Deirdre didn't recognize put her hand on Deirdre's arm and air kissed both her cheeks. Along with the kisses came a familiar blast of rose and jasmine mixed with musk. Probably Joy. "Deirdre darling, I was so sorry to hear about your dad," she said. The voice Deirdre knew: this was once-upon-a-time brunette Marianne Wasserman, her high school's queen bee. "You haven't changed a bit," Marianne added.

Deirdre wondered how Marianne could tell since Deirdre had on a coat and head scarf and sunglasses. The crutch, probably. "Marianne," she said. "It's so sweet of you to come."

"You remember Nancy Kellogg?" Marianne said, indicating the woman standing behind her. Deirdre never would have recognized the once-chunky redhead who was now a blonde, too, and skeletal.

Deirdre slapped down the bitchy voice in her head. It was nice of the two of them to show up, even if they hadn't known her father at all and even if they hadn't seen or talked to Deirdre since high school.

Nancy gave Deirdre's hand a wooden shake. "We thought Joelen might be here," she said, rising up on her toes and looking around. *We.* That made Deirdre smile. Apparently she and Marianne were still attached at the hip.

"Oh, there's Henry," Marianne said. "Hi!" She waved at Henry, who was on his way over to join them.

"Joelen Nichol," Deirdre said. As Henry joined the group she shot him a look that she hoped conveyed *don't contradict me.* "Gosh. I haven't heard from Joelen in ages. No, I doubt very much that she'll be here. But you are, so you never know."

"Hello, Henry," Nancy said.

Henry colored slightly. "We should go in," he said. "Come on. Let's get out of the rain. The service is supposed to start soon."

Henry started to pull Deirdre up the path to the chapel. Deirdre waggled her fingers at Marianne and Nancy and mouthed *See you,* even though she knew that was unlikely. "Sounds like they know you," she said to Henry under her breath.

"Knew me. Briefly. Nancy wanted to be in pictures."

"Polaroid pictures?"

Henry chuckled. "I told you, I was an asshole. Where's Mom?"

Turned out Gloria was already inside. She was sitting in the front row, which was cordoned off for family. Mourners had already filled about half the chairs in the chapel. Some Deirdre recognized as family friends. Others anyone would recognize. Gene Kelly. Ernest Borgnine. Ray Bolger. They'd all worked with her dad.

As Henry walked Deirdre down the aisle, simple piano chords accompanied Ella Fitzgerald's sweet, silvery voice on the sound system. "With a Song in My Heart." Deirdre's eyes teared up. She'd helped pick the music.

Henry walked her up to the casket. Deirdre ran her hand lightly over its smooth coffered lid. The words *I'm sorry* echoed in her head. For blaming him all these years. For not accepting him for the complicated human being he was. For not getting down off her high horse, as he'd have put it, and just enjoying their time together. And for what she was about to do: run out on his funeral

386

service. She knew it wasn't respectful, but respect had never been her father's strong suit either. Besides, she was sure he wouldn't have wanted whoever killed him to get away with it.

She sat between Henry and her mother. A movie screen was set up in the front of the chapel. When she turned to look behind her again, the rows had filled and people were standing at the back. Frank Sinatra was on the sound system now, crooning about how he'd done it *my way.* Her father might have argued with that choice — he'd always said Sinatra was a thug and a bully. But the lyrics were perfect for a man who, facing the final curtain, would have thought he'd been king.

A little while later, the lights dimmed in the chapel and the hum of voices went silent. The screen at the front of the room lit up with the words ARTHUR UNGER 1926– 1985, white lettering on a royal-blue ground. There was a long pause to allow stragglers to file in, and then the back doors shut and the slides began. First was a stiff, old-world portrait of Arthur as a baby in his bearded father's arms, surrounded by his mother and three older brothers. Then, Arthur sitting on the front stoop of a New York City brownstone with one of his brothers.

Arthur, handsome and muscled in bathing trunks at a pool where he'd spent summers as a lifeguard and sometime emcee at a resort in the Poconos. As a bridegroom in a dark suit, Gloria in a tailored suit, too, carrying a bouquet of roses. Both of them looked impossibly young and handsome and — Deirdre tried to find the right word — tentative.

Silence, piano chords, and Nat King Cole's smoky voice began singing. "Unforgettable" . . . Her father would have found the choice entirely too mushy, but it was Deirdre's cue. She made sure that her scarf and sunglasses were secure and leaned over to her mother and then to Henry. "I'll be right back," she told each of them. Without waiting for a response, she grabbed her crutch and made her way to the back of the chapel.

With her sunglasses on and the lights low, the audience was pretty much a sea of indistinct faces. But when Deirdre pushed into the lobby where it was brighter, she recognized the one person still out there: Detective Martinez. She appreciated that he was keeping a respectful distance from the mourners, and fortunately he was preoccupied writing some notes and didn't notice her until she was nearly to the ladies' room.

"Miss Unger?" She heard his voice as the restroom door closed behind her.

The white-and-blue Mexican-tiled room with gleaming brass fixtures was empty. No one stood at the sinks. No feet were visible under the doors to the stalls. Music from the service was muted but still audible.

Deirdre really did need to pee. While she was in the stall, she heard the door to the room creak open. Deirdre raised her feet so they weren't visible. It wouldn't be Detective Martinez. All he had to do was wait for her to reemerge. She hoped it wasn't Marianne Wasserman, concerned as she was about Deirdre's mental status.

Then she heard a woman's voice. "Zelda?"

"Thalia?" Deirdre lowered her feet. "Hang on."

"There you are," Joelen said when Deirdre opened the stall door. "How do I look?" She turned around to show off a tan raincoat over a short black dress. Her hair was done up in a French twist. She turned her toes out and gave the black umbrella she was holding a Charlie Chaplin twirl.

"Perfect," Deirdre said. "But better when you're wearing this." Deirdre took off her coat and gave it to Joelen. Joelen took off hers and they swapped. Deirdre unwound her scarf and tied it around Joelen's head. Dropped her sunglasses into the pocket of the coat that Joelen was now wearing.

"Thanks for sending Tyler over to get me," Joelen said. "He's pretty cute, though I can't say I remember him."

"Well, he remembers you."

Joelen smiled. "Story of my life, but never with a happy ending."

"So far."

Joelen opened up her large black leather handbag and pulled out a blond wig. Deirdre took it from her, shook it out, and started to put it on her head.

"Wait. First you need to put this on." Joelen took out a net cap with banded edges. She snapped it over Deirdre's curls, then tucked in stray strands of hair, just like in a bathing cap.

Bing Crosby and Frank Sinatra were playing on the sound system now, singing a soused duet and proclaiming *What a swell party this is*. That meant the slide show was past its midpoint.

"Hurry up," Deirdre said, "before they send someone in looking for me."

"Don't have a cow. Hold still." Joelen eased the wig over the cap and tugged it a bit sideways, then back the other way.

"There. Done." She stood back and assessed.

Deirdre turned to face the mirror and considered her own reflection. Blond bangs and shoulder-length curls framed her face.

"How do you like it?" Joelen said. "Seriously, you should consider going blond."

"I look like me with a wig on."

"That's because you know you." Joelen got out a comb and teased some of the hair on top, then smoothed it all around with her hands. "There. Fabulous."

Deirdre looked into Joelen's reflected eyes. Suddenly she was right back in Joelen's bathroom, sitting on the fluffy pink fur-covered stool and watching Joelen do her hair and makeup for Bunny's party, just hours before both of their worlds imploded.

"What?" Joelen said.

"Why did you confess if you didn't do it?"

Joelen's eyes widened. "I thought you wanted me to hurry and get back in there."

"Was it to protect your mom? Or my brother?"

After a few beats of silence, Joelen gave a tired laugh. "Does it matter at this point?"

"I don't know. It might. What if what happened twenty-two years ago isn't finished playing out? What if my father's murder is connected to what happened to Tito?" Deirdre turned to face Joelen. "So please, did you kill him?"

Joelen shook her head. She put her finger to her lips. "*Shhh,* don't tell anyone." She paused. "Did you?"

"Did I . . . ?" For a moment Deirdre was too shocked to even form a response. "Are you kidding? You're telling me that you don't know who did it?"

"Let's just say I wasn't sorry he got killed and I'm not sorry I confessed." She glanced toward the door and lowered her voice. "I thought I was protecting my mother. It worked out. I only wish that had put an end to it."

Before Deirdre could ask *Put an end to what?*, she heard a familiar piano introduction, then horns, then Louis Armstrong. "Oh, Lawd, I'm on My Way." They'd picked it not for the lyrics but because her father loved it, and because it was so deeply sad and hopeful at the same time, and because if her father had had his druthers, he'd have wanted a jazz funeral procession that stopped traffic and marched right down the middle of Avenue of the Stars in Century City, once a back lot of the studio where he'd done his finest work.

The song was the last in the medley accompanying the slide show and Deirdre's cue to get going. "Here. Take my crutch," Deirdre said, and gave it to Joelen.

Joelen gave Deirdre a pair of oversized white-rimmed sunglasses and a black umbrella. Deirdre put on the glasses and gripped the umbrella handle — flat instead of a hook. She took a few tentative steps, using it like a cane. The tip, with its corklike rubber fitting, didn't slip on the tile floor.

"Looking good," Joelen said, tightening Deirdre's head scarf around her own head and putting on Deirdre's sunglasses.

"Front row, second seat in on the left," Deirdre said. "Break a leg."

"You break a leg, too," Joelen said, giving Deirdre a hug. "Be careful, okay?" She took Deirdre's crutch and, faking a limp that made her look like Quasimodo, started for the door. "Too much?" she asked over her shoulder.

"Yeah. Dial it back, just a smidge."

CHAPTER 41

Deirdre cracked open the restroom door just in time to catch a glimpse of Detective Martinez following Joelen into the chapel. So far so good. As soon as he was gone, she hurried through the lobby and outside. The umbrella made a surprisingly serviceable substitute for her crutch.

The limousine met her as she reached the end of the walkway. Its front passenger door swung open. She got in. Tyler reached across her and pulled the door shut. "Everything okay?"

Deirdre took off Joelen's sunglasses and dropped them in her coat pocket. "So far so good."

Tyler pulled out into the street and headed back toward Westwood Village. "You were right, by the way. There's no record of a new warrant to search your house. And there's nothing in the West LAPD blotter about any mugging yesterday in or near your lawyer's office building."

"You don't think Detective Martinez was ordered up from Central Casting, too?" Deirdre said hopefully.

"No. He's real. And very competent."

Minutes later, they were double-parked in front of Sy's office. "Your car's up on the second level," Tyler said, offering Deirdre her car keys. "Why won't you tell me what you're doing? Maybe I can help."

"I'm not *doing* anything. I'm just waiting to see who shows up. I'll be invisible."

"Invisible?" He sounded skeptical. "Why do you have to do this alone?"

"I just do." Sure, something could go wrong. She was willing to put herself at risk. She wasn't willing to risk putting yet another person, someone she cared about, in danger. Her thoughtless actions had already harmed Sy. And she wasn't about to go to the police. Not yet, anyway. She was already considered a suspect, and as Sy said, once they had a suspect they did their job and built a case. "Besides, you need to go back for Gloria and Henry, and to rescue Joelen if it turns out she needs rescuing."

"Here." Tyler gave her a slip of paper. "This is the number of the car phone in this rig. Promise you'll call if you need backup. I don't want anything to happen to you."

Deirdre leaned across and kissed Tyler on the cheek. "Thanks." She got out of the car and entered the building, then turned and watched as Tyler pulled the limo away from the curb and drove off. Then she turned back. Centered herself. Reviewed her plan.

First thing she'd do would be to go into Sy's office, unlock the drawer, take out the envelope she'd left in it, and put it on top of the desk in plain sight. Then she'd settle into the closet and wait. She'd photograph, not confront, whoever came. Wait until the person was gone so she could safely emerge from hiding. Develop the snapshots, take her evidence to Sy, and together they'd bring it to the police.

Deirdre started up the stairs. The tip of the umbrella thumped each time it connected with the glazed tile floor. She was halfway down the second-floor hallway when she froze. The door to Sy's law office was ajar. Someone was already there.

She tucked the umbrella under her arm and used the wall for support so she could approach the door silently. The door hadn't been broken in, so whoever it was knew how to pick a lock and disable an alarm. She stood very still, just outside in the hall, listening for sounds. Footsteps. A cough. Anything that would tip her off to whether the person was still there.

She crept closer. Nudged the door open a bit more. It was dark in Vera's outer office. No one was in the room. But the door connecting to Sy's office was open. Creeping even closer, Deirdre heard a thump. The sound of a drawer being slammed shut? She fought the urge to flee. Instead, she forced herself to push the hall door open a bit wider. The hinge squeaked and she pulled back, waiting for someone to emerge. When no one did, she slipped inside, crossed the room, and closed herself in the supply closet.

She waited, her heart banging in her chest, afraid that any moment she'd be discovered. But still, there was silence.

Through the gaps between the louvers in the closet door, Sy's office looked empty, too. But now she heard a shuffling sound. Footsteps? She felt for the camera she'd left on the shelf and took it down.

A black shadow crossed directly in front of her. Deirdre reared back, banging her head against a shelf. The person had been moving fast and was backlit. She'd have to wait —

The phone rang.

Deirdre aimed the camera at the desk where the light on the telephone was blinking. She looked through the viewfinder.

The phone rang again. The figure came back into her field of vision, moving away from her toward the desk. A man.

Click. She took a picture.

The man picked up the phone. After a pause, he said, "I know." *Click.* Deirdre's grip tightened around the camera and she took picture after picture of the man's back, the camera whirring after each click.

He sat in the desk chair. "It's not here," he said. *Eets not hyere.* Deirdre froze. She knew this man's voice. This was no intruder. It was Sy, sitting at his own desk in his own office. He must have been released early from the hospital.

Deirdre didn't want to pop out of the closet and startle him. That was all he needed with his cracked ribs and concussion. So she crept from the closet, through Vera's office, and continued out into the hall. Pretending she'd just arrived, she rapped at the outer office door with the umbrella handle and called out, "Hello?" When Sy didn't answer, she rapped again and started through Vera's office to the open connecting door. "Anybody here?"

She entered Sy's office. He was still at his

desk, now talking heatedly into the phone. When he paused, Deirdre came up behind him. "Sy?"

Startled, he swiveled to face her and did a double take. "Deirdre?"

"I didn't expect you to be here," she said, taking off her wig and the cap underneath it and shaking out her hair.

In a quiet voice, Sy said into the receiver, "I have to go." After a brief silence, he added, "I will let you know." He hung up the phone, leaned back in his chair, and gave Deirdre a wry smile.

It took a moment to register. No bandage around Sy's head. No stitches down the side of his face. No blood in his eye. He rubbed his chin, his pinkie ring catching the light. "Tests were all coming back normal. I told them I had enough. All those tubes and wires — too much for bumps and bruises."

Bumps and bruises that had miraculously vanished. Deirdre followed Sy's gaze to the foot of the deer antler coat rack. There sat a bulky briefcase that hadn't been there an hour ago. It was the same one that Sy had brought over to her father's house, the one from which he'd pulled her father's will, the one that had supposedly been stolen when he was attacked.

"The police recovered it," Sy said, answering the question Deirdre hadn't asked.

"Really?" Deirdre wanted to believe him. She wanted to believe that Sy thought he'd been mugged. That he was here in the office because he was a tough guy who'd lost patience with overcautious caregivers. That, throughout her father's life and even after his death, Sy was still her father's best friend, the surrogate uncle who'd always been there for her and Henry and always would be. "Did they catch the guy?"

"No, but they found my briefcase" — and there was just a heartbeat of hesitation, Sy's tell — "just around the corner in a Dumpster."

Sure they did. Deirdre leaned against the desk, feeling sick. Because there beside Sy was the envelope she'd locked in the drawer, the title scrawled across it in black marker. It had been torn open, and the blank sheets of paper that she'd tucked inside were strewn across the desktop.

CHAPTER 42

Sy rocked back in the desk chair and gazed at Deirdre across tented fingers. "I never thought you, of all people, would walk out on your father's funeral."

"I never thought you, of all people, would betray him."

Sy barely blinked as he held her gaze. "Oh, Deirdre. I do wish it had not come to this."

"And what exactly is *this*? You went to a lot of trouble to make us all think you'd been mugged." She knew from his bemused expression that this time she'd gotten it right. There'd been no mugging, and no police officer (phony or otherwise) showing up at the scene. Only a well-connected "victim" who could get himself checked into a tiny private clinic that specialized in cosmetic surgery where, for a fee or perhaps as a favor to one of their regular clients, the staff would pretend to care for "injuries" that had been conjured courtesy of smoke and mirrors, as Bunny would have said, along with a little help from Wardrobe and Makeup.

"I am sorry," Sy said, and he did seem genuinely saddened. "You have been caught up in this from the beginning. We tried to disentangle you. Really we did. And it *was* taken care of. Until your father decided to write a tell-all. I warned him not to. It was not worth it, no matter how much publishers were offering him."

"Publishers were making offers?"

"And a producer was eager to option the rights, according to Arthur at least. No one had actually read it, as far as I can tell. Thank God for that. And of course he hadn't finished writing it. But if there was one thing your father knew how to do, it was pitch."

"So do you really think anyone would have wanted to read it?" Deirdre asked.

"Are you kidding? It has everything. Old Hollywood, glamour, sex, intrigue, and violence. Details about a true crime that captured the imagination of a generation of moviegoers. In other words, a blockbuster. And I'm fine with that. Arthur can have his bestseller. Bunny will have her comeback. I can make all that happen. But the manuscript needs a few tweaks before it can go public. I'm already working on that. And in the meanwhile, I can't have a copy of Arthur's draft floating around."

"Arthur's draft?"

"So where is it?"

"It's in the mail."

"You mean this Xerox copy?" Sy crossed the room to his briefcase, opened it, and pulled out a FedEx envelope. He held it up so Deirdre could see her own handwriting on the mailing label. Deirdre's mouth went dry.

"I had you followed. So where's the original?" He shook the envelope at her.

"The original? Good question," Deirdre's words came out a rasp. "Because as you can see, that's a Xerox of a carbon copy. I've never seen the original. Knowing my father, I'm guessing he gave it to someone to read. Someone whose judgment he respected. Whose integrity he trusted. You."

Sy didn't bother to contradict her.

"And of course, you recognized the potential for disaster. Bunny's audience could forgive her for murdering a murderous boyfriend, but not for seducing a sixteen-year-old boy."

"Yes." Sy rubbed his chin. "It would have been a public relations nightmare. I tried to reason with him. But your father let his ego get in the way. I'm sure you can imagine."

Deirdre could. Serene in his own sense of entitlement, Arthur would have blown off his oldest friend's concerns.

"He was going to reveal details Bunny had been sure he'd never tell," Sy said.

"But he didn't know who killed Tito. He thought it was me or Henry."

"It was."

For a moment Deirdre felt short of breath. "But you told me —"

"I told you it wasn't you. Henry killed Tito."

"Henry killed Tito?" Deirdre parroted the words, but her brain wasn't taking them in. "He didn't."

"He did. He came over late that night after the party. Bunny met him. Tito discovered them together."

"But Henry told me Bunny stood him up."

"Henry lied. He's been lying for so long, I'm not sure he even knows what the truth is."

"Henry?" Deirdre felt the air go out of her. She groped behind her for a chair and sat. "It had to have been self-defense," Deirdre said, her voice sounding wooden.

"Of course it was self-defense. No jury would have found your brother guilty. He was a kid who'd gotten in way over his head. He was ready to confess. But Bunny couldn't let that happen. She'd have been pilloried for having an affair with a teen-aged kid. So she called your father and when she saw him driving up, she ordered Henry to take your father's car and drive you home. She promised him that she'd take care of everything. Which she did. She called me.

"Months later, when the news stories had finally died down and Bunny had given birth, she told Arthur that the baby was his grandchild. They struck a deal. She had me draw up a trust that your father agreed to pay into until Jackie turned twenty-one, and your father agreed he'd never tell a soul that Henry was Jackie's father. In return, Bunny would make sure the police never found out that Henry and you had been in the house at the time of the murder. She'd make sure the police never found these."

Sy rose to his feet and walked over to the coat stand. He bent, picked up his briefcase again, and brought it over to her. Deirdre knew what she'd see even before he got there — the stained yellow dress, looking no more soiled than when Bunny had taken it from her. Lying on top of the dress was the bone-handled knife. The splash Deirdre had heard had been just another of Bunny's tricks, playing to her audience's expectations.

"By the time I got to the house," Sy went on, "she'd switched knives and wiped the one that killed Tito on the dress you'd been wearing earlier that night. Always thinking ahead, you can say that for her. She showed your father the knife and the dress. Promised to give them to him after he had finished paying into the trust. Your father thought he was protecting you and Henry both. These can still be handed over to the police . . . if it becomes useful to do so. You can be sure that will never happen if you just give me the last copy of the manuscript."

"You thought the manuscript was in his office, didn't you?" Deirdre said. "That's why you set the fire."

"Not me personally. But yes, I hired someone. I had no idea that your mother would be up there looking for the manuscript herself, or that you would come back when you did. The important thing" — Sy grabbed Deirdre's arm and pulled her close to him — "is that you give me the last copy of that manuscript. Now."

Deirdre's shoulder throbbed as Sy's grip tightened. "Is this what you tried with Dad?

406

When persuasion and reasoning and arm-twisting didn't work, you bashed him on the head?"

Sy winced and loosened his grip. "It does not have to be this way. Your father wanted to tell his life story. He wanted to be the star. Give me the manuscript and I will do everything in my power to see that it is finished and well published."

"Too bad it has to be posthumous and filled with lies." Deirdre wrenched free and backed away.

"Not lies. Omissions."

"Henry?"

"Erased."

"Can you explain one thing to me? She could have had anyone in Hollywood. Why Henry?"

Sy seemed taken aback by the question. "He was young." Sy shrugged. "She wasn't." He shook his head. "Bunny wants what she wants, and she is used to getting it. Your father, too, in his way. He thought he was entitled to write whatever he damned well pleased. It was pure, shortsighted hubris on his part. Bunny couldn't let that happen. Too much was at stake."

"Cerulean," Deirdre said, the word sounding like air leaking from a balloon.

"You know about that?"

"Bunny had the art for the ad framed in her dressing room. All very hush-hush, or so she said."

"Selling a dream to a vast and untapped audience: women of a certain age." Sy held up his fingers as if he were framing the slogan. Like her father, he was a pro at pitching an idea. "It's going to be huge. Television ads. Free samples in the Oscar gift bags. International tour. She'll be on Johnny Carson. Barbara Walters. *Good Morning America.* She'll be getting scripts again."

"Arthur's memoir would have soured everything," Deirdre said. "Except for Walters. She'd have wanted her even more. What's more fun than a public shaming?"

"You understand. I tried to convince him of his folly. What she would do if she found out what he was up to."

"And she did find out, didn't she?"

Sy didn't say anything. He didn't need to.

"So what happens now?"

"If I'm writing it, then you give me the last copy of your father's memoir and I fix it."

"And if I don't?"

"Ah. Then Susanna comes forward and challenges your timeline. She tells the police that you left the gallery early and she finished the installation alone. Susanna, not Shoshanna, by the way."

"Susanna? You . . . ?"

"Didn't you think it was just a bit far-fetched that a prominent Israeli artist would want his work shown in a third-rate San Diego art gallery? So desperate, in fact, that he would pay for the privilege? *I yem Avram Sigismund,*" Sy said, affecting a thick accent. "*I yem very well known in Israel, but I hev to show my verk in the United States. . . .* Lucky for me, your partner cannot tell a Russian from an Israeli accent. And you still were not suspicious when, right after that, an arts reporter you never heard of calls and wants to feature your gallery in an article?"

"You bastard."

Sy looked genuinely wounded. He sat back in his chair. "I wasn't trying to hurt you. When your father told me you were going to help him get ready to move, I needed to make sure he would be alone the night Bunny and I came over to reason with him. It was a conversation I could not afford to have interrupted. I had no idea Susanna would get creative and have you paper over the gallery's windows. Or that Bunny would want to come back . . ." Sy's face fell.

"Or that I'd pick up the shovel on my way

up the driveway the next morning."

"Yes. I do wish you had not done that. But let's not dwell on missteps."

The scary thing was, the scenario Sy was spinning sounded entirely plausible. Whether Deirdre had gotten to the house in time to kill her father would come down to her word against Susanna's, and her fingerprints on the murder weapon sealed it.

On the other hand, Susanna wasn't real. "How hard do you think it will be for me to discredit someone who's not even a real artist's assistant?"

"She is not. She is a rather mediocre actress. A good detective could demolish her story, and a defense attorney worth his salt could poke holes in it. But it will never come to that because after she comes forward and it becomes clear that you will be arrested and charged, you will find a quicker, cleaner way to extricate yourself." Sy paused and thought for a moment, his gaze snagging on the umbrella she was using for a cane. "A car accident, I think."

Deirdre felt as if ice water were trickling down her back. "You'd kill me?" she said, though she could see from his expression that he was dead serious.

"I am very fond of you, and it will make me very sad. So let's not find out. But there

410

is a great deal at stake. Millions this year. More millions for years to come. Not to mention the legacy of a great actress who is far more ruthless than I. Surely we can come up with a better ending."

A better ending. As if her father could spring back to life like TV's Bobby Ewing in *Dallas.* Instead this would be the ending in which someone gets away with her father's murder.

"Step one is not negotiable," Sy said. "You give me the last copy of Arthur's memoir. In return, Susanna backs your story that you left the gallery late. And I do everything that I can to make sure you are not indicted for your father's murder. As you know, I am very good at my job." Sy picked up a chewed-on cigar from the ashtray on his desk and stuck it in the corner of his mouth. "Then we discover your father's memoir among his papers. Finished, of course. And edited slightly. But basically his life with a never-before-revealed, eyewitness account of the events surrounding Tito Acevedo's murder.

"Most of the story will be a familiar to you. The glamorous party. You were sleeping over. Your father came back to get you. Wonderful stuff, how he comforts Bunny in her distress. She practices the confession she plans to deliver when the police get there. We take out the part where they move Tito's body from Joelen's bedroom. It just makes things more complicated than they need to be."

"Is that where Tito was killed?"

"According to Bunny" — Sy raised his eyebrows — "and on this I take her at her word, Henry burst into her bedroom, yelling at Tito to leave her alone and brandishing a knife. But he did not have the nerve to use it. Tito chased him. Henry hid in Joelen's bedroom, but Tito came after him. It was pure chance that Tito was the one who ended up dead. Pure chance that you were not there. Tito died in the bed you had been sleeping in."

Deirdre closed her eyes and for a moment she was back in Joelen's bedroom, smelling hairspray and feet and ripe pungent sawdust in the cage where Joelen's pet guinea pigs lived. *I thought I was protecting my mother.* That's why Joelen said she'd confessed. In the end, her confession had protected Bunny and Henry both.

"Like I said, we leave all that out," Sy went on. "Before the police arrive, your father drives off with you. Next thing he knows is the morning headlines: Joelen's confession and arrest for murder. We add a third act.

The trial. Bunny's triumph in court. Happy ending: Justice is served. In its way."

"And Henry? Is he in the movie?"

"Who's Henry?" Sy chuckled, the sound rumbling deep in his chest.

"What about Jackie?"

"A mere footnote. Bunny will endorse the book. Publishers will be crawling all over one another to get their hands on it. Movie rights will go at auction. You and Henry will cash in. And Bunny will go back to her favorite private clinic, Beverly Medical Center, for more plastic surgery in preparation for her product launch and a starring role in the feature film. Arthur will be dancing in his grave. The changes to his story will seem minor. Believe me, he would not have cared."

"If he didn't care, then why are we here talking about this? Why is he dead?"

"Because he would not bend. Do not make the same mistake, Deirdre." Sy's jaw stiffened. "So, which will it be?" He raised his index finger. "Susanna goes to the police and tells them you had plenty of time to drive to Beverly Hills and kill your father?" He raised another finger. "Or I get the last copy of your father's memoir and turn it into a bestselling book and blockbuster movie. Arthur, played by" — he thought for a moment — "Dustin Hoffman. You? What's her name, the blonde in *Footloose*. Joelen? Maybe they'll cast an unknown. Cameos by famous aging stars, all of them publicity whores."

Deirdre held up three fingers. "Or I go through his papers, the way he asked me to. Sort. Cull. Inventory. Preserve. Certainly his memoir, even if it's unfinished, gets preserved."

"I'm running out of patience," Sy said, reaching into the desk drawer and pulling out a small silver handgun. "Do I get the manuscript or don't I?"

It wasn't the gun that scared Deirdre. It was the cold expression on Sy's face as he looked her squarely in the eye.

Chapter 43

"I cannot believe you tossed it over the side of the road into the canyon," Sy said from the passenger seat as Deirdre pulled her car out of the parking garage. It was all she could do to keep her sweaty hands anchored on the wheel. "You did not think someone would take it?"

"Not where I left it." After her talk with Henry the night before, she'd driven around for an hour looking for somewhere to hide the manuscript. It had been much harder than she'd thought it would be to find a secure spot. Finally it had come to her: people didn't mess with roadside shrines.

"I have never needed to use this before," Sy said, looking down at the gun in his hand. "I bought it for Elenor but she would not take it."

"Guess it's not her weapon of choice," Deirdre said.

Sy ignored that. He braced himself with

his other hand on the door as Deirdre rounded a corner a little too fast.

"I drove all over," Deidre said, "thinking I'd leave it in a backyard, under some bushes, buried in mulch. But these people" — she pointed up one of the driveways, where a gate led to hidden backyards — "have gardeners. Automatic sprinkler systems. Motion sensors and alarm systems."

She heard a clicking sound and glanced across at Sy. He was cocking and uncocking the gun that he held in his lap, pointing at her leg.

The car brushed the curb and Deirdre jerked the wheel. There was a deafening pop. Deirdre screamed and locked her hands on the wheel as the car slew to one side of the road and then to the other. A sulfurous smell. Was she hit? She slammed on the brakes and steered into the skid, narrowly missing a parked car.

At last she got the car under control. She took a quick glance down into her lap. In it were beige plastic shards. Pieces of dashboard.

Her heart pounded like a jackhammer and her fingers ached. That's when she realized Sy was gesticulating at her. Waving his hands, including the one holding the gun. Saying something. Shouting probably. Bu her ears were ringing.

Finally the ringing abated. She looked across at Sy. He was calm now, staring at the gun, white as a sheet. "Gun is loaded," he said.

No kidding. Deirdre's forehead and the back of her neck were coated with cold sweat, and she felt as if she couldn't breathe. As if there weren't enough oxygen in the car to fill her lungs. She rolled down the window. Took some deep breaths.

She glanced across again at Sy. He looked as terrified as she felt. He had the bluster to threaten, but maybe not the nerve to pull the trigger. Either way, as long as he had that thing in his hands he was dangerous.

Her heart still pounding, she turned north on Beverly Glen. The two-lane residential street, most of its houses hidden by tall bushes, climbed slowly. Deirdre steadied herself. *Keep on talking.*

"So then I thought, maybe I could hide it somewhere in a park," she said as she drove past a small park, barely big enough for a few picnickers to lay out their blankets. "In a public restroom or behind a storage shed or in a trash bin. But I couldn't trust it to remain unnoticed for long. So I thought: How do they do it in the movies? They stash things in lockers in bus or train stations.

But do they still have storage lockers? And is there even such a thing as a bus or train station within striking distance of Beverly Hills? Which got me thinking about a locker at a country club."

Her ears popped as they climbed higher and higher. Farther up, the houses were more modest and the road narrowed. Finally she turned onto Mulholland right behind a red Porsche that was moving fast. Deirdre kept on its tail, hoping she was making an impression, that the driver would remember her if anything bad happened.

"Which could have worked except I don't belong to a country club."

Sy held on to the door. He looked like he was about to be carsick. The gun was still in his hand, pointed at her, his finger still on the trigger.

"It's not much farther," Deirdre said. "Would you quit messing with that thing? I know you don't want to shoot me while I'm driving."

"I do not want to shoot you at all."

Deirdre turned tighter than she needed to coming around a bend. Tires screeched and Sy braced himself against the door. But still he held on to the gun. The turnout was just ahead. At least in a few moments they'd be out of the car.

She still hadn't caught her breath when she pulled the car off the road and into the same parking area where she'd spun out, day before yesterday. There were no bikers there today, just a battered, orange-and-white VW bus and an older couple standing at the opposite end of the overlook, taking in the view of the Valley.

Dust settled around Deirdre's car. She started to open the door.

"Not yet." He had the gun steady and pointed directly at her. "First, where is it?"

Deirdre swallowed. "It's over there." She pointed to the tree twenty feet down off the side of the road, its base crowded with mementos of people who'd been injured or lost their lives.

Sy took the keys from the ignition, grabbed Deirdre's umbrella, and got out of the car. He motioned for her to get out, too. She did. He looked around, casting a nervous glance in the direction of the couple. They weren't paying attention to anything but the view.

"Suicide Bend," Sy said, reading the sign and edging closer to the guardrail. He looked over, then gazed up toward the tree branch where the car bumper twisted in the wind. "I guess you are not the only person who got hurt here."

Deirdre limped over to the stretch of guardrail closest to the tree. "I threw it from here."

Sy stared down the steep incline. "Go get it."

"I can't —"

"Then you should not have thrown it." Sy passed her the umbrella she'd been using in place of her crutch.

Deirdre sat on the guardrail. "Or we could just leave it there and it will be our little secret. I'll never tell."

Sy gave her a long, steady look. "You know I cannot risk that. Think of this as part of your role as your father's literary executor."

Deirdre almost laughed. What she was about to do was a gross perversion of the role her father had bestowed upon her. "You're only going to change what he wrote."

"It will still be Arthur Unger's story. Boy from the Bronx makes good. Think about how he would feel if the choice were between dooming it to obscurity or twisting it a bit and making it a smash."

"You must have tried that argument out on him."

"And I think he would have come around. Eventually. But not everyone is as patient as I am."

The worst part was, Deirdre knew Sy was right. She set the tip of the umbrella into the wet soil at the top of the embankment and swung her legs over. Next to the teddy bear and beside a fresh bouquet of flowers, she could see the glint of shiny foil in which she'd wrapped the manuscript. If she gave it to Sy, no one would know that the father of Bunny's son had been a sixteen-year-old kid. Henry could go on pretending to be a friend of the family, taking his son under his wing like a big brother. No one would know that Henry killed Tito.

What would her father have wanted? She knew the answer to that. He'd have wanted to be played by Jack Nicholson.

What mattered to Deirdre? That took her a few moments.

She turned back to Sy. "Will you tell me one thing?"

"Maybe."

"Did you kill my dad?"

"No." Sy's voice was firm. She wasn't sure if it was regret or annoyance that flickered across his face. "But I will say that I did, if it comes to that. I will be very convincing. People who confess to protect people they love can even come to believe the lie."

"Bunny killed him, didn't she?" Deirdre said.

Sy's expression didn't change, but that told her all she needed to know.

Deirdre stood, set the tip of the umbrella in the harder-packed soil farther in from the guardrail. Carefully she began to descend toward the base of the tree.

■ ■ ■ ■

Almost Two Years Later, Wednesday, March 11, 1987

■ ■ ■ ■

CHAPTER 44

Silver-haired Johnny Carson bounced a pencil on his desk and raised a hand in a salute to his audience. "My guest tonight is one of the most glamorous movie stars of all time. When her name was on the marquee, bam, they came. Her new movie is about to open, and it's both a public and a very personal triumph. Would you please join me in welcoming the one, the only" — the camera shifted to a robin's-egg blue curtain that drew aside — "Elenor Nichol."

Orchestral fanfare and long, sustained applause exploded as Bunny, her eyes wide, red lips glistening against white teeth, stood framed by the curtain. She wore a slinky black gown. A diamond brooch sparkled at her slender waist, and diamond chandelier earrings grazed her porcelain shoulders. Her black hair was piled high on her head, with tendrils curling down her back.

"She looks spectacular," Deirdre said,

watching the show from the bed she now shared with Tyler in their arts-and-crafts bungalow in Los Feliz Village. Deirdre's share of the income from her father's book and the movie deal had been enough for half the down payment on the house and a year's rent on a storefront on Hollywood Boulevard where she'd soon open her own art gallery. Deirdre and Henry had given a share of their earnings to Gloria, who'd opened a yoga and meditation studio at a hot springs resort between Death Valley and Las Vegas.

On TV, Bunny put her hand over her mouth as the applause continued. She seemed genuinely overwhelmed. Carson got up and offered her his hand, then gave a mock bow all the way down on one knee, like he was waiting to be knighted. Bunny smiled as he stood, offered her his arm, and led her over to the guest chair.

When the applause died down, Carson sat and rested his arms on his desk. "As you can hear, you've been missed."

"Thank you. This means so much to me." Bunny leaned forward as if sharing a confidence, her cleavage swelling. "You're all so kind. You know, I never really meant to leave Hollywood. I just needed time." She shifted in the chair, crossing her leg so that her thigh peeked through a slit in the skirt. "Time to find myself."

"And I trust you have," Carson said, glancing at her leg and giving the audience one of his trademark smirks. Then he smiled graciously at Bunny. "We're glad to have you back. You're a true movie star legend."

"You make me sound like an anachronism." She gave him a sly look. "But I am happy."

"Is it your work or something personal?"

"Probably the work. But who can tell? Regret can be very disabling. It took me a long time to learn to let it go."

He smiled an impish grin. "Screw regret."

Bunny gave a *naughty boy* shake of her head. "Am I being good? Am I being bad? Am I this? Am I that? Who cares? Let it all go. I've learned to live with my past. But I do have a few scars." She widened the slit in her skirt to expose her knee. "Can you see my boo-boos?"

"You want to show them to us?"

The audience howled.

Bunny smiled. Blushed.

Carson spread his arms, like he couldn't help himself. "Might there be a new man in your life? Because behind every great woman is a great behind."

The audience laughed, and Bunny turned

to them. "Now you all have to stop egging him on."

As the audience response faded, Johnny's look turned serious. "Okay, so you've let it go. You've . . . um . . ." He bounced a pencil on the desk.

"Finished my *film.*" Bunny turned to the audience, spread her hands, and was rewarded with applause.

"You want to talk about your film? What's it called?"

"You know what it's called."

"Notorio," Carson said, and music swelled, violins in a syncopated tango with flourishes from a snare drum. A movie poster came up. There was Bunny in the same long black dress, waves of long black hair framing her face, wrapped in a dance embrace with her Latin lover. Deirdre could hear Tito's voice whispering in her ear. Yes, it was about the connection.

"Notorio," Bunny said. "With Tito Altavista."

"Tito?"

"Just a coincidence."

"In Hollywood, there's no such thing as coincidence."

"He's a young Fernando Lamas."

"Fernando Lamas."

"It was a great experience."

428

"With Tito Altavista?"

She looked toward the audience. "Yes."

"Have you ever worked with Fernando Lamas?"

Bunny ignored that. "The movie opens in Los Angeles tomorrow."

"And are you having fun with this new movie?"

"I never do anything I don't enjoy," Bunny said without a hint of irony. "Not anymore."

Johnny raised his eyebrows. "I can certainly relate to that."

Bunny tucked her knee demurely back into her skirt.

On the screen now was the cover of Arthur's book. Johnny said, "I understand the movie is based on a book written by an old friend of yours."

True to Sy's word, as soon as Deirdre had given him the manuscript, Shoshanna/ Susanna had showed up to confirm Deirdre's story. Shortly after that, the shovel mysteriously disappeared from police evidence, and a few months later, Arthur's death was ruled *by misadventure.* Six months later, Arthur's memoir, *One Damned Thing After Another,* was published. The movie's publicity rollout had pushed it onto the *New York Times* bestseller list.

"Yes. Arthur Unger is" — Bunny gave her

head a sad shake — "*was* a writer. A huge talent. One of Hollywood's greats. And one of its most underappreciated. Maybe now the Academy will recognize his work."

The book cover faded and was replaced by a head shot of Arthur himself taken back in the early days, the kind of black-and-white publicity still that the studio had taken of all its contract talent. Then the picture of Arthur faded, replaced by a still from the movie, Bunny and Jerry Orbach in Bunny's pink bedroom with the actor Tito Altavista dead on the floor with a knife sticking out of his abdomen.

Jerry Orbach wasn't Jack Nicholson or Dustin Hoffman — not A-list enough to share the limelight on the *Tonight* show with Bunny, which was probably just as well. But he was smart, handsome, and a terrific actor. A Broadway song-and-dance man, too. Arthur would have appreciated that.

On TV, Carson asked Bunny, "I understand you worked with Mr. Unger on his book."

"Yes. We collaborated before his tragic death."

Collaborated? That made Deirdre laugh out loud.

"In fact, we talked about it the very day he died. Ironic, don't you think?" Bunny pursed her lips. That brazen admission took Deirdre's breath away.

"And I understand Arthur Unger was not just a friend of yours," Carson said. "His book gives an inside look at the most tragic event in your life, a murder almost twenty-five years ago that got worldwide headlines. People still haven't forgotten. It's something you have never talked about publicly before."

"And I'm not starting now."

"So if we want to know —"

"Go see the movie. It's always better than real life."

The camera held for a moment on Carson's face, his eyebrows raised in dismay. "You heard what the lady said. See the film. And with that . . ." he said and pointed off camera.

The TV went to commercial, and there was Bunny again, wearing another low-cut, slinky black dress adorned with diamonds. Deirdre had the odd sensation that she was in Bunny Nichol's dressing room again, the mirrored walls reflecting and reflecting back infinite images of the glamorous star. It wouldn't have surprised her if the doorbell rang to reveal yet another Bunny, this one in person. Except Deirdre hadn't seen or spoken to Bunny Nichol, not since Bunny had pretended to toss the bloodied dress and the knife into her pool. Joelen had ended up brokering the sale of Arthur's house for $1.1 million. That someone had died there in mysterious circumstances only increased the interest in the property. It was, after all, Hollywood. Deirdre and Joelen hadn't spoken since the closing.

During the commercial for Cerulean, violins, piano, and finally an accordion swelled to a tango rhythm. A tall, slender man dressed all in black moved slowly away from the camera toward Bunny, took her in his arms, twirled her once, twice, then bent her backward. The scene dissolved to a close-up of Bunny raising a bottle of Cerulean as if in a champagne toast, arching her head back and spraying her neck with the perfume. In smoke, words wrote themselves out on the screen in front of her.

Because

you're a woman

"Cerulean," Bunny's voice whispered as the words dissolved into a skim of mist that took over the screen and slowly dissipated to reveal a bottle of the perfume.

Deirdre turned the television off.

"That woman is a piece of work," Tyler said.

"She is that," Deirdre said.

"And she makes it sound as if the story is all about her."

"It always is."

Deirdre had been invited to a screening of the movie. She and Henry had gone together. The movie echoed *Sunset Boulevard* without the grit and irony, with the screenwriter aging and the Hollywood star young and glamorous. Arthur's life story was relegated to a few meager flashbacks.

In the movie's climactic scene, Tito works himself into a jealous rage. He hits Bunny repeatedly, then grabs the strand of pearls she's wearing around her neck, twists it tight, and starts to strangle her. Bunny's mouth opens in a silent scream, her eyes go wide, and her face turns red. Joelen, played by Winona Ryder, screams at him from the bedroom doorway to stop. Tito drops Bunny and pivots toward Joelen, fingers flexed.

Bunny screams. She sees Joelen has a knife. Tito does not. He lunges for Joelen.

The camera lingers on Tito's face. Stunned. On Joelen's face. Shocked. On Bunny's face. Horrified. Then the camera pans back as Tito drops to the floor, rolls over onto his back, his glazed eyes staring up at the ceiling.

In the movie, there was not a whiff of Deirdre's presence at the house that night.

No trace of Henry's role in the tragedy, either. Henry still had no idea how close he'd come to being thrust into the limelight. Charged with murder. Revealed as the father of Bunny's son.

After they sold Arthur's house, Henry quit his job at the motorcycle dealership and used his share of their earnings to buy a one-story fixer-upper on a canal in Venice. In the garage, he'd opened a small recording studio.

Audio of Bunny's testimony before the coroner's jury had played as the movie's final credits rolled. Sy had gotten Arthur a posthumous screenwriting credit, even though he'd never actually touched the screenplay.

"How would your father feel about the way she hijacked his story?" Tyler asked.

Deirdre paused. How would Arthur have felt? He knew writers got no respect. That his job was to put words on the pages of scripts that directors and actors inevitably rewrote, mangled, or ignored. But now he had a bestselling book. A major motion picture. Earnings that could have easily have paid for a bigger swimming pool and a credit that might yet garner an Academy Award nomination. He was still in the game.

"He'd have been thrilled," Deirdre said.

AUTHOR'S NOTE

Like any young girl growing up in Beverly Hills, I was fascinated by the 1958 murder of Johnny Stompanato. I was ten years old, and I can remember poring over the pictures and articles that ran in the newspapers. The house where it happened was just a few blocks from where we lived, and Cheryl Crane, Lana Turner's daughter who confessed to stabbing her mother's gangster boyfriend to death, was just four years older than me.

Readers may recognize the crime as one of the inspirations for this book. But in researching *Night Night, Sleep Tight,* beyond rereading news accounts that ran at the time of the crime, I deliberately avoided learning anything about the people involved in the real crime. Instead I took the murder and its trappings, along with my own visceral response to it years ago, as a jumping-off point for an entirely fictional story with

fictional characters I could build from the
ground up.

ABOUT THE AUTHOR

Hallie Ephron is the bestselling, award-winning author of suspense novels. Her novels have been finalists for the Edgar, Anthony, and Mary Higgins Clark awards. With *Night Night, Sleep Tight,* she takes readers back to early-'60s Beverly Hills, a time and place she knows intimately. She grew up there, the third of four daughters of Hollywood screenwriting duo Henry and Phoebe Ephron, contract writers for Twentieth Century Fox who wrote screenplays for classics like *Carousel* and *Desk Set.* Ms. Ephron's novels have been called "Hitchcockian" by *USA Today,* and "deliciously creepy" by *Publishers Weekly.* Her award-winning bestseller *Never Tell a Lie* was made into a movie for the Lifetime Movie Network. Her essays have been broadcast on NPR and appeared in magazines including *More, Writer's Digest,* and *O: The Oprah Magazine* ("Growing Up Ephron"). She writes a regular crime fiction book review column for the *Boston Globe*. Ms. Ephron lives near Boston with her husband.

The employees of Thorndike Press hope you have enjoyed this Large Print book. All our Thorndike, Wheeler, and Kennebec Large Print titles are designed for easy reading, and all our books are made to last. Other Thorndike Press Large Print books are available at your library, through selected bookstores, or directly from us.

For information about titles, please call:
  (800) 223-1244

or visit our Web site at:
  http://gale.cengage.com/thorndike

To share your comments, please write:
  Publisher
  Thorndike Press
  10 Water St., Suite 310
  Waterville, ME 04901